NO PLACE *Like Home*

ORLINDA VALLEY
SERIES
BOOK THREE

DONNA R. MADDEN

Also By Donna R. Madden

More Than Enough series
More Than Enough
Your Love is Enough
You Are Enough
Orlinda Valley series.
No One But You
No Love Like Yours
No Place Like Home

To everyone who makes home a little better.

NO PLACE
Like Home

Chapter 1

Rowan

Twelve years of my life had been spent in a uniform, waking at the ass-crack of dawn to do PT, traveling to all parts of the globe to support peace—now, with the sign of a pen, it was over, and I was on Interstate 40 heading east toward Tennessee—toward home.

My phone rang through the speakers of my Jeep Wrangler as I inched my way closer to the Tennessee state line. One glance at the caller ID told me it was Trevor, my best friend since middle school. I clicked the answer button just as someone cut me off on the highway. "Son of a bitch, what the fucking hell?" I yelled out the window.

Trevor's laugh filled the interior. "Damn, Rowan. I'm guessing you're having a good drive?"

"Oh yeah. It's been nothing but a party," I said as I swerved into the left lane and sped up to pass a white minivan. "Been a pretty simple drive until now, but this traffic fucking sucks." I laid on the horn as another car swerved into my lane. "Has everyone lost their fucking mind and does no one work anymore?" I sighed as the

Welcome to Tennessee sign loomed over the road. "At least I'm finally in Tennessee. Only a couple hours left." I had planned on making a career out of the military, staying in until I could retire, but the past couple years things had become less fun. I found that I suddenly wanted to settle down, and Orlinda Valley called to me.

I chuckled. I hadn't been home in five years. I've been avoiding it like the plague—for no other reason except I use to hate it. Now here I am, heading back to the past. No job, no plans, just hope for the future.

"Tennessee's the place to be in the fall. You came at the perfect time."

Trevor's voice jarred me back to our conversation. "I don't know if I agree with that. But, anyway, you didn't tell anyone I'm coming in this early, did you?"

"Nope. Hold on."

I heard Trevor's voice move away from the phone speaker, talking to someone else. He was probably serving customers at Jerry's Pub in our hometown of Orlinda Valley, where he was bartender and part owner. It had been an old hole-in-the-wall bar for as long as I could remember, and when Jerry, the past owner, finally had enough, he sold it to a group of firefighters itching to do something fun and different. Trevor was one of those firefighters, now living both his dreams of saving the town from the occasional fire and owning a bar. From what I'd been told, they'd turned Jerry's Pub into a thriving business, and now it's the popular place to be.

"All right," Trevor said, returning to the call. "So, have you decided where you're going to crash?"

"Since you can't promise your couch to your best friend who's been off keeping your sorry ass safe, I asked Kai when we talked last night if I could stay with them. But they're still under construction, so they don't have space."

"I still can't believe they didn't ask you to be in the wedding."

"Fuck that. It's a wedding, the guy doesn't know me at all, and I didn't know when I'd be able to get home. Anyway, he told me I could stay at Kora's since she's no longer using her place. As long as Mom doesn't come over to check on things, I should be good until I'm ready to make my presence known."

Kora was my cousin, and we were as close as siblings. She and Kai met a little over a year ago and were getting married in two weeks. I was glad she finally found someone to spend her life with. From what I knew about Kai, the man who drove into town one day and right into her heart, he was every bit the man she deserved.

"You know this wouldn't be such a big deal if you'd've come home more often."

"Yeah, whatever. Doesn't matter now. I'm home for good."

"Home and unemployed. You know Bryson's going to love your irresponsible attitude," Trevor said.

I shook my head as I passed a semi. I was the youngest of three boys. Bryson was the middle brother. He was loud, obnoxious, and always the life of the party. Jamison was the oldest. A widower and single father, he was serious and loved by all.

Twelve years ago, I turned my back on multiple scholarship offers to play football, because I couldn't imagine spending four more years in school when I had no clue what I wanted to do with my life. Not to mention, I needed to get away from home, and away from the knowledge that I was the only McKendry brother without a plan. The Army had been my out. It was the one thing Bryson and

Jamison hadn't pursued, and something I could do on my own that would make my parents proud.

"I don't give a fuck what Bryson thinks. Even if I found a cure for cancer, he'd have issues with something. I don't live my life for his praise anymore." I hit the gas to speed past a semi as we started an uphill climb, but it was all for nothing. As I crested the hill and turned a curve, I saw nothing but a sea of red brake lights, and I slowed to a crawl. "Shit. Traffic is stopped dead. Fuck me. Look, I'll talk to you tonight. If I ever get home."

"Sounds good. Stop by the pub when you're ready to get out. I'll be here."

The line went dead. I clicked the end call button and turned up the classic rock channel. I might have grown up near Nashville and enjoyed country music, but one thing I got out of the military was that when you needed mindless music to keep your thoughts from wandering too far, rock 'n' roll was the only way to go.

Even though the music was loud, the windows were down, and we were going a whopping ten miles an hour, my mind did wander. I probably should have at least let my mother know I was going to be home early, but I knew she'd make a big deal out of it and then get excited about me mending bridges with Bryson and all that shit, and I didn't want to go there yet. I hadn't even told Summer, my closest friend aside from Trevor. We talked every week—hell, sometimes multiple times each week. She was going to be pissed when she saw me. She hated surprises.

As the traffic crawled along, I thought back to the first time I truly met Summer. It was a hot and humid June day when we were in middle school. Trevor and I kayaked down the Red River and banked our kayaks at the "swimming hole", the place where the river widened and became deeper. A rope hung from a limb of a large tree that grew out over the bank of the river, and people could jump from a small rock ledge and swing into the water. It was a great place to relax in the sun on the shore, wade in the shallows, or swim past the drop-off, and it was always crowded with local kids taking advantage of the long, humid summer days.

Kora and her best friend, Darlene—now my sister-in-law, married to Bryson—were there with a girl named Summer, whom I'd seen with them many times but had never really talked to before. Near as I could tell, Summer was trying to kill fish—though she insisted she was "skipping rocks". Either way, she sucked at it.

I walked up next to her, picked up a nice flat rock, leveled it to the ground and let it soar. It hit the water and skipped off the top five times before finally going under. "You're a fucking show off," were the first words I remember her saying to me. I had never heard the f-bomb out of a girl's mouth before and was shocked into a stupor. I instantly realized her language was one hundred percent *Summer*, and that I had found my newest best friend. The rest of the day was spent tossing around the football, rowing around in Trevor's and my kayaks, and trying to teach Summer how to skip rocks. She never could get the hang of it. By the time I left for the Army after graduation, she was still unsuccessful, and there were fewer fish in the river because of her attempts.

It was almost five o'clock by the time I took the ramp off the interstate toward Orlinda Valley. The country breeze whipped through my hair as I tapped my hand in rhythm to the music blaring from my speakers. I turned down a back road to take an alternate way to Kora's, because I wasn't ready to drive through downtown yet. I was sure I'd see someone walking or driving who would recognize me, even in this Jeep, and it wouldn't take long for word to get back to my mother that I was home. I was already risking being seen by my mother staying at Kora's, since Kora's five-acre property was adjacent to my family's land. My mother had sold her the lot years ago, and she had lived there until recently when she moved in with Kai.

I turned off the road onto the gravel driveway, and the tiny brick ranch house came into view. It was the house my parents had lived in when they were first married, on the twenty-five acres of farmland they'd bought along the Red River. Once their family grew, they built a bigger house on the adjacent property, and Mom lived there still.

I followed the driveway to the rear of the house and pulled in next to a car I didn't recognize—not that that was a surprise, since I'd been gone for five years. But Kai hadn't mentioned that anyone else would be staying here. On the other hand, maybe he wouldn't have told me about them because he didn't know I was arriving a week earlier than planned.

I sent Kai a text telling him I arrived early and waited for an answer while the song that was on ended and another began. When I got tired of waiting, I figured I had a choice: I could either stay here or go say hi.

"Oh well. Hope the person's friendly." I grabbed my duffle bag from the back seat—I'd get the rest of my stuff out later once I decided what to do with it. I knocked and waited, but there was no answer. After knocking again with the same result, I found the key under the flowerpot where Kai said it would be, and let myself in.

The house had an open floor plan, so I could see the kitchen and living room from where I stood near the door. Off to the right was a short hallway which held the bathroom and the only bedroom. I glanced around and saw no evidence of anyone staying in the house.

I shrugged and dropped my bag on the floor, then pulled a glass from the cabinet, filled it with water, and took a deep drink as I leaned against the counter.

I stood tall and craned my neck toward the music I heard coming from the bathroom. *What the hell?* My eyes darted toward the closed bathroom door. Someone *was* here. I could hear what sounded like a woman talking—or was it singing?—but it was hard to make out.

Should I tell whoever it is they have company? I thought, then shook my head. Why should I? Whoever it was, they probably weren't supposed to be here, anyway. I squared my shoulders as the door swung open.

The occupant—yes, it was a woman—strolled out, her body wrapped in a short white towel that barely covered her ass and showed off her toned, sun-tanned legs. She had another towel twisted around her head which bobbed side to side, and she wiggled her hips in tune to the music. The view from here was well worth my price of admission. *Damn. Welcome home, Rowan!*

She spun to the music as she released the towel from her head and let out a blood curdling scream as soon as her eyes focused on me. Her hand grabbed the front of the towel as it came loose and fell down her front giving me a brief, but much appreciated, glimpse of some amazing cleavage before she pulled it up again.

My brows popped, and the grin I'd started when she wiggled her way out of the bathroom now filled my face.

"Holy flying fuck," she raged, her voice laced with venom and eyes wide with shock. "You scared the living shit out of me, Rowan."

Summer. She still looked amazing and had a mouth that would embarrass a sailor. Nothing had changed, and I loved that about her.

"Damn, Summer. That mouth of yours and that show you just gave me in that get-up you're wearing would get me hard if you weren't my best friend."

I placed the glass on the counter and crossed my arms over my chest.

Her beautiful face reddened with rage and her chest strained against the towel as she seethed. Yep, she still hated surprises, and clearly the fact that I'd surprised her had pissed her right the hell off. A pissed Summer was an entertaining Summer, and her mouth and no-bullshit attitude were things about her I could always relate to. She'd always been beautiful in her own way—all female, yet able to wield the harsh words and bitchy attitude that made so many guys afraid of her.

Not me, though. I loved that about her. If it hadn't been for her, my status as the youngest of three boys would have sent me off the deep end a lot earlier than it did.

That, and she made me feel things no one else ever had.

I looked her up and down again. She'd been athletic in high school, and from what I could see of her now—which was quite a lot because of that very skimpy towel—her legs were still long, tan, and fit, and her skin golden and smooth. Her hair hung in wet waves down her back but appeared to be almost back to her normal light-brown color. And, of course, her deep cleavage still looked amazing as ever.

"What the hell are you doing here?" she snapped, her voice losing its edge. She stood up taller, the scare she'd gotten now totally resolved and her take-no-shit attitude one hundred percent back in place.

"I could ask you the same thing." I pushed away from the counter. "Kai gave me permission to stay here and told me where to find the key. He said the house was empty." I strutted toward her, my gaze traveled up and down her body.

I talked to her every week, but a phone camera was not the same as talking face-to-face. Seeing her in person was so much better. Seeing her in person in a towel and getting a quick flash of booby goodness—well, *that* was a bonus.

Summer held her ground, her stance strong and her hands on her hips. "Kora gave me permission and told me the same thing. It's her place, so her word holds truer."

I shook my head. "Well Summertime, it looks like we may have a problem. It's good to see you, though." I opened my arms and raised my brow. She rolled her eyes and walked into my embrace.

She smelled like she always had, like honeysuckle, coconuts, and sunshine. The perfect scents of Summer.

For the first time since I left the Army, it felt good to be home.

Chapter 2

Summer

I walked into the bedroom with a slight bounce in my step, though I sure as hell wasn't going to let Rowan know he did that to me. He had a way of always making me happier simply by being in his presence. I threw on a sports bra, tank top, and yoga pants, then joined Rowan back in the living room.

"I'm going to fix me a coffee. Want anything?" I asked him.

"Got a water. Thanks."

As I waited for my coffee to brew, I studied Rowan's back as he looked at photos on Kora's mantle that she hadn't packed up. His fitted army-green T-shirt defined his muscles, the sleeves hugging biceps that bulged slightly as he picked up a picture. His dark hair was cut short and tight on the sides and longer on top—still perfectly neat and tidy, like it always had been. His complexion was tanned, showing he'd spent time outdoors, and a slight five o'clock shadow darkened his strong jawline. My eyes traveled down his back to his ass, which filled out his jeans nicely.

Yeah, he was my best friend, but I'd be blind if I didn't notice how amazing he looked. He turned, and when his large brown eyes caught mine, I could swear they glimmered as a smile grew on his face.

I returned the smile and cleared the sudden frog in my throat. "Sure, you don't want anything?" I asked him.

"Nope, I'm good." He sat on the couch, his back to me once again.

I finished fixing my coffee and plopped down next to him. I took a sip and smiled over the top of my mug. "So, did you lose track of time in your quest to keep America safe? The wedding's in a couple of weeks. I thought you weren't coming home till right before."

"Nope. I know what the date is. Had a chance to get home and thought I'd surprise everyone." Rowan chuckled, the sound deep and relaxed. He'd nestled in the corner of the couch with one arm draped over the back, and while he'd looked good from behind, this view was even better. His smile ticked up a notch. "Looks like so far I succeeded."

I placed my mug on the table next to me and slapped his arm resting over the back of the couch. "Yeah, dumb shit. You could say that." I closed my hand over his forearm. "It's good you're home." I leaned in and hugged him around his neck.

Now that I was fully clothed and not scared as shit because some person who shouldn't be in my kitchen was gawking at me in a towel, I could enjoy the hug, and the feeling of familiarity returned. Rowan was here in the flesh—finally.

Rowan was more than my best friend. He'd been like a brother to me. We'd been inseparable in school, to the point that other guys were scared to approach me because they thought we were an item.

We hadn't been, even though I had to work hard at getting even Kora and Darlene to understand that—while secretly admitting to myself that sometimes I'd wished we were. But I'm not a relationship type of gal. And, besides, he was never in need of a girlfriend, since every human with two legs and tits was lined up to date him. Friendship was perfect from where I sat.

He squeezed me back, his hug solid. My entire body relaxed against him, and I didn't miss the sigh that escaped his lungs, or the way he seemed to slump against my shoulder. I held him a little longer. I could feel his heartbeat slow through his tight shirt. My insides fluttered as the scent of him—masculine and outdoorsy—soaked into my senses.

I patted his back. "Hey." I pulled away and held his arms so I could look him in the eyes, which had grown distant and serious. "Is everything okay?" His gaze darted around my face like he was searching for something. I cocked my head.

"Yeah, everything's perfect." A smile lit up his face again, and he trailed his fingers through the wet hair hanging over my shoulders and sucked in his lips. It was obvious his thoughts were far away. He was here, looking at me, yet he wasn't. He closed his eyes briefly and when he opened them, the distance was gone.

He stood and picked up his duffle bag from the floor. "I'm going to throw my bag into *our* room, hop in the shower, then unpack. I hope there's room for my stuff in the closet. It's going to be a tight stay." He winked and walked away.

Again, my gaze followed him. I couldn't lie. He looked good, probably better than ever. A warmth stirred deep in my gut. I swallowed, ignored the feeling, and got to work straightening up the place. I picked up a spare bra and pair of panties from the floor of the bedroom and moved clothes around in the dresser to give him a drawer and some space in the closet. I wasn't sure how this was going to work, but I didn't think it would be for long. At least it didn't look like he brought much with him.

I exited the closet at the same time a towel-clad Rowan entered the bedroom.

My mouth went dry. *Fuck me.*

My eyes traveled over his perfectly chiseled chest down to the spattering of hair at his navel. I promise I never let that trail of hair lead my eyes to the secret spot where it vanished beneath the towel—the towel that hung loosely on the alluring curve of his sculpted hips and waist.

He dried his hair with a hand towel and gazed around the room.

My body needed to get a grip. It wasn't the first time I'd been alone with a barely clothed Rowan. At the river in our swimsuits, we wore less, but that was a young teenage Rowan, and this man who stood in front of me was more of an Adonis than the Rowan I remembered.

I quietly cleared my throat so I could speak. "I emptied a drawer for you." I gestured toward it. "And made room in the closet."

"Thanks. I didn't bring much, so this will work just fine."

Just then a knock on the door took my attention away from Rowan and the thickness of the air in the room. I pointed. "Gotta get that."

He stepped out of the way.

I brushed past him and breathed for the first time since I got to admire him in a towel.

"Hey." Kora let herself in the house.

"Hope we're not interrupting anything," Kai answered as he closed the door behind them.

"Yeah, about that." My voice was thick with irritation, and my eyes held Kora's.

The smirk that filled her face was too much. Kora, my best friend since forever, always wanted Rowan and me to hook up. In Kora's demented mind, Darlene was with Bryson, and if Rowan and I were a couple, we would all be one big happy family.

"Kora, enough," I said as I held her gaze and crossed my arms over my chest, willing her to get the message that Rowan and I *weren't* going to happen.

"There's my favorite cousin," Rowan's deep voice bellowed from behind me. He strutted past and wrapped Kora in a tight bear hug and twirled her in a circle. As he passed, the smell of sage and cedarwood lingered in the air.

Kai's face lit up as Kora's laugh filled the room. Those two were disgustingly sweet together.

"Rowan." Kai stepped forward and greeted him with his hand out.

Rowan grasped Kai's hand and patted him on the shoulder with the other. "Kai, it's so good to meet you in person." He glanced at Kora. "From the glow radiating off my cousin, you must make her pretty happy."

"I try."

Kora brushed her hand through the air. "Enough with that. What the hell are you doing here this early? I about went into a panic when Kai told me you were coming in and were staying here." She looked at me, then back to Rowan, then to me. "Sorry, Summer. This is a tiny miscommunication."

I raised my brow. "That's the understatement of the century."

"Yeah, I wish I could have one of you stay with us," Kai said, "but I promised my sister that she could, and our other two bedrooms are filled with shit—Kora's stuff in one and building materials in the other."

"It's all good," Rowan said, waving his hand in the air as if sweeping away their worries. "I'm sure Summer won't mind sleeping on the couch, or maybe she could go to my mother's house. She has plenty of room."

"I was here first, so you get the couch. And there's no fucking way any time this century that I'm going to Tonya's." Tonya and I were like oil and vinegar. We didn't mix and irritated each other to the core. Kora and Darlene always said it was because we were two peas in a pod, but I never agreed with that. "She's your mother. I'm sure she would love to have her baby stay with her. And if not, you've got two brothers with extra space, *and* five empty acres of your own itching to have someone live on it. I'm sure you can find somewhere to go."

"Yeah, well, I can't stay on my property until I have a place to live," Rowan said as he crossed his arms over his chest and leaned back against the counter. "Jamison and Lilly have weekly sleepovers that I don't wish to be a part of. Darlene and Bryson—yeah, that's asking for World War Three—and my mother, well, she's my mother. I didn't leave home to come back and stay with her. I was looking forward to staying here at this cute little house, enjoying time to myself."

"Yeah, well *my* house is under construction due to mold," Summer retorted, "so I'm out of there for the next few weeks. If *you* want a bed, you'll have to go to your mom's. Just saying."

"You two can hash out who's sleeping where later," Kora said as she put her arm around my shoulders. "Summer, you need to put on something more appropriate. It's Saturday night and we're going to

Jerry's Pub. Time for dinner and some drinks. I'm sure there will be lots of people ready to see this guy."

"I told Trevor I'd stop by as soon as I got settled, so I'm game," Rowan said.

"Fine," I answered. I stalked to the bedroom but turned at the doorway and pointed toward Rowan. "I'm getting dressed. There's no lock. Stay out."Rowan grunted. "Good to know. I'll have to keep one eye open tonight. You might sneak into my bed and have your way with me while I sleep."

I huffed out a breath and slammed the door behind me. Then I searched my closet until I found my favorite well-worn blue jeans and threw on a white crop top and my cowboy boots. I added some serum to my now-dry wavy hair, combed my fingers through it, touched some mascara to my lashes, and was ready to go.

When I got to the kitchen, Kora had some shot glasses and my tequila on the counter.

Lemon drop time—our favorite drink. She poured us shots, dumped some sugar on a plate and got the already cut lemons and limes from the refrigerator. The guys each grabbed a lime and salt, but Kora and I dipped our lemon wedges in sugar.

"Here's to Rowan," Kora said as she raised her glass. "Welcome home."

We all tapped our shot glasses together and tipped them up. Damn, it tasted good.

"Well, why don't we take this to the pub?" Rowan said. "I need to see Trevor." He threw his arm around my shoulders. "I haven't partied with y'all in way too long." I knew he was speaking to both Kora and me, yet his eyes never left mine.

Again, warmth filled my gut.

It'd better just be the tequila.

Chapter 3

Rowan

"Hell yeah, Rowan!" Trevor's voice rang out above the noise of the small dinner crowd at Jerry's Pub as he strutted out from behind the bar toward me. We wrapped each other in a guy hug, with loud claps on each other's backs and a whoop of excitement. It had been five years since I last saw him—my oldest friend, my brother from another mother. Seeing him felt good. I'd needed this more than I realized.

"Come on, let me get you a drink." He led the way to the bar. I sat on a stool, followed by Kai, Kora, and Summer. "What's your poison, man?"

"Your best beer that's not an IPA," I answered.

"You got it." He pounded on the bar twice and turned away to fill glasses with beer from the tap. I took in the bar I'd only ever heard about and seen glimpses of in grainy phone photos. The fire-fighter theme was impossible to miss, from the fire hydrant and beer mug logo to the firefighter paraphernalia hung around the room, tastefully combined with Orlinda Valley High School sport memorabilia and a hell of a lot of orange. Beige walls framed the space, complemented by rich wood fixtures, sturdy booths, and high-top tables scattered throughout. On the other side of the large room were double garage doors and a wall of windows that looked like additional seating and a covered patio. The bar stretched along one entire wall, lined with stools that looked well-worn by regulars. At the far end, the kitchen bustled with activity, sending out mouthwatering aromas that had my stomach growling immediately—a sharp reminder that I hadn't eaten much all day.

Trevor placed my beer in front of me and went about getting everyone else's drinks. Kai also got a beer, and the girls ordered that lemon drop thing again. I shook my head and chuckled then picked up my beer and took a long sip. "Y'all did a great job on this place," I said to Trevor.

"Thanks. It's been a lot of elbow grease to get it done, but it was well worth it."

An older man who looked to be in his sixties, with short gray hair cut tightly around his ears and a gray mustache, walked toward us with his arms loaded down with food.

"Here you go. Burgers for the men, and nachos supreme for the beautiful ladies." He set the nachos in front of the girls.

Kora smiled widely at him. "Thank you, Terry. It looks and smells delicious."

"You're more than welcome, Kora." He placed a burger in front of Kai. "Here you go, son."

Kai nodded politely, but his face didn't light up nearly as much as Kora's. "Thanks, Terry."

"And this is for you," he said as he placed a burger in front of me.

Summer made the introductions. "Terry, this is Rowan, Tonya's youngest son."

The older man turned to me. "Well, good to finally meet you. Tonya talks so much about you. Army, right?"

"Yes, sir."

"Well, welcome home. I'm sure your mom's glad you're here."

"She will be, once she knows," Kora said. "It's a secret."

"Well, she won't hear it from me." Terry motioned like he was locking his lips and walked away.

I fixed my burger and took a bite. The flavors melded together into the best burger I think I'd ever tasted. "Damn," I mumbled as I took another bite, then another.

"Shit, Row. Looks like you haven't eaten in days," Summer said.

"No, just today," I said between bites. "Been on the road all day and only stopped to grab snacks at gas stations, then I got to the house and became distracted by a towel-clad beauty singing like she could be the next Taylor Swift." I waggled my brows at Summer, which earned me a swat on the shoulder.

Call me crazy, but the glare she shot me sent heat straight to my gut. I couldn't stop the smile that filled my face, even as I finished the last bite of my burger and washed it down with a sip of beer.

"Good, isn't it?" Trevor gestured toward my plate. "What else can I get you? Another beer? Summer, Kora—margaritas?"

I finished my beer and nodded. Travis took the empty bottles and plates and left again to refresh our drinks. I turned to Kai. "So, that was your father?"

"Yep," Kai said. "He helps Nico in the kitchen and is doing a surprisingly good job."

"You call him Terry, not Dad."

"Again, yep. Long, boring story. Not worth telling."

Just then, Darlene's voice echoed over everyone else's. "Oh, my gosh. Rowan?"

I stood from the stool. "Hey, Darlene." I wrapped her in a hug and wasn't surprised to see Bryson, my brother—her husband—right behind her.

"It's so good to see you!" She squeezed me like she meant it, then laid her hands on my shoulders. "When did you get in? Why didn't you tell us you were coming in so soon? Have you told your mother yet?"

I laughed at her million questions. "I got in a little over an hour ago. I didn't tell anyone because it was sudden. And no, not yet." Then I turned to my brother and my jaw clenched. The last time we saw each other was our father's funeral, and we had to try hard not to beat the shit out of each other—but that's how it always was with us. We never got along, and as we got older things just kept getting worse.

"Bryson," Darlene said stepping away from me. "Isn't this amazing? Rowan's home."

Bryson shook his head, his face a mask I couldn't read. "Well, the prodigal son returns. I'm speechless. I had no idea you'd bless us with your presence this far away from the wedding. I expected you the day before."

I glanced at Darlene as if to ask, *is Bryson for real?* She gave a small shrug.

Bryson took a step closer, and a smile crept up his face. "Seriously, bro, I'm glad you're home, and I know Mom and Jamison will be ecstatic." He wrapped his arms around me and gave me a couple pats on the back. I did the same.

I didn't feel any of the love in his hug I had from everyone else's. Worse, I didn't feel much at all. I'm sure he noticed the same thing. It was ridiculous. We were brothers and grown adults. We should be ready to bury the hatchet and keep the past in the past. "They will be once they find out," I said.

He stepped away and gave me a good look-over. "You seriously didn't tell them? But you talk to Jamison every week."

I shrugged. "It was last-minute."

"Well, they'll know soon enough. This is Orlinda Valley. News travels fast. Anyway, I guess I need to watch how I act this time around. You're quite a bit bulkier than last time you were home. Not sure I could take you anymore."

Seriously? We hadn't seen each other in five years, and that was the first thing he wanted to say to me? "I missed you too, brother." I stepped away from him, feeling my anger already rising to the surface.

Luckily, Kai distracted us. "Come on, let's go grab a table on the patio. There will be plenty of room for all of us."

Everyone grabbed their drinks and followed, but I stayed behind and took a seat at the bar.

"Hey," Summer pushed her shoulder into mine. "You're not going to leave me with them, are you? Since you're home, I need you by my side. They may not pick on me much with you around."

I pursed my lips. Suddenly I didn't feel like being with a crowd. "You go ahead. I'm going to hang here with Trevor for a bit. Catch up."

"Yeah," Trevor agreed. "You aren't the only one who hasn't seen this guy in a while. At least you talk with him more than me."

"The phone works both ways, dipshit," Summer said as she sat on the stool next to me. "Maybe you should get away from this bar or your cows and learn how to socialize."

I chuckled. Summer never could stand Trevor. He was too country for her, but their banter always made for some good entertainment.

"Trust me, Summer, I socialize just fine. Just because I'm not pissed off at the world and don't wear a permanent scowl on my face means nothing."

She narrowed her eyes and took a sip of her margarita. "Good drink, Trevor. At least you have *something* you're good at."

"Yep, you've never complained about my ability to make a drink."

"Damn straight."

I chuckled at them and said, "It looks like you two finally found some common ground. Guess I *have* been gone a long time."

Chapter 4

Summer

I never understood what Rowan saw in Trevor. They were total opposites. Rowan was good-looking, athletic, outgoing. Trevor was country through and through. He ran his family's cattle farm, listened only to country music, and had a strong Southern twang that irritated me straight to my soul. Of course, Kora had a thing for him also. They started dating junior year and broke up when Kora left for college, so Trevor has always been around.

I listened to the conversation between Trevor and Rowan. Trevor was updating him on some people we graduated with, but there was something off in Rowan's manner. I thought something was bothering him when he was sitting on the couch at the house, but I couldn't put my finger on it. Now he seemed really off, and it couldn't have just been seeing Bryson again.

I finished my margarita. "Trevor, I'll take another. Frozen this time." If I was going to sit with Rowan at the bar, I figured I might as well have Trevor refill my drink, since Kora took the pitcher with her.

Trevor worked his magic on my drink and placed another beer in front of Rowan. "Maybe you should slow down," he said. "You don't want to face Bryson with too much alcohol in your system."

Rowan's gaze was blank—empty. "Thanks for the warning," he said.

Trevor held my gaze for a long beat, shrugged, shook his head, and walked away after saying, "I'm glad you're home, buddy."

I studied Rowan as we sat in silence. It had been a bit since I'd seen him without a phone screen between us, but I don't remember him ever looking quite like this. "Rowan," I said and placed my hand lightly on his arm. "What's going on? What's bothering you?"

He turned and his large brown eyes searched mine. His were slightly blood-shot, but I wasn't sure if it was due to the drinks or emotions.

His gaze bore into mine, then traveled over my face. I could feel him studying me intently, and my heart stuttered when his eyes stalled at my lips for a brief second before meeting my eyes again. He brushed his hand lightly against my cheek, and across my chin.

My breath hitched in my chest. What was going on? This wasn't the first time he'd ever touched me like this, yet I'd never had these reactions before. I had to remind myself that he was my best friend. The one I could always count on, especially after my parents' divorce.

His hand rested on mine. "It's so good to see you, Summer. You have no idea how much I've missed you."

His voice was thick and masculine. Much more serious than I'd ever heard him, except for when his father passed away.

Just then, a voice boomed over the country music coming from the speakers. "No way. Is that my little brother? Kai said there was a surprise here, but Rowan?"

I jumped out of the way as Rowan leaped from his stool and beelined for Jamison, the oldest McKendry brother. The whoop they let out as they wrapped each other in a pounding hug was so loud I was sure all of Orlinda Valley heard it. Laughter and hard man-slaps echoed throughout the pub. The melancholy, intense expression had been wiped clean from Rowan's face at the sight of Jamison, and his light, carefree attitude had returned.

"Rowan, what the hell are you doing here?" Jamison said as he pulled away from Rowan. "You're two weeks early."

"What, want me to go back to Texas?" Rowan joked.

"Hell, no." Jamison put his arm over Rowan's shoulders. "You're here and that's all that matters." He squeezed him in a side hug and put him in a headlock, which Rowan easily wrestled his way out of with laughter and chiding.

"Hey, Lilly," Rowan said as he pushed Jamison away and brushed his hands through his hair to fix it.

"Hey, Rowan," she answered, giving him a hug, then stepping back toward Jamison, who automatically wrapped his arm around her waist. "This is an amazing surprise."

Rowan's gaze went back and forth between them, and his grin grew even more. "No, *this* is an amazing surprise." He gestured between the two of them. "It's good to see you, Lilly, and you two look happier in person than on the phone."

Jamison pulled Lilly closer, and she gazed up at him. "Yep, all's going crazy-well," Lilly said. Jamison brushed his lips against hers in a quick kiss.

I felt like gagging at the intense sweetness that oozed from Lilly and Jamison. "Yeah, that's wonderful and all," I said, "but now that you're here, Jamison, and Rowan's out of the funk that Bryson caused, why don't we go join everyone else on the patio? I'm sure you can rein in the bullshit that is Bryson." I picked up my margarita and grabbed Rowan's hand. Being with Kora and Jamison would keep him in this much happier mood.

"Trevor," Rowan said, "is there anyone who can take over for you so you can welcome your best friend back home?"

"Shannon will be here in a bit. Once she's clocked in, I'll come over. You good?" He gestured to Rowan's almost empty beer.

"Yep. I'm good for now." He finished off his bottle, placed it on the bar, and followed me to the patio.

We found seats around the crowded table near Kora and Kai. Keeping Rowan as far from Bryson as possible was a necessity. I was not in the mood to play referee.

"So, Row, what got you home earlier than expected?" Kora asked.

Rowan shook his head. "Just had a chance to leave early and took it. Thought I'd surprise everyone."

"Well, it worked, and I'm glad you're here," Kora said.

"Me too," Trevor agreed as he placed a tray of shots in the middle of the table. "It's gonna be great having you home even for a little bit." He put an arm around Rowan's shoulders. "Everyone grab a shot. Girls, there's tequila and lemons with sugar for y'all."

Kora, Lilly, and I grabbed tequila and dipped a lemon slice in the sugar. A lemon drop had always been our drink of choice—well, other than a margarita. And Darlene held up her water and a sugared lemon. Being about four months pregnant kept her from indulging.

Trevor passed shots around the table and waited with his arm in the air. "Here's to amazing friends, love, and everyone being together. Welcome home, Rowan!"

I smiled wide and echoed him. "Welcome home, Rowan." I clicked my glass to Trevor's and Rowan's, and everyone did the same.

I watched Rowan. He seemed happy, but I couldn't miss that his smile didn't quite reach his eyes.

Eventually, the guys went to play cornhole, and we women were left at the table.

"I haven't seen Rowan in forever," Lilly said. "I guess the last time was at Carl's funeral, and before that . . . Well, it's been a while."

Kora took a sip of her margarita and added, "Yeah, that's the last time we all saw him. He was never one to come home."

"And before you say a word, Summer," Darlene pointed her finger at me, "I know Bryson's part of the reason he left and one of the main reasons he stayed away, but it's time they both grew up. The past is in the past."

I tried to glare at her, but my heart wasn't in it. I knew she was right. They needed to move on. "I couldn't agree more, Dar."

"So, what exactly happened between Rowan and Bryson?" Lilly asked. "I know they never got along as kids, but what was so awful that he left home and hardly came back?"

Darlene and I held each other's gaze. Either of us explaining things would result in a very one-sided account.

Luckily, Kora jumped in. "We had just graduated high school, and Bryson had come home from college. We were all at the river, and Darlene and Bryson just hit it off. They started seeing each other and, to make a long story short, it came out through a lot of yelling and fist-throwing that Rowan liked Darlene, and then he started acting like a baby . . .”

I narrowed my eyes.

“What, Summer? You know it’s true.”

I hated this story. The thought of Rowan liking Darlene always made bile rise in my gut out of jealousy, even after all this time. *Move on, Summer.* I shook my head and said, “Yeah, you’re right. But Bryson didn’t have to be a complete dick every chance he got.”

“Maybe,” Kora added, “but it was just a way Bryson could irritate Rowan, and it worked.”

I pointed at her. She totally hit the nail on the head. “Exactly! He was an asshole then and continues to treat Rowan like shit and has never apologized.”

“Maybe he should have apologized for how he acted, but apologies were never one of his strengths,” Kora agreed. “And apologizing isn’t something either one of them ever did. Add that to their disdain of each other and—”

“Okay!” Darlene put her hand up. “Please stop talking about my husband. Yes, he may push Rowan’s buttons too much, but he never wronged him in any way.”

“I know,” I agreed. How could I not? Rowan and Darlene had never been an item, and it was obvious from the very beginning that Bryson and Darlene were perfect together and disgustingly in love. Our talking about it wasn’t going to fix it. “You’re right. Now, let’s hope they grow up, and let’s get drunk.” I passed shots around and Darlene filled her water glass. “It’s weird, you not drinking with us,” I said. “Soon Kora will be baking a baby also, and I’ll have to drink by myself.”

“‘Baking a baby’? Seriously, Summer?” Darlene said.

I nodded. "Fuck yeah, I'm serious. Everyone's moving on and leaving me out here by myself." I picked up my shot.

"Hey, you got me," Lilly said.

"Bullshit. You're attached at the hip to Jamison."

"There's no ring on this finger," she said wiggling her hand in the air.

"Yeah, not yet. Give it time," I grumbled.

Kora smirked at me. "You won't be alone. Rowan's home now."

"Yep," Darlene agreed. "And he's looking pretty good. Who knows what could happen."

I eyed them both. "Take your shots and shut the hell up," I said as I downed the clear liquid and glared at Kora and Lilly until they did the same, both with stupid grins on their faces.

"What's wrong, Summer?" Kora asked. "Do you have your eyes on someone and been keeping it a secret?"

"That's what I was wondering," Darlene said, sharing a look with Kora as they both giggled.

"Or maybe she's irritated because she's going to give in to the angst between her and Rowan and finally do something about it," Kora said.

"God, that would be awesome," Darlene agreed. "Summer getting laid, having a few orgasms. Yeah, she needs that. It would help her relax a little, and she could use some relaxing."

"Who could use some relaxing?" Rowan asked as he and the guys joined us back at the table.

I eyed Darlene through narrowed eyes, sending a silent threat that she'd better not answer that question.

She raised her brows and hid her giggle by taking a drink of water.

But it was Lilly I should have been worried about. "Kora and Darlene were just letting Summer know she needed to relax, and getting laid would help."

I slammed my hands on the table and jerked my gaze toward Lilly. "Are you fucking serious?" I bellowed. "Damn, I expect that type of shit from them," I jabbed my finger toward Kora and Darlene, "but you, Lilly, are supposed to be the nice one."

Everyone got a hearty laugh, and I glanced at Rowan. He smiled, lifted his brow, and took a gulp of his beer. At least he didn't seem to know they were talking about him. I rolled my eyes and waved to Barb, our server.

"Yes, darlin'," she said in her thick southern drawl.

"More tequila shots, please," I said.

"One for everyone?" she asked me.

"I don't give a shit about any of them. Just get me a couple and keep them coming." I grabbed Rowan's beer to wet my dried throat while I waited. "And another beer for him." I held up the bottle.

"You got it, sugar," Barb said as she walked away.

"A few more shots and you'll be nice and relaxed Summer," Bryson said.

I held up my middle finger, and he howled with laughter.

"God, you're a dick, Bryson," I said, and nudged him away from me. Why was I friends with these people, again?

CHAPTER 5

ROWAN

"Umm, Rowan," Jamison said as he glanced at his phone. "Did you ever tell Mom you were in town?"

I placed my beer on the table. "I never got around to it. It's been one big whirlwind of surprises and activity since I got in. Right, Summertime?" I nudged Summer with my elbow and lifted my brow.

"Oh, yeah," she said. "A hurricane-whirlwind of surprises, if that's even a thing."

I laughed and winked. I could be mistaken, but it looked like her face gained a little color. A blush maybe?

"Yeah, well," Jamison said glancing between the two of us, "you'll be getting around to talking to Mom pretty soon. She and Diane are on their way."

I blew out a heavy breath. I loved my mom, but did she have to come here? *Now?* "How did she hear I was home?"

"Bro, it's Orlinda Valley, not a huge metropolis," Bryson said.

"Yeah, and you *are* the town hero," Trevor said. "Football god, war hero."

"Trev, football god? War hero? Seriously? It's been ages since high school, and I wasn't in war. Just deployed. Not all that exciting."

"It doesn't matter," Kora chimed in. "You came home, showed up at the pub, and your mother found out you were here from someone else—not you. She's not going to be happy."

"Right?" Summer added. "I told you to go see her before we came here. Now she's going to bring her loud mouth to our night."

I wasn't sure, but it sounded like she cursed under her breath.

"What loud mouth are you talking about, Summer, dear?" My mother was here. "And look who came into town. Didn't let me know he was showing up for the wedding early and totally ignored me."

I stood up, grinned, and held my arms wide. "Momma."

"Don't you dare *Momma* me, Rowan Charles." The scowl she shot me might have gone straight through my heart if she had magical powers. Lucky for me, she didn't—that I knew of.

I wrapped my arms around her, anyway, and rested my head on top of hers. "Momma, please forgive me. I wanted to surprise you, but Summer and Kora insisted I come here with them first. They wouldn't let me say hi to you."

"Bullshit," Summer exclaimed. "Don't listen to him Tonya."

"Figures you'd throw us under the bus," Kora said with a laugh. "Just like old times."

I backed away from my mom and raised my brows as I looked down at her. Her blue eyes were still as gentle as I remembered, yet they held a small glint of hell-raising in them. Yep. She was my momma. All heat and gossip—but I was her baby and got away with everything.

She slapped my arms off of her.

Okay, maybe I wasn't getting away with this.

I held up my hands in surrender. "Sorry, Mom. I screwed up. But I wanted this to be a surprise. The only one who knew I was coming home was Trevor."

She whipped her head toward him and he held up his hands. "Momma T, I wasn't the only one who knew he was coming home. He told Kai also." Trevor pointed at Kai.

Smart. Blame the one they all love. That would calm her down.

"And now *I'm* getting thrown under the bus," Kai said. "Tonya, I did know, but he begged me not to tell anyone. He wanted it to be a surprise, and things would have worked out perfectly if Kora didn't tell Summer she could stay in the guest house."

"Okay, okay!" Diane, one of my mother's best friends, cut in. "All this is getting confusing and chaotic." She turned to my mother. "T, just forgive your boy and welcome him home so I can have my turn, or I'm going to push you out of the way so I can give this handsome Army soldier a hug."

"The hell you say, Diane," my mother retorted. "But fine."

"See, Rowan," Diane said. "Nothing's changed here. I'm still always right."

My mother laughed her laugh that was more like a cackle, wrapped me tight in her arms, gave me a good hard squeeze and kiss on the cheek, then grabbed a stool from the table behind us. "Scootch your ass over, Summer. I'm sitting next to my son.

"Damn, Tonya. If you give me a minute . . ." Summer cursed under her breath again as she slid her stool to the side. "Diane, are you two staying awhile? I thought you had a book club meeting at Kaye's. Y'all were talking about it today at the salon."

"Yes we do. We won't be here long. We were on our way and stopped to get snacks and wine at the store when Mrs. Ledbetter told us she heard Rowan was home. T couldn't wait, so here we are."

"That's right. My baby's home and I needed to see why he didn't let me know, but it's all good." She patted my arm. "Now, how do we get a glass of wine around here?"

Trevor stood. "I'll take care of you both. Two white wines? I just got a case in from the winery."

"Of course," said Diane.

"Great. I'll grab two glasses." Trevor left for the bar.

"So, Rowan, what brought you home two weeks early?" asked Diane.

I lifted my beer and took a drink. It started going down really easy, probably because I'd already had more than I needed.

I watched Trevor as he poured drinks at the bar. Since everyone was here, there was no time like the present. If I could stall a little more until Trevor came back, I wouldn't have to tell them the reason more than once.

"Well?" my mother asked.

Trevor was on his way back with a tray of two wines and more beers. He passed them around to everyone, settled back in his chair, and I took a big breath.

"I was going to wait and let you know after the wedding, but since everyone's here and I got to come home early . . ." I took a deep breath. "I am officially a free man."

"You're what?" Jamison asked.

"What do you mean?" Bryson asked.

Summer sighed heavily. "It means he's no longer in the military, dumbasses." Her gaze fell on mine. "I knew you were considering not resigning, but what the hell? You didn't say a word to me, and you tell me everything."

"You knew he was considering getting out and you didn't say anything to us?" Jamison asked.

"He asked me not to," Summer said. "And it's not like I tell y'all everything we've ever talked about." She rolled her eyes.

"Summer," my mother started, "you shouldn't keep some-thing—"

"Mom. Everyone, please. Let me explain." Good lord, this was crazy. "I know I should have given y'all a warning, but once the numbers were totaled, I found out I could take leave now and then be out officially in November." I held my hands up. "So, I took it and I'm free."

"But you love the Army," Summer said.

"You wanted to make a life out of it," my mother added.

"I know. You're both right, but I was tired of being away from home. I left when I was eighteen. It's been twelve years, and I'm ready to be home."

It was Bryson's turn to speak up, and there was a hard edge to his voice. "You were in such a hurry to get away and hardly came home at all. Now all of a sudden you want to be here?"

Summer sat up tall and opened her mouth, ready to say some-thing I'm sure would have been a bite at Bryson, but I shook my head, laid my hand on hers, and she backed off. "I know, Bryson. I burned a lot of bridges over the years, but I'm ready to repair things. I'm not that immature eighteen-year-old anymore."

He and I stared at each other, and his harsh gaze finally softened, then he focused on the label of his beer bottle.

I continued. "I have an interview with a company that has offices in both Texas and Nashville the week after the wedding." I shrugged. "I'm hoping they offer a job in their Nashville office."

"I think that's awesome, man," Trevor said. "It'll be great to have you home."

CHAPTER 6

SUMMER

Tonya and Diane left soon after we toasted Rowan with a free round of drinks. Thank God. I loved them both, but Tonya—she's loud, and always takes over the conversation.

"Alright, y'all," Rowan said, "it's been great being here, but I'm beat and have had more than my limit of alcohol. I've gotta get home. If I beat Summer, I get the bed and she'll be on the couch."

I snapped my head toward him. "Bullshit. We've already discussed this. That bedroom's mine. The couch is all yours, buddy."

Kora laughed. "If it makes you feel any better, Rowan, it's a comfortable couch. And, again, if you don't like it, you can always go to your mother's. She would love to have you."

"True," Rowan agreed. "But I'm not ready for that tonight."

Trevor stood. "Well, y'all didn't drive here, not that either of you'd be in any shape to drive home, so I'll take you. You can fight out who gets the couch on the way." He started toward the bar. "Just give me a minute to check on things and I'll meet you outside at my truck."

It wasn't long until we were pulling into the driveway of Kora's little ranch house.

"Thanks, Trev." Rowan reached for the door handle but didn't open it. "Want to come in and get a coffee? It's still early."

"No thanks, man. I'm going to get home. Five a.m. comes early."

"You still taking care of your grandpa's cows?"

"Yep. Sure am. I'll see you soon. Stop by sometime."

"Sure will, man."

I pushed on Rowan's shoulder. I'd had too much to drink and really needed a cup of coffee. "Can you open the door and get out already? Y'all two can talk later. It's not like you're going anywhere anytime soon."

"Okay, Summer." Rowan chuckled as he opened the door. "Thanks again, Trev. I'll call you."

I left Rowan at the truck as he and Trevor said their goodbyes. You'd think it'd been forever since they'd talked. Well, maybe it had been. Whatever.

I unlocked the door. The tequila and random other drinks I had were getting to me and my head was a bit fuzzy. I put a coffee pod in the Keurig.

When I heard the kitchen door close, I asked, "Row, want a cup?"

"I'd love one. Make sure it's strong."

"You got it." My cup finished brewing and I put another pod in the Keurig and got the half-and-half and sugar while Rowan found popcorn and threw a bag in the microwave. Once coffee was made and popcorn popped, we got comfortable on the couch, the bowl between us. We sat together silently, sipping coffee and munching on popcorn. My head calmed a bit as the caffeine, salt, carbs, and fake butter hit my stomach and filled my veins.

I watched Rowan turn on the television and search for something on one of the streaming services. His face was a bit flushed from the alcohol, but he looked good. Happy.

"Damn, Row, you're making a mess." I picked up popcorn that fell on the couch and tossed it in my mouth. "You might have gotten older, and I'm sure a bit stronger, but your popcorn eating habits haven't changed at all. You're still a slob."

"Not true." His eyes never left the television. "We used to eat popcorn with Coke. Now it's coffee." He lifted his mug. "My habits have changed."

I thought about what he said. We used to eat popcorn and drink Coke just about every Saturday afternoon on his parents' couch. It was our thing. Sometimes we'd even go to the movies just for the popcorn, drenched in movie theater butter. "Popcorn's better with Coke than coffee."

"Yeah, but coffee's now a necessity." He gestured to the TV. "Check it out." *The Conjuring* was on. "Brings back memories. This movie scared the shit out of you when we saw it in the theater."

The main character opened the basement door and fear clenched my stomach. "Yeah, can't say much has changed." I turned my body so I was totally facing Rowan and tucked my legs up under me. There was no way I was watching this movie. "So, you couldn't tell me you changed your entire life's goals? You had to treat me like just another one of your friends? I thought we were different."

He turned to me and waited a bit before he spoke, his gaze traveled over my body. I resituated myself on the couch, suddenly uncomfortable.

"Not like I had a chance to say anything. You took me off-guard dancing around in a towel when I walked in, then we were interrupted by Kora and Kai." He turned back to the show.

I wasn't going to let him ignore me and I didn't want to hear the music from the movie, so I leaned over him and grabbed the remote before he could react, pushing the power button to shut off the TV.

"Hey! What the hell, Summer. I was watching that."

I threw the remote onto the carpet. "Now you're going to talk to me. If you're here for more than the next two weeks, what are we going to do about this living situation?"

"Your house should be finished soon, right? Then you'll be gone, and I'll be here. So, technically, I think that makes you the guest and I should get the bed, as this is my house."

My eyes narrowed. Was he serious?

"Or," he raised his brow in a challenge. "We could always share the bed. Wouldn't be the first time."

"Not happening. Not this time, anyway." There were times, back when we were in high school, when I would be at his house and wouldn't want to go home. After my parents' divorce, my mother often drank too much and yelled a lot. I'd stay at Darlene's and Kora's most nights, but sometimes I'd just crash at Rowan's.

My mother never asked where I was, and as long as my father wasn't bothered by me, he didn't care what I did. My parents were so wrapped up in their own shit—mom drinking away her depression and dad fucking any woman who would take him. I had to have an escape, and, luckily, I had amazing friends with great families.

The nights I was at Rowan's house, we'd both sleep in his bed, but he'd sleep on the top of the covers with me under them. We were always clothed, but it made me feel safe to be able to be there with him.

I walked to the closet by the front door. "I was the first person here, so this is my place, and you're the guest. My house will be ready in three weeks. Until then . . ." I pulled out an extra pillow, a sheet, and a blanket. "You'll need to get comfortable right here." I threw everything at him one item at a time, then turned and left him sitting there with the grin that always grinded its way into me.

"Come on, Summertime. You look angry. Don't be. It's me." He spread his arms wide, and his grin broadened.

That damn grin. It always irritated the hell out of me. It was the grin that would get all the girls chasing after him, but it just pissed me off.

Until now. The slight flutter deep in my gut surprised me just enough to piss me off more. I groaned in frustration. "Good night, Rowan." I turned and walked away, but his chuckle followed me.

***

"Dammit." I had been tossing and turning for I didn't know how long. This was ridiculous. I flopped on my back and plopped my arms down hard on either side of me. I stared up at the ceiling. "It's just Rowan, and this bed is plenty big enough."

I threw back the covers, plodded heavily toward the door, and opened it. "Hey, ass, are you awake?"

"I am."

His voice didn't even sound remotely tired. How irritating.

"I can't sleep. Want to talk? We can sit up in my bed and watch TV."

"You want to sleep with me? Summertime, I don't know if that's a good idea. We're just friends. I don't want you to get the wrong impression."

Even though I heard the joking tone in his voice, a rock lodged in my gut. What was I thinking? "Whatever. I was just offering, but if you're stuck on being a dick, you keep your sorry ass on that hard couch." I slammed the door and cursed under my breath. I might not have been able to sleep, but that didn't mean I was in a mood to deal with his sarcasm, which of course he thinks is cute. I think it's fucked up.

I fluffed the pillows behind my back and turned on the television. I'd found a rom-com and had just gotten comfortable when the door to my room opened. "Summertime, you need to relax and not take everything so seriously." Rowan joined me on the bed and threw his legs on the comforter. He was wearing blue flannel lounge pants, a white T-shirt, and carried two bottles of water and a package of my favorite chocolate chip cookies. He handed me a water and opened up the cookies.

"You're not going to eat those in my bed."

"Technically, not your bed. And, yes, I am." He popped an entire chocolate chip cookie in his mouth and exaggerated chewing it.

The sound of the crunchiness grated on my nerves. "Don't you dare get any crumbs on the sheets."

"Of course not," he said with his mouth full. "That's why I put the entire cookie in my mouth at once." He took a drink and grabbed another, shoving that one into his mouth whole too. Then he offered me the bag.

I sighed heavily. "So, you're eating in my bed. Are you going to sleep here also?"

"You did ask me, so why the hell would I say no? I've never turned down a beautiful lady." He brushed my hair over my shoulder and wiggled his brows.

I chuckled as I took a bite of the cookie. "That, I believe."

"Saying I'm a ho?" he asked, feigning shock. "If so, I've got to say, I'm offended."

I rolled my eyes and focused once again on finding something to watch. "I doubt that offended you, but you've never hurt for a lady's attention."

"Well, there's one lady whose attention I've never had in that way."

I froze as my heart did a slight stutter, and I stared at the screen without registering what was on. I turned slowly toward him, my eyebrows raised. "Excuse me?" I asked. If I gave off my typical air of not giving a shit, maybe he wouldn't realize how that statement affected me. How my heart picked up speed and my stomach did that churning thing again.

Our eyes locked for a brief second before one corner of his mouth turned up. "You seem a little shocked. You should know I've always thought you were beautiful."

I rolled my eyes. "Yeah, and you look good too. Stating the obvious means nothing. That's how we could be friends all these years." I turned my attention back to whatever the hell was on and took a bite of the cookie.

Damn him. If he thought I was going to give in to that sexy grin and his come-fuck-me eyes, he was *so* wrong. Now to get my body to climb on board.

Chapter 7

Rowan

Summer froze and if I wasn't mistaken, her breathing halted for a brief second. I held her gaze and was almost swallowed up by her large hazel eyes. They were so unique—light brown with a hint of gold around the pupil. When she was pissed, though, they turned darker, almost black, like she was burning from the inside out. Luckily, I didn't get that gaze just now. Maybe that was a sign.

She turned from me and put her attention back on the screen, but I couldn't tear my eyes from her and took in her profile. Her nose still had a soft graceful curve that I use to trace with my finger to make her smile. Her cheek was just rounded enough, though right this minute it held an indentation in the center—a tell-tale sign she was biting the inside, deep in thought. Maybe I shouldn't have told her I thought she was beautiful, though I do and have since we were teenagers.

God, I've loved her for decades, and I've often wondered if she could sense it. The times I'd stare a bit too long when she wasn't looking, or recently, how I'd talk shit about the latest guy she was dating, or even the times I delayed hanging up when we FaceTimed.

Damn, this was not a time to go there. I wiggled my way under the comforter and sheet. "Summer, find something you want to watch, and don't mind me."

"Wait, you say that and then get comfortable in my bed?"

"What did I say?" I asked.

"That you've always thought I was beautiful."

I should have realized she wouldn't let that comment go. I was sure her guys-are-shit-and-aren't-to-be-trusted senses were tingling. Hell, with her this close, I had to admit my senses were also tingling, and not in a this is my best friend kind of way. "Good night, Summertime. I didn't mean anything by it. Just joshing you like usual."

She rolled her eyes and smiled. "So, I'm not beautiful?"

I shrugged. "Not if it puts me back on the couch."

"You're a dick."

I chuckled. Things were back to normal. "Damn, this bed is comfy. So much better than the couch."

"I'm glad you approve," Summer said. "Keep on your side, and don't steal the covers."

"Well, you make sure to keep your hands to yourself and don't take advantage of me. It's been a long day and I'm exhausted. I have no energy to fight you off." I rolled away from her. I didn't need to feel her body or heat at all. I was already having issues keeping my dick under control.

I closed my eyes, and a vision of her from earlier came to me. As I lay on the couch, having rejected her offer of the bed, I'd watched her ass as she walked away. It had always been a perfect ass, but it looked even better now with years of maturity behind her. I sighed deeply.

"You good?" she asked.

"Yep," I answered. "Though sleeping in lounge pants is something new for me. I usually sleep in boxers—or better yet, let it all hang out."

"Not tonight, you don't. If you want to stay in here, you'll keep your pants on."

"Gotcha. Good night."

"Good night."

I closed my eyes, suddenly exhausted.

"Hey, Row?"

"Yeah?" I answered, my voice already heavy with sleep.

"I'm glad you're here."

My heartbeat settled in my chest and a smile filled my face. "Me too, Summertime."

Tonight would have been the perfect time to tell her the real reason I came home, but I'd be seeing her every day, and had nothing but time now. Tomorrow was another day. We could talk then.

I snuggled down into the pillow. Her quiet laugh at the television screen relaxed me and guided me to sleep.

"Something smells amazing!" I said, my voice scratchy and frog-like after I woke up the next morning. I stretched my arms over my head, scrubbed my hands over my face, and felt the mattress give a little.

"It's about time you woke up," Summer said as she sat next to me on the edge of the bed, two coffees in her hand.

I pushed to sitting and combed my fingers through my hair. "Good morning." I took the coffee from her and took a sip. Rich and creamy. "Thanks."

"Don't thank me. Just get your lazy ass up." She slapped my legs.

I pulled my feet from under the blanket and placed them over her lap.

"Come on Rowan. I hate feet and you know it."

I chuckled. "Summer, when are you going to stop with your grumpiness? When you smile and have fun, you're so much prettier."

"First off, it's seven a.m. Too early to be happy. Second, I'm not grumpy. I just don't like your freaking fungus feet all over me."

I lifted my feet toward her face and wiggled my toes. "Lick 'em, Summer," I said in the sexiest voice I could muster this early in the morning. "You know you want to."

She pulled my toe so hard it cracked. "Ow. Fuck." I jerked it away. "What did you do that for?" I sat up taller.

"If you would have kept your fungus to yourself, you wouldn't have had that happen to you." The corner of her mouth ticked up and she hid her face in her coffee mug.

I watched her as she sipped her coffee. Her brown hair was stacked on top of her head in a messy bun, and some pieces of hair hung loose. Her face was just how I liked it best—void of makeup. Her hazel eyes popped more when fakeness didn't hide them. "You look good, Summertime. Relaxed. And even though you try to hide it from everyone, you look happy and content."

She blinked a couple times, her way of taking in a comment she didn't want, then smiled. "Thanks. Maybe it's the company. I'm really glad you're here, Row. Even though you do snore."

I chuckled. "Bullshit. I don't snore."

"Prove it." She lifted her brow in a challenge and walked out of the room.

I shook my head, got out of bed, hopped in the shower, and got dressed.

When I walked into the kitchen, Summer was standing by the counter eating a bagel. "Made you breakfast," she said as she gestured to the plate next to her.

See, she *was* a caring person. She might try to make the world believe she didn't give a shit about anyone or anything, but Kora, Darlene, and I knew that was just a cover. A safety device she put in place years ago. But she cared. When it came to her friends, she cared a lot.

I filled my coffee and took a seat. "Thanks for the bagel."

"Of course," she answered, not taking her eyes from her phone.

"So, what do you say we go to the river today?" I asked.

"The water's a little chilly. It's October."

"Yeah, but it's supposed to be seventy-eight and sunny. Come on. Just sit in the sun, listen to the water. I miss it."

"Fine," she said.

"Great. I should probably say good morning to my mother first, then we can get out of here."

"Well, she's not home," I said as I peeked through the kitchen door of my mother's. The kitchen was dark and empty. I shrugged and slung my arm over Summer's shoulders and led her back down the path between my mother's house and Kora's property. "You're my witness I stopped by."

The morning was already perfect. There was something about Tennessee in October. Even though today was going to be slightly warmer than average, the humidity was non-existent and the sun was bright.

"Shit." Summer stopped abruptly and I about fell over her.

"What's wrong?" I looked at her then followed her gaze down the path.

A rooster—an enormous rooster with brown feathers, a long black tail plume, and a large red comb and wattle—was there on the path, blocking our way. "I thought Kora took her chickens to Kai's already," I said.

"She did. Except him. Big Red."

"He's a large, good-looking cock. Don't tell me you're scared of cocks, Summer." I chuckled and wiggled my brow as I continued walking, but Summer didn't react at all to my joke. She grabbed my arm and jerked me to a hard stop.

"It's a chicken, Summer. What's the big deal?"

"He's not a chicken. He's the devil dressed in chicken feathers. He's pure evil and out for blood."

I laughed. Couldn't help it. From what I saw, it was nothing more than a rooster.

Just then, he crowed—a loud, jarring crow that echoed against the trees and along the openness of the field.

"See. He's the devil, and he's warning us we're in his way," she hissed.

I studied her, then reached up and placed my hands on either side of her face, gently forcing her to look up and meet my eyes. Hers were round and full of fear, but she didn't fight me. "Summer, you're acting insane. It's only a rooster, and if he's a little upset, he should be. All his women were taken away from him, and he was left behind." I left Summer and walked toward the rooster. "I feel sorry for him."

I grew up around chickens, and there's never been a devil-clad rooster that I haven't been able to put my chicken-whispering powers to work on. I crouched low with my hands up, showing him they were empty. He started prancing around and fluffed out his neck feathers, rooster-speak for, "Watch out, I'm big and scary."

"Rowan, don't! He's going to—"

I put my hand out toward Summer. "Shhh, shhh, Summer," I whispered. She needed to be quiet. I was determined to get this rooster.

He let out another crow as I closed in. Just a few more slow, quiet steps and I'd pounce and grab him, holding down his wings, and I'd be able to pick him up without him flying away. I froze for a second, a step away.

Then I pounced—and he jumped and flapped his wings and hit me square in the chest with his talons. "Fuck!" He kept at it. One thing when you have wings, your jumps tend to keep you in the air. He kept hitting me with those fucking spurs he had on the back of his feet, and the squawk that came from him was ear-splitting.

I did the only thing I could. I rolled in a ball and covered my head with my arms as he continued his demonic assault.

"Oh, my God!" Summer screamed and I could hear her running toward me. "Get the hell out of here, you fucking devil rooster! Get away!"

I peered through my arms, and she was shooing the devil-rooster away with a stick. I stood to my feet, brushed dirt from my pants, and watched in awe.

She swiped at him time and time again, but now he was attacking the stick. She kept at him, though, with crazy in her eyes—no other way to describe it—shouting cuss words and swinging that stick like her life depended on it.

Laughter broke free from deep in my gut.

She stopped her assault on the rooster, and Big Red, realizing he'd won the battle, shook his feathers out and strutted off across the yard, swinging his fluffy feathered ass.

"What are you laughing at?" Summer tossed the branch at me and crossed her arms across her chest.

I tried to dodge it, but was laughing too hard and it hit my thigh. "Ouch," I looked up at her and tried to scowl but failed at that also. The complete and total pissed-off expression she was throwing at me made me lose it again, and I doubled over, laughing so hard my gut started to ache.

"See if I save your sorry-ass life from that devil-chicken again. Next time, I'll let him talon you to death." She stomped back up the path.

I took in deep breaths and jogged after her. When I caught up, I laid my arm over her shoulders. "Come on, Summertime. What if I'm injured?"

She stopped in front of the door of the ranch house. "You can't call me that when you've been a dick. That's only when we're friends." She opened the door and walked into the kitchen. She sighed and said, "Are you hurt?"

The sweetness and concern in her voice melted my heart. I lifted my shirt to check. "Nothing too serious." I had a few scratches and a little blood, but I wasn't going to lose sleep over it, unless . . . "Do you think I'd be safer if you nurse my wounds?" I shot my brows up.

Summer glanced at my abs and lifted her gaze to mine. I might have been mistaken, but was that a little bit of lust I noticed for a split second?

"I think you'll live," she said, then walked toward the bedroom. "I'm getting my bag, then we can go. I'll drive."

So much for concern. I pulled my shirt down. "So, we aren't friends, and you're not concerned about my injuries, but you still want to hang with me today?" I said as I grabbed water from the fridge and filled a small cooler I found in a cabinet.

She glared her famous Summer-glare at me as soon as she returned to the kitchen, then grabbed some snacks from the cabinet and threw them in her bag. "Yeah, I feel sorry for you. Your only friend works too much at Jerry's Pub. If it wasn't for me, you'd be pitifully wandering after your brothers like you did when you were young." She held the door open. "Get your ass moving. I only have until two. Some of us actually have to work and pay our bills."

CHAPTER 8

ROWAN

We filled up on sandwiches at the Quick Shop, a small convenience store with the best sandwiches this side of the Mason-Dixon Line. When you're stuck with limited choices in small-town America, the Quick Shop becomes a delicious option.

I relaxed as Summer drove us through town and toward the river. She pulled onto what used to be Mr. Johnson's road, formally named Johnson's Path Lane. It had been a pothole-filled driveway, but was now filled in with crushed gravel, sans potholes. When we got to the crest of the hill, a large two-story brick house stood back along the tree line, a two car garage off to the side. As we passed the house, I could see a fenced-in area with a small barn and what looked like a chicken coop. Chickens pecked around the yard.

"Just so you know," Summer said, "the creek bed is now owned by Kai, and this is their house."

"Damn. This is Kora and Kai's place?"

"Yep. They're still working on the inside—paint and Kora's touches—but it's mostly done." She pulled past the house and the road wound down toward the creek and a turn-around with ample parking. I grabbed the cooler of drinks from the trunk after we got out, then followed behind Summer.

"Wow, this is amazing," I said. What used to be just a pebbled bank down to the river now had a sandy area with a brick firepit in the middle of it. Five Adirondack chairs surrounded the firepit, facing the creek. "Kai's done an incredible job." I sat in a chair and spread my legs out in front of me.

Summer did the same, placing the bags of food between us. She handed me a sandwich and bag of chips.

"Thanks," I said, and we ate in silence.

It was peaceful here. The only sounds were birds chirping and the babble of the water as it ran through the river in front of us. Occasionally, I heard the sound of goats and the crow of a rooster. "Kora's animals add a bit of country charm to the quiet of the river," I said.

"I guess," Summer agreed. "The goats are pains in the ass, though. They're always escaping from their enclosure and tend to get all up in our shit."

The sounds of crushing leaves issued from behind us. Summer turned. "Speak of the devils."

The crushing of leaves became hooves on rocks, then soft swishing as they reached the sand. "Baa."

"Watch your sandwiches. They will eat anything."

Suddenly there were three goats in front of us, stretching their necks toward our food. Summer reached in her bag and took out some carrots. She threw them and the goats jumped away to get their snacks.

I laughed. Couldn't help it. I've never been a big fan of goats—well, farm animals in general—but I grew up with them and was not surprised that Kora would have three. She always loved coming over and helping Mom with ours. I knew they had names. Kora always named all her animals. When we were young, my father would buy a few head of cattle. He always warned her not to name them, but she never listened and spent much of her high school years refusing to eat beef. "So, who do we have here?" I asked.

"Well, the black one is Baby Goat. And those two are Percy and Jackson. I can never tell which is which, but I don't think they really care."

"Kora named her goats after her favorite books like she always said she would."

"Yep. Of course she did. Her chickens are named also. Edgar is the rooster she brought with her, and two of her hens are Allana and Poe. There are more literature names, but I don't know them. I think she's crazy. Just give me the eggs and forget the names."

I laughed as I finished my sandwich. The goats had finished their snacks and were laying in the sun, looking relaxed. "So, Summertime, will I be meeting that guy you told me about on the phone?"

"Derrick?" She shook her head. "Hell no. That was one date. Honestly, I think I scared him a little." She grabbed a bottle of water.

"You?" Again I chuckled, and again she gave me her fuck-you look, and I lost it. After I'd caught my breath, I smiled over at her. "I have not laughed this much in a while. Thanks, Summertime, for brightening my day."

"Glad I could be of assistance," she said in a snarky voice as she stretched out, laid her head back, and closed her eyes.

I couldn't take my eyes off her. Her hair glistened in the sunlight, and she looked like an angel—which made me snort. Summer could be anything she wanted, but an angel she was not. She was naturally pretty, and when she relaxed and didn't have a scowl on her face, she was more than that.

She was breathtaking.

She turned toward me and smiled—and I suddenly remembered to breathe again.

"Can I ask you something?" she asked.

"Of course." I copied her. I stretched out and closed my eyes if for nothing else so I could block her beauty from my mind—not that I didn't have every bit of her face etched in my memory. At least the rays of the sun felt good, and I focused on that.

"Why did you start calling me Summertime?"

I shrugged in answer to her question, though I knew exactly when I started calling her Summertime, and why. I remembered it like it was yesterday.

It was the summer before our sophomore year in high school. We were hanging at the river—right here, just like we always did. Summer wore a bikini—not quite the skimpy kind that would make me uncomfortable in the near future, but still a bikini—and the look of her newly forming breasts under the skimpy cloth, the way her ponytail shimmered under the summer sun, and the scent of the coconut and honeysuckle sun block she had me apply to her back, all became what I would think of whenever I thought of summertime.

Eventually, her carefree, take-no-shit attitude that always left me in awe of her would be what I compared all women to, and would keep me from being able to commit to anyone in any relationship. No one ever measured up to my perception of the perfect woman, because Summer was who I based perfection on.

I considered my answer carefully. "You've always been Summertime to me. I never wanted to forget what it was like when we hung out by the river the summer before our sophomore year. You were finally out of your extreme goth phase you went through and smiled more, especially when it was just the two of us."

I opened my eyes, and our gazes met. My heart leaped and picked up speed. "You were always happiest when we were here. The smile on your face and color of your skin was a perfect combination—perfectly Summertime." I moved my sunglasses on top of my head so I could see her better. Her hazel eyes were more golden today. They usually were when she was relaxed—happy. Our gazes held.

I watched as her tongue brushed lightly against her bottom lip, then she sucked in her top lip and bit down. A familiar longing I hadn't felt in a while rose up in my belly and caused the crotch of my shorts to tighten. How I wished I could read her mind. What was she thinking? What was she feeling? She was always good at hiding her emotions and feelings, while I always wore them like a badge for the entire world to see. "What?" I asked.

I could never tell what she was feeling, even now. She held her feelings deep within her, keeping them hostage, not sharing anything with anyone. She held my gaze a bit longer. My heart hammered in my chest.

She swallowed hard—I saw the movement in her throat. "I'm thinking we need to take a walk in the river." She slipped off her shoes and pulled water shoes from her bag, throwing a pair at me. "I found these in the closet. They're probably Kai's. Put them on." Then she jumped from her chair and waded into the river.

ial

CHAPTER 9

SUMMER

That had gotten way too intense. Electricity had shot sparks throughout my entire body and caused my nerve endings to scream. I'd had tingles from my head to my toes.

This was crazy. No. No. No. This was *Rowan*. I can't be having these feelings toward him. Not now. Not after all these years.

But damn, the way he looked at me, and the story of how he started to call me Summertime . . . I sighed and continued my walk through the water while my thoughts drifted. I'd wondered briefly that summer whether we might finally admit our feelings for each other, but when sophomore year started, he had an amazing season on the football field, and became the most wanted guy in the school. Then that snotty-ass cheerleader bitch he started seeing made sure we didn't talk much, and I decided we would always be better off as friends.

Now, though . . . What the hell *was* that? What was going through his mind, and why the hell did my body react the way it did? When he looked at me like that . . . Damn, I didn't even want to think about what I saw in his eyes. He was Rowan, and if something was ever supposed to happen between us, now would be a stupid time. I needed a *single* friend. I needed to always be able to count on him. This—whatever this was—had to stop.

We waded into the creek—which, technically, wasn't a creek at all, but a narrow part of the Red River. The water was chilly in the shallows, but it didn't take long to get used to it. The farther in you went, though, the deeper and colder it got. We waded just around the bend to where the river widened and became the swimming hole.

"Shouldn't we watch the goats?" Rowan asked.

I brushed my hand in the air. "No, they'll be fine. They'll probably still be there when we get back, unless Kai comes home."

We stopped where the water was still at our shins. Rowan reached down and pulled out some rocks. "Did you ever learn to skip rocks, or are you still a fish murderer?" He sent one stone skipping along the top of the water five or six times before it fell under.

"Don't know. Haven't done it in a while." He laid a flat rock in the palm of my hand, and a zing of awareness pulsed through my body. I pulled away from his touch and turned my attention to the task at hand: skipping this damn rock. I cocked my arm back, kept it even with the water like I remembered him showing me years ago, and let it fly. It landed with a hard *kerplop* and sunk immediately. I pursed my lips. "Shit. I guess that answers that."

"Here." Rowan said as he choked back a laugh, his face giving away his amusement.

I narrowed my eyes.

"Sorry. Let's try this again." He handed me another rock. "Remember what I always told you." He went behind me and placed his left hand on my waist while his right hand guided my right arm through the air. "Gently, now. Keep your arm straight, and when you let it go, aim for the top of the water."

I turned to adjust my stance, and my shirt slipped above the waistline of my shorts just far enough that his hand touched my skin. Our eyes met. The warmth of his fingers brushing my skin sent a now familiar, yet unwanted, shot of electricity through my core.

My eyes popped wide. Did he feel that? I searched his face and saw nothing, and when he spoke, he broke whatever this moment was between us. "Be gentle, and you'll do it." His voice was soft in my ear, his breath brushing the side of my face.

It took me a second to realize he was talking about the rock. I cleared my throat to help focus my brain, pulled my arm back, horizontal with the ground, and sent my rock soaring. It skipped twice before falling under the water. "Yes!" I yelled. "I've never been able to do that. You're an amazing teacher, Row." I turned quickly—and found he was much closer than I thought.

He grabbed me around my waist and the air left my lungs.

I tipped my head back to be able to see him, and his eyes stayed on mine for a split second before glancing at my lips. *Damn*. My heart needed to slow down and remember who this was. This was Rowan. Maybe if I continued to remind myself of that, my body would get the message.

My eyes—the traitors—fell to his mouth, which was inching closer. I could feel his breath, soft and warm, as his lips hovered over mine. My heart thumped wildly and my eyes fluttered closed.

The goats bleated a greeting back at the beach where we left them, but I didn't care.

Then, "Summer? Rowan? Are you out here?"

Shit. The spell, or whatever that was, was immediately broken. I pulled away and puffed a breath. "It's Kai. Come on." I turned away without hesitating because I didn't want to see the look of rejection that crossed Rowan's face any longer than the quick glimpse I just had. I needed to put space between us. What the fuck was going on? What were we doing?

I made it back to the bank in record time. I didn't even look back to make sure Rowan was following. Didn't have to. I heard his light splashes in the water behind me.

"Hey, Kai," I greeted him. "Rowan wanted to come to the river."

"No problem. Looks like y'all had company." He gestured toward the goats that were now walking slowly back to the property.

"Yep," Rowan said as he caught up to me. "They were friendly." He stood close enough I could feel his arm brush against me.

"Yeah, they are. Wasn't the water cold?" Kai asked.

"Little bit," Rowan said. "But as soon as your legs get numb, it's all good. I was showing Summer how to skip rocks. She never really learned how to do it."

"Yeah, but I did it," I said with what I hoped passed as excitement at my accomplishment. I grabbed my phone from my bag, avoiding all eye contact. "Shit. It's one thirty. Glad you called us, Kai. I've got to get to Shear Perfection." I slipped off my water shoes, dried my feet, and put on my socks and sneakers. "You want me to drop you off at the house first?" I asked, finally making eye contact with Rowan.

The look on his face—maybe hurt or desire—made me wish just briefly that we could have finished that kiss.

"If you don't have any plans," Kai said to Rowan, "I'd love for you to hang out a bit." Saved again by Kai.

Rowan glanced at me then back to Kai. "Sounds good. I'll see you later, Summer." There was something in his eyes—like all the words I knew he wanted to say, but now was not the time.

I nodded once. I sure as hell didn't trust my voice. Taking advantage of the distraction, I turned away and picked up my bag and the remnants of our lunch.

"It'll be good to get to know the man who stole my favorite cousin's heart," Rowan said.

I could tell he was joking, trying to make light of things, but there was a slight hesitation in his voice. Someone who didn't know him as well, like Kai, wouldn't have detected it, but a good friend, like me, absolutely would.

"I'd love to see the house and the palace barn where the goats live," Rowan said.

Kai chuckled, and then he and Rowan led the way up the path toward the truck.

CHAPTER 10

ROWAN

S ure, I wanted to get to know Kai, but . . . *damn* his timing.

I watched Summer drive away. I would have waved, but she never looked up. If we just had a few more uninterrupted minutes . . . I puffed out a breath, and with it the irritation that filled my gut. I've got to do something about this tonight.

Kai gave me a quick tour of the outside as he led the way to the fenced-in area and let the goats back in. "There's no way to keep these little shits from getting out." He leaned toward me. "Don't let Kora know I called them that."

One of the black-and-brown goats glanced at Kai, bleating a protest, and head-butted him in the thigh. "It seems like you need to worry about the goats more than me," I said, laughing.

"Percy, quit." He pushed the goat away and Percy yelled at him again, then bounded after his brothers.

"How can you tell him from the other one?"

Kai shook his head. "I can't, but from what I can tell, Percy's the one always causing trouble." We entered their small barn, where he filled their food trough and gave them fresh hay. "There. Now maybe they'll stay put—until their mom gets home, at least."

I followed him outside. There were six chickens pecking at the ground and a rooster not far away, keeping an eye on us. "I met Big Red, the rooster Kora left behind."

"Yeah, we couldn't catch that ass, and the injuries we would've sustained weren't worth it. That one," he gestured toward the one watching us, "was easy to catch, keeps the girls safe, and doesn't get all into being a cock."

I laughed. "Next time Summer tells me to stay away from Big Red I think I'll listen to her. He *is* an ass, and I have the wounds from the encounter to prove it."

"I don't doubt it," Kai said. "So how are you and Summer dealing with the one bed?"

I thought back to last night, sitting on her bed, eating and joking together—how much I enjoyed being that close to her, even though we were fully dressed. It brought back memories of when she'd stay at my house when we were teenagers, and we'd talk until all hours.

But Kai didn't need to know all that, so I said, "You know, I'm letting Summer think she's in charge for now, and that keeps her happy. A happy Summer is much easier to be around than a pissed Summer."

"I can see that. Summer's a trip." We walked past the front of the house and into the backyard. "I thought Kora was a spitfire when I first met her, but Summer has her beat, hands down."

"No truer words have ever been uttered," I agreed. "How many acres do you have here?"

The yard was flat and open all the way back to the tree line. Sod had been laid down, covering the areas they'd finished building on.

Past that, you could barely make out the river behind the trees and the field on the other side of the river. It had always been an amazing piece of property, but now with a new house and some TLC, it was even better.

"Twenty acres, give or take." Kai slid open the patio door and I stepped into the kitchen, which opened out to an enormous great room with eight-foot tray ceilings that made it look even larger. Floor-to-ceiling windows in the kitchen made the outside feel like it was inside. I followed Kai through the great room to the base of the stairs that welcomed you at the front door. A convenient coat closet stood to the left of the entry.

"Kai, this is . . . Well, 'nice' doesn't pay it justice. It's amazing."

"Thanks."

We continued through a bedroom on the bottom floor with a large connecting bath, still full of construction supplies. "Will this be yours?"

"Nope. Just an extra room. Eventually, it'll be an office, or maybe a spare bedroom. Kora's hoping her dad will come visit occasionally. The master's upstairs."

The upstairs hall had windows that let in outside light, and an amazing view of the spacious yard and tree line. Kai led me to the right. "This end has a small room for an office and two spare rooms, eventually to be filled with babies." He winked and continued his tour.

The office was smaller than the two rooms, but still big enough for a twin bed, if needed. The spare rooms were both spacious with large closets and a Jack and Jill bathroom. Like everywhere else in the house, windows filled the rooms with light.

I followed him back down the hall.

"This is our room," he said as he opened the door.

The room we entered was huge. I walked to the three large windows that filled the back wall. The view was amazing. "Kai, wow. I'm sure Kora loves this."

"She does. This is where I proposed to her, back when the house was just a skeleton."

After spending a little more time admiring the upstairs and the view, we made our way to the kitchen. Kai leaned against the counter. "Water, beer, sweet tea, or coffee?"

"Beer would be great."

"I was hoping you'd say that." He grabbed two bottles from the fridge, a High Water IPA and a Summertime Lager. I chose the lager. "Interesting choice," Kai said, and his mouth ticked up.

"Interesting how?" I asked as we opened our beers and got comfortable at a high-top table out on the patio.

Kai paused a beat, his gray eyes studying me. "No reason." The smirk that he didn't care to hide pissed me off.

I glanced at the label of the beer in my hand, which depicted a sun rising behind a lake and the word "Summertime" in bold lettering. I sighed. Yeah, a little too much of a coincidence. "I hate IPAs, just so you know."

"Gotcha," Kai said, but this time he hid the smirk behind his beer.

How irritating. "The women all think you're a saint," I said. "I'm calling bullshit. What are you insinuating?"

"Fine," he said, that smirk still on his face. "Darlene and Kora are always teasing Summer about you and her, because it's fun to get a rise out of her, but I don't know . . ." He took a drink of his beer. "You could have had any drink you wanted, and you chose the

Summertime Lager. And, to be honest, you both looked like I interrupted something when I called you at the river. Just observations."

Did I want to go there? I didn't even know Kai—not well, anyway. I studied the logo on the bottle some more. Summertime. Brown hair and hazel eyes popped into my mind. *Shit.*

"Fine, I get it," Kai conceded. "Discussing you and Summer is off the table. Let's just talk about you and forget about Summer. How was the Army?"

The tension I had felt building in my chest since Summer drove away eased a bit, and I was thankful that Kai was willing to change the subject. We small-talked about the Army, and I told some stories from when I was deployed. We laughed and had a good time.

"It's great to have a chance to get to know you in person," Kai said. "Kora talks about you all the time. Things you did growing up, adventures you had. Trevor's missed you also."

"Same here. And, so far, I'm glad I'm home."

"I can see why. This town's amazing—I felt welcome right away. And your mother and the ladies . . ." Kai shook his head. "Gotta love them. I don't get why you didn't come home more often."

I chuckled and turned toward him. "No one told you why I left?" I emptied my beer.

"I know from Kora that after high school you chose the military and walked away from a scholarship to play football. I know that you and Bryson had words over it. He thought you were going to waste your life. I also know that you and Bryson always had a rocky relationship, and when he started dating Darlene, who you secretly liked, that made things even worse." He sat forward. "I also know that Kora and Summer protect you fiercely, even though Darlene's in the middle of you and Bryson. I also know that your mother misses you, and Jamison thinks you hung the moon—if you don't mind an outdated saying."

"You know a lot," I said. "Most of it on point. Walking away from a scholarship was hard, but staying here and living beneath the shadow of the McKendry brothers was something I didn't want to do. And I was more pissed at Bryson for dating my friend than someone I actually liked. I was never really interested in Darlene." I stared out over the yard. The one who had my heart wasn't easy to deal with, generally swore off relationships, and had become much more distant our senior year.

"Look, one thing I won't do is judge someone for their past. Trust me, mine has issues I'd rather ignore." He gestured to my beer. "Want another?"

I nodded, and he left to get two more bottles.

"This is probably my new favorite," I said when he handed me another Summertime Lager.

"Yep, a new brand from the local craft brewery. Trevor keeps it stocked at the pub. It's seasonal, so it'll be gone soon. You need to grab it before it gets away."

Was he talking about just the beer? "Excuse me?"

"What?" he asked, his smirk back.

My pulse raced. I bit my tongue and looked at the sky. Clear blue today, just a few stray clouds.

"Hey, guys." Kora's voice floated in the air as she walked around the back of the house and joined us on the patio. "It's my favorite cousin."

She gave me a tight hug. I chuckled. "Kora, it's not like you have a lot of choices."

"Not true," she said. "Bryson could be my favorite."

"Not likely," I answered.

"You're so rude." She nudged me in the shoulder with her palm as she turned to hug and kiss Kai.

I'd never felt like a third wheel before—but now . . . Yeah, a little. "Do you need privacy? I can leave."

Kora got comfortable on Kai's lap. "Sounds like something Summer would say," she said as she took a sip of his beer. "Maybe she's already rubbing off on you."

"They did spend the afternoon together." Kai said. "I found them at the river. Well, I called them, making sure it was them, and they showed up looking guilty."

Kora's face beamed. "No way." She turned to me. "Row, are you and Summer finally giving in to the sexual tension that's always been between you?" She turned to Kai. "They've been avoiding the obvious since high school."

God, here it starts, and I've only been home a few days. I took a deep breath. "Kora, stop. You know the deal."

"What?" she asked, all innocence.

"There's nothing between me and Summer."

"Okay, you're right. But you want there to be."

I closed my eyes to get a rein on her bullshit. "What? We can't just be friends?"

"Of course you can, if that's all there was. But come on, Row. I know you. I know you both. That's not all there is."

This was *so* not the time. I didn't want to talk about this, so I said, "I thought you had an important wedding job for me. Now's a great time to fill me in."

Wedding talk. I knew Kora couldn't resist, and thankfully I was right. The subject of Summer and me was over—for now.

Chapter 11

Rowan

"**M**om, you home?" I yelled as I walked through the back door of my childhood house and was greeted with a delicious, garlicky smell wafting through the air. A salad had been prepped and sat on the counter in the same white ceramic bowl painted with vegetables that my mother had always used for salad. I grabbed a green pepper off the top as I looked around the kitchen.

The last time I was home, for my father's funeral, my parents had been in the middle of redoing the kitchen. Jamison told me Mom stopped the work after Dad's death, but Jamison made sure to get it finished. It looked great now. The cabinets, walls, and appliances had all been updated, and Mom had made sure the large space was open enough to seat our family of five, plus friends and extended family.

In the quest to find my mother, I walked through the kitchen, the formal dining room, then the foyer that no one used because they all came in the back door—and stopped dead in my tracks when I got to the living room, where I finally found her.

She was bent over, her palms on the floor, her knees at an almost ninety-degree angle to compensate for what appeared to be a lack of flexibility. Her butt was in the air—sort of—and her breathing sounded labored.

"Mom, what the hell are you doing?" I glanced at the television where the thin, hot woman was in a much better-looking position. Her strong ass was up for the world to view—and enjoy—with straight knees and palms flat on the floor. She looked long, strong, and elegant, with a body that went on for miles.

Yep, Mom was struggling.

"Downward dog," she said, her voice strangled as she hung her head upside-down. "It's a yoga position. Gotta keep up my sexy fig-ure." She slowly stood with an almost inaudible *ooff*, and stretched her hands high in the air. "Almost done. Getting ready to cool down." At that, she laid on the floor—well, more like plopped with an added grunt—then placed her feet together. "Dinner will be ready soon. Can you take the lasagna out of the oven and set the table?" She glanced at the television and attempted to copy the woman by laying on the floor, her hands over her head.

My mother. Gotta love her. "Sure, Momma. Just the two of us?"

"Nope, four."

"Four? Who else is coming? Jamison and Lilly?" They would have made it five, since they also had Darcie, Jamison's five-year-old daughter—no, make that six, with Lilly's five-year-old also.

"Nope. Summer and Terry."

"Terry?"

"Kai's father. He's just a friend—don't get your boxers in a twist. We have dinner every Thursday night and go to bingo after. I invited Summer, because, well, I felt sorry for her. Bless her heart—she looked dazed today at the salon and wasn't her typical self. She never once gave me shit about anything I said to her. It was weird and disturbing." She closed her eyes and continued breathing. "Now, shhh. I've gotta get into Shanti."

Okay, whatever that meant.

She folded her hands over her chest and her breathing became deep. I left her and set the table. Luckily, things were approximately in the same place as they were when I was home last, so it wasn't hard to find anything.

Just as I finished setting the table and laying out parmesan, salad dressing, and the side dishes, Terry entered the kitchen.

"Rowan, right?" He held out his hand in greeting.

"Yes, sir." I had only met him briefly at the pub the other night. I studied his face as I shook his hand. He was thin and balding, and his skin wrinkled around bloodshot blue eyes, which were similar in color but not as shockingly crystal-gray, blue as Kai's. I couldn't picture Kai looking like this as an old man, so he must have taken after his mother.

"Terry, so glad Nico gave you the night off so you could join us," my mother said as she entered the kitchen. She carried the lasagna to the table, along with a knife and spatula. "Terry, go ahead and sit down in your usual place at the end. Rowan, sit by the windows." My mother placed salad on her plate and passed the bowl to me. "Salad first, then I'll cut into the lasagna."

"What if I don't want salad?" I asked as I took the bowl from her.

She glared and pursed her lips.

I chuckled to myself. "Mom, you should be well-relaxed after finding your, um, Shitee—or whatever that was. Why do you look aggravated?"

"It's *Shan-tee*," she snapped, stressing each syllable one at a time. "Get it right." She rolled her eyes. "I am perfectly relaxed, thanks to the yoga, but you need your vegetables, so eat a salad and don't argue."

I put my hand up, "Got ya, Mom. Salad it is." Terry chuckled as I passed him the bowl. "Grab salad, Terry."

"Well, of course. Everyone needs their veggies," he said.

"Where's Summer?" my mother grumbled.

Just then the door opened, and Summer walked in. "Hey everyone." She briefly caught my eyes before she turned away, but enough tension passed between us that I knew we were on shaky ground. Great. Our friendship will forever be screwed up because of that almost-kiss.

My mother placed salad on Summer's plate. "Well, I'm glad you're here, Summer. I was worried you wouldn't be coming. I'm guessing you'll take salad?"

"Of course," she said as she sat down. "Everyone has to have their veggies."

I glanced around the table. "All of you? Really" I asked.

Three pairs of eyes looked at me, with questioning.

My mom used the dressing and passed it to Summer. "Here you go."

"Thank you, Tonya," Summer said.

I watched the interaction between the two of them while I slowly ate my salad. They both poured dressing the same way and started eating their salad after cutting the leaves into smaller bites. Their actions were so much alike. I glanced at Terry, but he was too busy eating and wasn't paying attention. Suddenly they both looked up and their eyes made contact with mine.

"Need something?" my mother asked, brows raised.

"Got a problem?" Summer asked at the same time. I tried to hold her gaze, but she looked back down at her food.

My mother glanced between the two of us while I sighed heavily. "Am I missing something?" she asked, narrowing her eyes. "It's suddenly pretty damn chilly in here."

Summer shook her head and looked at my mom but blatantly ignored me. "Nope. Not missing a thing, Tonya." She put her fork down. "That lasagna smells amazing. What are you waiting for? Get it cut. I can't wait any longer." Summer raised her empty plate, and my mom looked between us once more.

I huffed and fixed my stare on my salad, stabbed my lettuce and shoved a forkful into my mouth. Frustration filled my gut. I didn't know why I was thinking everything would be like normal when I saw Summer again after what happened this afternoon. I knew her like I knew the back of my hand. I shouldn't have been surprised that she was acting cold and aloof. I took some deep breaths. Maybe I should practice the Shit-nee, or whatever the hell it was my mom was doing earlier.

My mother filled our plates with large slices of lasagna. I thanked her and ate. The three of them held the conversation while I chewed and swallowed. Summer was avoiding making eye contact with me, and the longer we sat at the table, the more irritated I became. I stabbed at my lasagna and scraped my fork with my teeth. Summer hated that grating sound. Maybe I could force her to acknowledge me.

Another forkful—scrape. I glanced at her. She wouldn't be able to ignore this forever. I knew her too well. She kept her head deliberately turned in Terry's direction, but I could swear I saw her side-glance toward me.

Again, scrape. Okay, maybe I was being childish, but . . .

That one did it.

Her head whipped around, and her eyes met mine. I gave her a half-smile, the one I used for a silent question. Her gaze was unreadable, but I knew her well enough to be aware that what happened earlier was bothering her, and the fork-scraping was the last straw.

"Do you mind?" she muttered.

"So, you *can* talk to me."

She filled her mouth with a forkful of lasagna and stared at me.

Damn, she was hot when she was irritated.

"Well, I have no clue what's going on here," my mother said, as her head bopped back and forth between me and Summer before she turned her attention to Terry. "Sorry, Terry. These two have always been close, but it seems like something has gotten under their skin. If I didn't know better, I'd think there was unspoken sexual tension between them. Seems nothing has changed."

Summer and I both jerked our heads toward my mom.

She chuckled. "I know y'all don't like to hear that, but it's true. It was true when you were in high school, and it's true now, as far as I can tell."

Terry laughed softly, a resonant and clear sound, which contrasted his rough appearance. "Oh, yeah, it's still true."

"Be quiet, Terry, and eat," Summer said in a chopped tone. Then she turned her glare on me—but it was a normal Summer glare.

There she was. The tension she brought in the door with her was gone. Summer was back—the Summer I knew and loved.

I choked on that last thought and grabbed at my glass of water.

"You okay, baby?" my mother asked.

"Yeah." I pounded on my chest. "Just went down the wrong way."

I've always told Summer I loved her, and I did. She was my best friend. We've always been there for each other. Why did that bother me now?

"So, Rowan, let's change the subject," Terry said. "How long you home for? Do you have to go back right after the wedding?"

"That's right, Terry, you didn't hear," my mother said. "Rowan's home for good." A scowl crossed her face. "He's taken his life-long dream of a military career and flushed it down the toilet like the shit he pushed out this morning."

"Seriously, Tonya? We're eating here." Summer flapped her fork in the air and gestured toward her plate.

"You're fine, Summer. Don't act like you have a weak stomach."

"Mom, it's not a big deal." She opened her mouth to reply, but I interrupted, sharp and direct. "No. I understand you're irritated with me because I didn't tell you my plans."

I placed my fork on my plate. "It happened so fast. My time to re-enlist came up, and I'd been considering getting out, because the fun of the military was waning. I'm not a kid anymore. I want to settle down and have a family." I hesitated and kept my eyes on my mother. I sure didn't want to say exactly when and why I decided to come home. Not to my mother. And glancing at Summer might give away too much. "So, when it came time, I decided I didn't want to stay in."

My mother's look was full of concern. "It's all good, Momma. And you'll get to see me every day. Hell, I can stay here with you if you want."

"Are you sure you're happy with your decision?" she asked in a soft voice.

I reached over and grabbed her hand. "Yes, Momma, definitely. I've been gone since I was eighteen, and I've missed so much. I need to be home. There's nowhere else I want to be."

I glanced quickly at Summer. Her eyes met mine and we held on to each other's gaze for a beat. I gave her a smile, and she answered it with a small one of her own.

"Well, then," my mom said, "I'm glad you're home." She squeezed my hand.

I felt the love of my mother radiate through me. Coming home was a good thing. Maybe I really should move in with her, even if it was just for a short time. It would be nice to wake up and have her cook for me, and to be here at the end of the day. I'd been gone too long.

"But you can't stay here," she said quickly and started eating again.

I stared at her, shocked. "Why? You have two extra bedrooms."

"Nope. I don't. One is filled with tons of stuff for the wedding, and the other I have to get ready for your Uncle Nigel. He's staying with me now that Summer's taking up Kora's house. He'll be here Friday." She took another bite of lasagna and chewed before she continued. "So, you'll just have to stay on the couch at Kora's with Summer."

And there it was. I'd been thrown out of my childhood home. I guess it was back to sharing a bed with Summer.

CHAPTER 12

SUMMER

We had just left Tonya's and were on our way back to our house. Well, not *our* house. Kora's. Whatever. Dinner was delicious, as usual. I always loved being asked to stay for dinner growing up and was envious of Tonya's relationship with her boys and with Kora. The way she cared and loved on them made me despise my mother even more, since the only one she ever cared about after my dad left was herself. Tonya was always cordial to me—hell, she'd let me spend the night with Rowan without ever questioning us, and over the years she'd had her way of letting me know what she thought about a guy I was dating, or the latest color of my hair.

Even though she grated on my last nerve most of the time, she seemed to know when something was bothering me and showed concern in her own way. Her heart was in the right place, though her mouth didn't always follow.

Tonight was no different. I caught her eyeing us a few times. Her scrunched brows projected to the room that she was concentrating on whatever was going on between us.

Damn. I'd worked so hard to get over my feelings for Rowan. Spent years convincing myself I was fine with being in the friend zone. Even talked myself into believing that what I've been feeling toward him since he came home was just infatuation. Harmless. Temporary. Nothing I couldn't ignore.

But the second I'd stepped into that kitchen, an awareness of him hit me like a wave I never saw coming, stealing the air from my lungs. Every nerve ending woke up, tuned into him—sharp, restless, impossible to shut off.

God, it bothered me, and not in the way it should have.

"Here let me carry that," Rowan said as he tried to take the plastic container filled with Tonya's famous lemon pound cake with cream cheese glaze from my hands.

"I've got it." I jerked my hand away. What did he think I was? An invalid? I could carry half a cake.

"I know you do, but it's my favorite, and I don't want to hate you if you drop it."

"What, like this?" I pretended to trip and almost dropped the cake for real.

"Shit, Summer!" He grabbed my elbow and held me up.

There was that zing of recognition again. Damn. I pulled away and walked faster. "I'm fine. Thank you for being concerned." I turned toward him. "Or was it the cake you were concerned about, not me?"

"You know, I'm not quite sure." He winked and walked ahead of me, beating me to the house. He didn't even wait before he walked in and closed the door in my face. What a dick.

When I got inside, I placed the cake on the counter and got out a Diet Coke as Rowan threw a bag of popcorn in the microwave.

"Go turn on a movie. I'll be there in a minute," he said.

"Sure. What do you want to drink?"

"I'll take a beer. I think there's a bottle of Summertime Lager in there. I brought some home from Kora and Kai's."

There was, and it looked good. I put my open can of Diet Coke in the fridge and grabbed two beers, then got comfortable on the couch.

Rowan joined me and placed the popcorn between us. "Harry Potter and the Half Blood Prince," I said. "I love this one." I got comfortable and settled in to watch my favorite movie.

"Haven't you watched this movie a million times?" Rowan asked.

"Hell no," I said. "More like a billion."

Rowan turned toward me with laughter in his eyes. "I remember when we were kids, and you said you hoped your children would get their Hogwarts letter one day. Still wish that?"

"Nope," I said. The fun of the movie evaporated. "Not interested in kids."

"Well, maybe you should be. You know your internal clock is ticking."

My internal clock is ticking? Who the hell does he think he is? I grabbed a handful of popcorn and tossed it at him. "You're a jackass! And, remember, you're older than me. If my internal clock's ticking, then yours is screaming 'last call!'"

He laughed and I swallowed against a rock that had lodged in my throat.

"You know Summertime, we may joke around, but we aren't getting any younger. We are over thirty."

I glanced at him and the laughter was gone from his eyes, replaced with something serious I hadn't seen on his face but a couple times.

The first time was when we were freshman in high school and his grandfather had passed away. The second was junior year, when Melinda Johnson broke up with him for one of his teammates.

That one broke my heart also. I couldn't understand why someone would break up with Rowan. Now, of course, Melinda and that boyfriend were married and had two children and one on the way, so I guess it had been a good thing. But what do I know about healthy relationships? I've never had one—well except for Kora, Darlene, and Rowan's friendship. And that was why I needed to ignore whatever was going on between us. I couldn't risk losing what we already had.

"Hey," Rowan said, cutting into my thoughts. "You're a million miles away. What's up?"

I shook my head, my eyes glued to the movie. "Nothing. You looked at me all serious and . . . Well, it creeped me out." I took a sip of my beer. "Not used to you being like that."

"It's an important discussion."

I turned toward him. "How? How is our age and our biological clocks an important discussion? You're my friend, not my lover."

He swallowed hard and his gaze suddenly intensified in a way I'd never noticed. That pull toward him I'd felt at the river returned, and the awareness I had at Tonya's stood up and screamed at me.

My breath caught as his gaze moved over me— skimming my hair, brushing over my eyes, and pausing at my lips. Without thinking, I touched my tongue to my bottom lip and tugged it between my teeth.

His eyes snapped to mine again as the pull between us became stronger. Hot. Impossible to ignore. He edged closer. His hand reaching out, his fingers threading through a strand of hair that had come loose from my messy bun.

I should've pulled away. Said something. Stopped whatever this was. But then, his fingers tangled deeper, gathered more of my hair, and with a gentle tug, he drew me closer.

Suddenly his lips were on mine—and my traitor mouth, acting on its own, opened to his. When our tongues touched, it was like I'd been struck by lightning, and every one of my senses stood on high alert. He tasted salty from the popcorn, cold from the beer, and just plain delicious. It didn't take long before the fluttering in my stomach melted into desire. I placed my hand on the side of his face. He moaned and took the kiss deeper.

I was breathless when we finally separated—not only from a lack of oxygen, but from the kiss, itself. It was amazing, sexy—hot as fire. When my eyes fluttered open, Rowan looked different. Still my best friend, but something else also. "What the hell was that Rowan?" I asked, my voice little more than a whisper.

"Something I've wanted to do for forever." His hand brushed against my cheek as my brain registered his words.

"You've wanted to kiss me for forever?" I asked him. Was I in awe, or shock? I couldn't tell. But his words . . . What the *hell*?

He nodded and closed the gap again. This time when our lips touched, the kiss deepened. Became desperate. Urgent. His hand slipped behind my neck and pulled me closer.

My hands inched to his shoulders. My fingers grazed the short hair at the nape of his neck. This kiss unlike any I had ever know—hotter, more electric. My body responded as a tingle traveled from my stomach to the tips of my nipples and pooled between my legs. Every nerve ending screamed for more. Every part of me ached for his lips on them.

This had to stop.

This was Rowan, not just some guy.

What the hell were we doing?

I broke the kiss. Placed my fingers over his mouth. My eyes closed tight as I caught my breath and tried to regain control.

This was crazy. Stupid.

I opened my eyes and searched his face, his gaze. He looked flush and confused, but his eyes were filled with desire.

Dammit. This was Rowan. I held my hand up and got off the couch. "We can't do this, Rowan. Fuck." I turned away from him. I couldn't stand to look at him and feel the desire that sparked deep inside my core. I had to get away and try to figure this out.

"Summer." He reached out for me and started to get up.

"No, Rowan," I said, and ran toward my room.

"Dammit, Summer, stop." His voice was sharp, and his footsteps were close behind me.

I had to get to my door before him and close it, because I knew he'd push it open. We messed around like that all the time when we were younger. I could never keep him from pushing the door open then—and that was before he developed that amazing, fully muscled chest. Or the ridges of his perfectly sculpted abs. Or the mountains that were his biceps . . .

Sure enough, when I went to close my door, he'd beat me to it and held it open with one hand, his arm like an iron bar. "Summer, don't shut me out."

The desperation of his voice hit its mark, and I froze.

"I know, this is sudden," he continued. "For you, at least. But I've fought my feelings for you for years. Fuck—decades. Since I started calling you Summertime, I've had feelings for you."

My breath caught in my chest. No fucking way. What was he saying? I stared at him, confused. How could he have had feelings for me, all the way back in high school? When he was dating cheerleaders? It didn't make sense.

He stepped closer and caressed the back of my neck—my weak spot. Then his lips were on mine, and my entire body melted.

Melted into his kiss, his touch, his taste, his warmth.

A moan escaped from deep in my chest which only encouraged Rowan more. He stepped closer, into the bedroom. Both his hands held my head, and his mouth devoured mine. The sound of pleasure rumbling deep in his chest was entirely masculine, and fucking sexy. It caused all my women parts to leap up and take notice.

Luckily, he broke the hot-as-a-volcano kiss to take a breath, and I forced all my willpower to the surface. "Rowan!" My voice broke, and I pushed him away. "We can't do this, no matter how much we want to. You're the only good man I have in my life, and this would ruin it. I don't want to have a one-night stand with you. We would never be . . ." I couldn't finish my sentence because his look of pure desire tore through whatever was left of my protests.

"Good," he said. His voice rough with emotion. "Because I'm not her for a one-night stand, Summer. I'm here for you. All of you. You're all I've ever wanted."

God, I didn't need to hear that. My gaze drifted over his face. He was still breathing hard, and though he made the most irresistible puppy-dog eyes at me, I could see it—fear.

I couldn't take it anymore. "I'm sorry, Rowan. You know where the sheets and pillows are for the couch." My throat tightened as I pushed him out into the hall and closed the door.

CHAPTER 13

ROWAN

I laid my head on the door bracing my hands on either side. I placed my ear on the wood like that might help me hear her. "Summer, I'm sorry. Please open up."

I held my breath, but there was no sound. Was she listening on the other side, or had she already gone to bed?

I leaned my back heavily against the door. It didn't lock. I could've opened it, but I wasn't that kind of guy. Right now, it might as well have been an iron gate rather than a thin piece of wood.

God, I was an idiot. Summer had always made it clear she didn't want a long-term relationship. That's why I never made a move before. But after hearing about all the assholes she'd chosen over the years, I couldn't stay away. I had to tell her how I felt. I was done hiding it. Done pretending I was happy being *just friends*.

Since middle school when I first met her, her father's inability to be a decent human simultaneously made her life hell and caused a starvation for male attention—but also fed her fear of committed relationships. I should have stepped up sooner. I should have told her then how I felt, but high school guys rarely made good decisions, and my choices were focused on hot cheerleaders and the next party. Even though I liked Summer, I was happy with her as my Summertime—the friend I could always count on.

I sighed heavily and pushed away from the door.

Now, I couldn't be sure whether Summer felt anything more for me than friendship. The kiss told me maybe she did. My goal when I came home had been to talk to her about my feelings, and I was supposed to talk first and act later. Yeah, well, I fucked that up this way to Sunday.

I paced the living room, and paused occasionally to listen. No sound at all came from the bedroom. It was only nine thirty. There was no way in hell I would be able to get to sleep. I raked my fingers through my hair and sent a text to Trevor.

You busy? I've got to get out of this house

It took a while before I got his answer, and I about wore the floor out pacing as I waited.

Nope. Just left the pub. Heading home. Come on by.

I was out the door before I finished reading the last word. I flew down the driveway, turned the music up, and rolled all the windows down. The fresh air and heavy rhythm of the drums and base guitars occupied my brain and kept memories of Summer from taking up too much space in my head.

I drummed my hands on the wheel as I flew down the back roads of Orlinda Valley. Trevor lived about five minutes farther out of town. The night was dark, only lit by a tiny sliver of the moon, but I could find Trevor's place blindfolded.

Finally, the electrified fence that always signaled the start of Trevor's family's property came into view on the left side of the road. I slowed and turned onto a paved drive that led to Trevor's parents' house, then veered off of it onto the pothole-filled road that led to his double wide.

He owned at least thirty acres of his parents' hundred. They had cattle, pigs, chickens, and a few horses, and sold grass-fed beef and pork to locals, as well as to the country stores in Orlinda Valley and surrounding towns. Trevor loved being a farmer and a fireman, and now I guess he loved being a bar owner also. He was a country boy through and through—small-town life had always been his thing. Even though he played football in high school and took up firefighting, farming had always been his goal. And here he was, living his dream.

I pulled in front of the detached garage, walked to his back door, and knocked.

"Man, you don't have to knock," Trevor said as he opened the door. "Get your ass in here."

His house was an open floor plan. The kitchen and eating area, with a bar counter, opened to a large great room with a fireplace in the corner. He had two small bedrooms and a bath down one hallway. His spare room was his home office, hence the reason I wasn't staying here with him.

He grabbed two beers from the fridge—again, the Summertime Lager and an IPA. "I'll take the IPA," I said, probably too quickly. I might not like IPA, but I had to stay away from that other one tonight.

He raised a brow.

I ignored him and took it from his grasp, and we got comfortable in the living room.

"Trev, you've really made this place look good. When I was here for Dad's funeral, it was not much at all."

"Don't be so nice. What you mean is, it was a run-down shit hole. Yeah, I considered building, but it's amazing what pulling up old carpet, adding some new additions to the cabinets, and a coat or three of paint can do." He placed his feet on the coffee table and crossed his ankles. "So, what the hell happened with you? You sounded desperate."

"Sounded?" I asked as my brows creased. "I sent you a text."

"Yeah, well I heard your tone in the words—or, better yet, the words you didn't say."

I haven't been home in about five years, and I didn't come here to talk about the shit that happened tonight. "I'm not here for advice or to talk about me. I want to know what you've been up to." I sat back. Talking to Trevor had been a good idea.

"I've been up to nothing," he said.

I sat and waited for him to elaborate. When he didn't, I said, "The pub seems to be doing great."

"It is," he said.

"How's your shoulder?"

"Getting better. Now, back to you."

I chuckled. "Dipshit, don't do that. Let's talk more. Are you going to be able to be a fireman again, or are you done?" Trevor had injured his shoulder pretty seriously in a house fire about a year ago. He'd been lucky that was all he'd injured, as the roof had collapsed while he was still inside.

"I was just cleared, actually. My last surgery did what it was supposed to do, and I have full movement."

"No shit." I sat up and leaned on my knees. "That's awesome. So, when do you get back on the job?"

"Next week. I won't be going into the line of duty for a while, but once my shoulder gets stronger, I'll be able to do more."

"Good. You'll get back to your crazy schedule and make yourself happy."

"Okay, enough. I get that you're concerned about it, but why now?" He narrowed his eyes and stared at me.

Dammit. I sat back. "I haven't seen you in person in five years. Can't a guy just be interested in his best friend?" Suddenly, this couch was not comfortable. I crossed my ankle over my right knee and tried to look relaxed. I hoped I looked better than I felt.

"Fuck." Trevor slid to the front of his chair and leaned on his thighs. "You screwed Summer."

I chuckled. "Well, not the way you mean, but yeah."

"What?"

I leaned my elbows on my knees, placed my beer on the table, and scrubbed my hands over my face. I kept my eyes covered as I said, "I kissed her, and, damn, it was amazing."

"Fuck. Seriously? You finally did it?"

I kept my face covered and nodded.

He laughed. "I'm guessing that with you being here right now and looking like shit, things didn't go as you hoped. But it couldn't have been just a kiss. Summer would have been able to handle that."

I puffed out a breath, dropped my hands, and looked at him. "I told her how I felt about her. How I've always felt."

"Holy Christ almighty." Trevor smacked his hands on his thighs and jumped up with a whoop and holler. "I can't believe it. You finally bit the bullet. Took the plunge. Threw caution to the wind."

I cocked my head. "What the hell is up with you?" Knots pulled tight in my gut as I thought about my situation. "You realize it didn't go well. I'm here, and not at the house with her. She walked away from me. Told me we couldn't go there. Slammed her bedroom door in my fucking face."

Trevor stopped his excited pacing of the small room.

"Yeah," I said. "I ruined one of the best friendships I've ever had, which is exactly what I knew would happen."

"Dude, that sucks. But she's Summer. She won't let herself be happy. She loves misery."

"No, she doesn't," I snapped, my words edged with bitterness. I hated when people talked about her in a negative way.

He held his hands up to hold me back. "Slow your roll, Rowan. I know you've always been protective of her. But you haven't seen her. Kora and Darlene are the only ones who can make her smile and relax—well, so can Kai. The past couple years she's dated men who are more toxic than drinking water filled with rotten cow shit."

I popped a brow,

"Seriously. Trust me." He sat back down. "You wouldn't want to have rotten cow shit in your drinking water. That would be bad."

I rolled my eyes, not because I was surprised at what he was telling me, but because his farm metaphors have always been irritating as hell. "Let's change the subject." We sat in silence for a bit. I took one final swig of my drink and walked to his refrigerator to grab another one. There was one IPA and one Summertime. I took them back and handed him the Summertime.

"Fuck, no. That IPA's the shit. That one's mine. I just have Summertime because it was left over from when Patrick, Kai, and Bryson stopped over last week to help fix the fence." He chuckled. "It's perfect for you. Put your mouth on a Summertime that won't slam the door in your face." He cackled at his own joke. At least he cracked himself up.

"Dick." That only made him laugh harder. Nothing like a friend who can laugh at you and make you feel better. "I'm glad you're still getting enjoyment out of my heartache."

"Please, you've always made it so simple. Saying no to pretty girls has never been a talent of yours, even when your heart was with someone else. Seriously. Give her time—she'll come around. You're the only one who can chip away at that frozen exterior of hers."

We got quiet as we drank our beers, but I couldn't handle the silence after a while. "So. We are right back where we used to be. Unable to be with the girls we want. How are you doing with Kora getting married?" Even though he and Kora were over a long time ago, he'd had a difficult time letting her go.

Trevor nodded thoughtfully, taking a swig of his beer before answering. "Won't lie. When Kai first came to town, I didn't trust him. But, he's unfortunately almost perfect and treats Kora like a queen. And, just like the rest of the town, I couldn't help but like him. He and Kora could become the king and queen of Orlinda Valley if they wanted. Even his father has grown on me."

"Shit, I'm sure that took a lot of doing."

"You have no idea. But Terry's staying clean and sober, keeping up with his AA meetings, and working the steps. Can't complain."

Trevor stood and put our bottles in the sink. That Summertime Lager had gone down like water.

"So, what's your plan now that you're a civilian?" Trevor asked.

"Going back to Texas the week after the wedding for the interview. I'm not sure what type of job I'm looking at, but if I could be home, it will be worth it."

"It'll be good. You've always been successful doing anything. Whether it's helping people, saving the world, or being behind a desk. You'll do great." He slapped me on the shoulder. "If you want to stay here tonight. It's fine with me. I'll grab you a pillow and blanket."

It didn't take me long to decide. I took the pillow and blanket. His couch was just as comfortable as the one at Kora's, and anything was better than going back to the house to face the emptiness and coldness of not being close to Summer.

Chapter 14

Summer

"Dammit," I grumbled as I rolled over for what felt like the millionth time and checked my phone. Five a.m. Thank God it was finally morning. I threw my legs over the edge of the bed, brushed my hands roughly over my face, and stretched my exhausted body. Last night sucked. Memories of Rowan's warm, luscious lips on mine kept haunting my dreams. I breathed heavily and pushed to my feet. I needed coffee—bad.

I trudged heavily out to the kitchen and pressed the button to get my cup of coffee brewing. The counter became my leaning post as I waited.

I glanced at the couch. No Rowan.

My heart fell in my chest, and I forced myself to hold my head up because it suddenly felt too heavy. What the hell *was* that last night? His lips. The way he *looked* at me. The blaze of heat and desire in his molten-chocolate eyes made him more irresistible than ever.

"What the fuck were you thinking, Summer?" I yelled at the empty house. "He's Rowan, he's not irresistible! He can't be."

Yeah, tell my body that. Just thinking about him—his touch, my arms around his neck, his hands in my hair as he devoured my lips—made my body quiver and tingle. "Holy . . . flying . . . *fuck.*"

The Keurig beeped its completion. Thank you, God. I fixed my coffee and trudged to the shower, glancing again at the empty couch. He hadn't slept here last night. Of that, I was certain.

I froze. Where did he sleep, then? I hurried to the back door and yanked it open. It was a quiet, chilly, October morning—and his jeep wasn't in the driveway. Where the hell did he *go* last night?

A harsh rooster's crow disturbed the peace just then, startling me. I looked to where it came from, only to see Big Red perched on the roof of my car.

"Get the fuck off my car, asshole." I grabbed a rock from the ground and slung it at the rooster. He squawked and shit on my car before flying to the ground and strutting away.

"Stupid cock."

He answered with another harsh, arrogant crow, and I slammed the door. "Fuck the shower. I need to get out of here."

I brushed my teeth, threw on an oversized sweatshirt and yoga pants, and piled my hair on top of my head in a messy bun, then climbed in my car and drove.

Where to? I used to go to Kora's when I felt alone, but I was already here. Alone. Because she was busy playing house with her fiancé. Besides, right now she would be getting ready for work. So would Darlene and Bryson. Darlene and Kora taught at the elementary, and Bryson at the high school. And that was the extent of my friend group. Shit, my life was pathetic.

I drove through town, still quiet for the most part except for the parking lots of Orlinda Valley Pharmacy and the grocery. Soon the town would be bustling—well, bustling for the small town of Orlinda Valley.

The hair salon came into view. It was still early, and I'd done all my stocking and ordering yesterday, which didn't leave a lot of extra work, but I supposed I could get some cleaning done before Diane and Kaye came in. With that decided, I parked and set to work distracting myself.

I had music playing on the speakers, the towels washed and folded, and the floors swept and mopped when the back door opened.

"Summer," Kaye greeted me. "What are you doing here so early?"

I shrugged as I put the mop away, then walked into the kitchen. "I was up and didn't feel like staying at home, so I came in early."

"Well, it looks like you've been busy," Diane said. "You must have been here a while."

"Just long enough to wash and put away the towels and do the floors. I completed the inventory and ordering yesterday."

I spent the rest of my morning planning the schedule for next week—Kora's wedding week. We were doing hair and nails for the entire bridal party, the three flower girls, and mothers and aunts. It was going to be a busy week, and of course the book club ladies weren't going small on anything.

I loved my job and easily got lost in what I was doing until my first appointment came in at ten, followed by another at eleven. As soon as my eleven o'clock left, I set about cleaning my station, just when Kaye called from the kitchen. "We have subs, Summer. Come eat with us."

I swept the hair clippings into the wall vacuum and joined Kaye and Diane in the kitchen, grateful for their thoughtfulness. I hadn't had a bite to eat all morning, and the sandwich was delicious.

"So, how's it going with Rowan?" Diane asked. "Do you have enough space?"

"Tonya told us she wouldn't let Rowan stay with her," Kaye said.

"You know how stubborn she can be," I said between bites. I thought back to last night before Rowan left. "Rowan didn't spend the night at the house last night, though, and I haven't talked to him today. He wasn't home when I left." I said as I took another bite and washed it down with Coke. "Don't know where he went." I pretended to shrug it off like it didn't bother me and hadn't been what put me in a cleaning frenzy all day.

"Hmm. Maybe he decided to hang with Trevor," Diane said.

"Don't know, don't care. As long as he doesn't bring anyone back to the house, he can do whatever he wants. It was nice not worrying about who would be in the living room when I woke up this morning."

I guess I was believable, because they let it go. We moved on to inventory needs, and this week's schedule. The salon would be closed Saturday, because of Kora and Kai's shower-slash-housewarming, so I was working later than usual most every night to make up for the lost business.

It was after six by the time I got home. I was tired but felt better than I had that morning. Work had managed to keep me from spending my time obsessing over Rowan—who still wasn't home when I pulled in the driveway.

Whatever. I was over it and glad to have the house to myself.

Big Red greeted me with a loud crow as he perched on the fence. "Yeah, good to see you too," I muttered. I walked in the house, around the living room, and to the bedroom. There was no sign that Rowan had been here at all today. Where the hell was he?

My heart beat hard, and my stomach churned. So much for not giving a shit. I needed a shower to wash away the day's work—and these thoughts about my best friend.

I tried my best to wash away the exhaustion, dread, and—damn him—the *need* that filled my gut as memories of last night's kiss flooded me. But it didn't work.

Rowan's dark hair, deep eyes, chiseled chin, perfect features—and, okay, absolutely fucking amazing body—wouldn't leave my mind. In high school, sure, I wondered what it would be like to kiss him. But he was so far out of my league. He dated girls so different than me, that I never let myself fantasize about him. I was happy being his friend.

I froze in the middle of scrubbing shampoo in my hair. What did he say last night? He'd wanted to kiss me for forever. He'd had feelings for me for decades—ever since he started calling me Summertime.

I rinsed my hair and let the water surround me in warmth. It wrapped around my body like a shield, a comfort I hadn't realized I needed. For a few stolen seconds I imagined that the water could wash away these feelings. The pull. The ache. The unwanted emotions.

But it didn't work. My desire for Rowan still haunted my thoughts. I sighed and leaned my head on the cool tiles, which contrasted with the warmth of the shower soaking into my bones. What the hell do I do know? I don't believe in relationships, and I sure as hell don't believe in love. Maybe for some like Kora and Kai, Darlene and Bryson, Jamison and Lilly, but not for me.

"Dammit, Rowan," I said under my breath. "Why did you wait all these years to tell me how you felt? What would I have done if you'd have said something sooner?" I stared at the tile wall of the shower.

Back in high school I would probably have run from him. I didn't want anyone to care for me in that way. But now?

I climbed out of the shower, toweled myself off, wrapped my silk robe around my body and tied it in front, then wrapped my wet hair in a towel to dry. I cleared the mirror of steam and started brushing my teeth—then paused and stared at my reflection.

What if Rowan and I *could* work?

My body instantly reacted, that now-familiar tingle in all my sensitive places answering my question with an enthusiastic *yes*.

But then, just as quickly as the feeling came, it disappeared—replaced by the even more familiar doubt and fear. It didn't matter whether my body thought Rowan and I could work. I had to avoid relationships. I had nothing to give to a man but frustration and emptiness.

I finished brushing my teeth and ran my brush through my wet hair. I leaned on the sink, stared again at my reflection, and let out a sigh. "Don't let it get to you. It's Rowan." I felt refreshed, if a little sad, and left the bathroom.

"Hey." Rowan's deep voice made me jump.

I spun toward him. He sat on the arm of the couch, looking hurt and a little unsure. My heart picked up speed. "Dammit. You've *got* to stop scaring the shit out of me."

"Sorry," he said.

I ignored the look of concern etched in his face as my heart thumped in my chest. "Where the hell were you last night and all day? It doesn't look like you've been home at all."

"Why? Did you miss me?"

I *wanted* to say, "Hell yeah, I missed you. I slept like shit and considered opening the door more than once." But instead, I said, "No. I was just concerned when I got up and saw you weren't here. Then you still weren't here when I got home."

He stood and walked toward me.

I swallowed as my eyes wandered up and down his body, taking in how well he wore his boots, jeans, and flannel shirt. He looked like the small-town farm boy from long ago—except now the boy had become a man. A hot, sexy man who caused tingles to spread throughout my body with one look. I chewed on my bottom lip as he slowly closed the space between us with his hands shoved in his back pocket.

"I went to Trevor's last night. I couldn't stay here," he said as his gaze blazed trails over every part of my body it touched, and the tingling ignited into flames.

I crossed my arms over my chest, suddenly feeling very vulnerable—and very desired. His serious expression remained focused on me and was hot as fucking hell.

I couldn't stand his stare any longer. I couldn't focus, yet I couldn't look away. "Rowan, stop looking at me like that," I whispered, my voice tense.

"Like what?" he asked, now within arm's reach.

My pulse raced in my throat. I swallowed, then said, "Like you want to throw me down and fuck the shit out of me."

He took a step closer and dragged his finger down my chest, from my collarbone into my cleavage, where he paused a second before continuing down to the knot in the belt of my thin silk robe.

His eyes never left me as he replied in a husky growl, "What if that's exactly what I want to do?"

Every nerve in my body could feel the heat of his skin through the thin fabric of my robe as he slipped a finger under that knot.

"Then what are you waiting for?" I asked, my voice a sultry whisper.

His eyes jumped to mine and froze. He backed away slightly, eyes wide.

I said the words. I crossed the line.

I had lost my fucking mind.

There was no going back now. I wasn't about to let him slip away and stop whatever the hell this was.

I grabbed a fistful of his shirt and yanked him toward me, crashing my mouth to his. The kiss was deep, raw, and unrestrained as if I were finally claiming something that had always been meant for me—because I was.

I broke our connection after a moment, and, before I could stop myself, grabbed his hand and led him into the bedroom. As soon as the door was closed, I untied my robe and dropped it at my feet, daring him with my eyes to look away.

My chest rose and fell as my breathing quickened with desperation. Why was he just standing there, shellshocked? Did I make the right decision, or did I misread his actions?

Just when dread filled my gut and I thought about covering myself back up, he struck.

His lips locked onto mine, one hand sliding up my body to cup my jaw, and the other to the back of my neck. Cradling my head, he kissed me with a fierce, unrelenting passion, his tongue claiming mine.

I could do nothing but whimper with surprise. It took me only a nanosecond to recover, then I threw my arms around his neck and pulled him in even closer till I couldn't tell where his body ended and mine began.

His hands on my bare skin were rough, but oh, so perfect. One cupped my breast and pinched my nipple. I pulled in a breath.

He stopped the kiss and pulled away just barely. "Summertime," he whispered. The way he looked at me and the tone in his voice when he said my name sent a shock straight down to my most sensitive area.

My hands tugged at his shirt and struggled to get it off, to no avail. I stepped away, and he looked at me like I was about to run away again. "No," I said. "This," I gestured to his body, "is not going to work. Take it off—all of it."

He chuckled and stripped. First his shirt—Lord in heaven what a masterpiece—then his pants. He stood in his boxers.

"Nope. I saw all this yesterday. I need it all. Now."

His lips ticked up in a sexy-as-hell smile that I could now admit turned me the fuck on. Just like the rest of him—every last delicious inch. And as my gaze traveled down his body, I could tell I did the same for him.

"Summertime, you are more amazing than I imagined." He stepped toward me and brushed his hands against my hips and up my sides. Chills ran through me from head to toe. When he got to my breasts, he kneaded them, ran his thumbs over my nipples, then sucked one at a time until my legs felt like they might not hold me up anymore.

I needed to hold onto something. My hands found his ass and squeezed, pulling him toward me until his erection pressed against my stomach. Then I reached between us and took him in my hand.

He let out a hiss and his gaze met mine.

I couldn't make out the look in his eyes, but if he felt anything equal to what I was feeling, his body was on fire, and his heart was about to explode in his chest.

"I want you," he said as he lowered me onto the bed, kissing and licking a trail from throat to cleavage. "So, fucking, bad."

Suddenly, fear gripped my heart. Once we crossed *that* line, we would never be "just friends" again. There would be no turning back.

I grabbed his head and forced him to meet my eyes. "Rowan, are you sure about this? What if we mess up our friendship? What if we don't work? We will never be able to go back to how things were. This is going to change everything."

His brown eyes darkened as he gave me *that* smile and brushed my still-damp hair from my face. "Yes, Summer, it's going to change everything—and it's about damn time."

His mouth closed again on mine, and his kiss threw all my doubts to the wind.

I forgot my fears and questions. All I could remember was this—right here, right now. This was all that mattered, and it was amazing.

Rowan was talented in ways I never imagined.

He kissed me everywhere. His tongue and mouth made their way down my body and worshipped every inch of skin they touched.

Finally, his fingers slid down to my core and pushed their way into me, his thumb circling the most sensitive area and sending me straight to heaven.

I closed my eyes and leaned my head back. He had taken me to a world I had never visited and knew I didn't want to leave. Then a different warmth replaced his fingers, and I gasped and lifted my head. Rowan's tongue now demonstrated secret talents I hadn't known he possessed.

"Rowan," I gasped, struggling to sit up.

He pressed my chest down gently with one hand, his eyes peeking up at me. I could tell he was smiling. When he raised his brow as if to ask how he was doing, I laughed and laid my head back. After that, I could focus on nothing else but the heat and exploration of his tongue—until the pressure that built up from deep within me finally shattered. I gasped and yelled his name, riding waves of sensation to their delicious end.

He finally kissed his way back up my spent, satiated body, my skin still so sensitive to his touch. I'd shut my eyes tight as the warmth of that amazing orgasm filled my soul.

His mouth met mine in a kiss that was softer, gentler, than the lust-filled ones we'd shared earlier. I wrapped my arms around him and held him tight, then tried to roll him over. He understood and locked his arms around my waist, turning to his back and taking me with him. He was a rock under me—and I didn't just mean his chest and abs.

I sat up and straddled him. He'd closed his eyes, his perfect face and body the picture of relaxation. I brushed his cheeks with my hands and leaned in to kiss him. I didn't know if a man should be considered beautiful, but I didn't really care in that moment. In my opinion, he was the most beautiful person I'd ever set eyes on. I kissed his chin then licked his nipple. It was hard, like the rest of him.

"Summer," he shook his head as I continued my descent, and pulled me back up to face him. "I've been waiting so long for this. I need you now."

He'd been waiting for this? For me?

I spoke his name once, as a question, but he covered my mouth gently with his fingers. There was nothing more that needed to be said.

I leaned over to the nightstand and pulled out a box of condoms.

When he quirked his brow, I said, "They've been there for a long while. A present left behind by Kora. Promise." I pulled one from the box and shifted so I could see him—all of him. I reached out and ran my finger from base to tip.

Damn, I really needed to taste him. "Just a little," I said out loud. I leaned down and, before he could stop me, kissed the tip of his erection, then wrapped my mouth completely around him.

I didn't think it would be possible to be turned on any more than I was, but—*damn*—was I wrong.

He groaned and his cock pulsed. I could have stayed there forever, giving him pleasure the same way he'd given it to me, but he pulled me up.

I sat up all the way and took my time rolling the condom to encase all of him, watching his face. Then I lifted my hips and sunk down onto him—slowly—enjoying the sensation as he filled me.

Groans escaped both of us.

Fuck, if I died right now, I'd be the happiest woman on earth.

I closed my eyes and dropped my head back as his hands cupped my ass. I started to move, and we soon found a rhythm. His hands moved from my ass to my breasts and squeezed as I rocked on top of him.

I opened my eyes, and his gaze caught mine. My heart slowed its frantic rhythm, and a calmness enveloped me.

I was fucking Rowan. Rowan McKendry, my best friend.

"Hey." He raised his hands to caress my face. "It's okay. Come here." He rolled and I was suddenly under him, his arms on either side of my face. "This is perfect," he whispered breathlessly, picking up his own rhythm. "Don't overthink it."

I nodded.

He smiled and our lips met.

As we both fell apart, my world fell into place.

CHAPTER 15

ROWAN

"Where you going?" I asked Summer, groggy and a bit hoarse from our long, amazing night. I pushed up in bed and let the sheets fall low, barely covering the evidence of what I wanted to start my morning with—but, instead, I watched her slip on her shoes.

"I have to work, and I'll be at the salon till six. We're closed on Saturday, so I have a full calendar all week." She never made eye contact as she put on her earrings.

I jumped from the bed, wrapped my arms around her from behind, and kissed her neck. There was no way I'd let her ignore me this time. Not after last night. Not after she proved to every nerve ending in my body that wanting her for years was so worth the wait. "Damn, you smell good—and taste even better."

She froze in my arms. I could feel her body go rigid.

I bit down on my cheek and pressed my forehead against the back of her head. I had to keep my irritation contained. Damn her father and all her past relationships. She always shut down when things became more than—well, platonic. I couldn't let her do that to us.

"Don't shut me out, Summer." I brushed her hair over her shoulder and placed a soft kiss on her cheek.

Her body leaned against mine before she turned and placed her hands on my chest. My bare chest. Her warmth soaked right into my skin, and a smile ticked up the corners of my mouth. "Morning," I said.

"You're naked."

"You're beautiful." I placed a kiss on her lips, and she finally kissed me back—short, but sweet.

"I've gotta go, Rowan."

When our eyes met, I raised my brow.

A glimmer appeared in her hazel eyes, and she pressed her lips to mine, another quick kiss which left me wanting more—but she relaxed this time, became less rigid. My lips curled up against her mouth.

When we broke apart, she walked to her closet. "What are you going to do today?"

I shrugged and picked up my sweats from the floor, pulling them as I thought. "Look more into my plans. Visit Trevor at Jerry's Pub. Maybe go see Kai and Kora. Maybe wait for you to come home so we can continue last night's activities."

"Yeah, well, I won't be home tonight until late." She walked out to the kitchen, and I followed. "After work, we have a last-minute wedding to-do list Kora has us going over at Darlene's. Just a little more than a week till the big day, and lots to do." She grabbed her purse. "So, I'll see you later. Maybe you should wait up." She raised her brows, gave me a wicked grin, and walked out.

I leaned against the counter and ran my hands through my hair. "What the hell am I gonna do to get her to relax and realize she's worth it?" I didn't know, but I sure as hell needed a cup of coffee. At least that was something I could take charge of.

My phone pinged as I poured half-and-half in my cup. My mouth watered as I read the text from mom inviting me to breakfast. Mom's breakfast usually included something like homemade biscuits and gravy or maybe pancakes and bacon. There was no way I was saying no.

I took very little time showering and getting dressed, then headed down the path to Mom's. I passed Big Red, perched on the old wood fence that was used to prop up the blackberry bushes. "Morning, Red," I greeted the ornery rooster. He flapped his wings and let out a loud crow. "See. We're becoming friends."

I laughed as he crowed again and jumped off the fence in the other direction.

I walked across my mother's patio and into the kitchen. The smell of bacon and maple syrup filled the air.

"Uncle Rowan, you're here." Jamison's daughter, Darcie, red curls bouncing, jumped from her chair and into my arms.

"Hey there, princess." I hugged her tightly. "Look at you." Her large, hazel-green eyes and head of red curls made her look like a tiny version of her mother, who had passed away about three years ago. "You are so much bigger in person, but shouldn't you be in school?"

"And you are more handsome in person, Uncle Rowan." She sniffed. "I have a cold, so I stayed home today." She coughed as she hugged my neck again.

Emotions clogged my throat. Darcie was five, and this was only the third time I'd seen her, the second being the time two years ago when Jamison and my mother came to see me at the base for a weekend. If it hadn't been for our weekly FaceTime calls, Darcie would be like a stranger to me.

I cleared my throat and willed the emotions to disappear. "You better not get me sick," I said as I put her down in her chair. "How's school going this year?"

"Hold that thought, sweet girl," my mom said as she placed a plate of pancakes and a plate of bacon on the table. "Sit and we can talk. She has so much to say about school, but we need to get eating first. She will talk our ears off."

"School's fun, but I forgot I'm not supposed to be talking to you. I'm mad at you, Uncle Rowan."

I froze as I reached for the syrup. "Why?"

"My daddy said you were home, but you haven't come by and said hi to us yet. Uncle Bryson said it's because you were ashamed of your family and didn't want to be around us, but I don't think that's true. Is it true? Did you not want to see me?"

Bryson, seriously? I sat up tall, anger bubbling up in my gut, but my mother's glare calmed me down.

"Sweet girl," my mother said, "Uncle Bryson did not mean that. Uncle Rowan loves us and had a very important job. That's why he couldn't come home."

"Yeah, I know he was in the Army and keeping us safe from enemies foreign and domesticate."

I laughed and almost blew some pancake crumbs across the table. How could I not? Darcie was five years old going on fifteen and talked a mile a minute, but *domesticate*?

"Darce, who told you that?" I asked as I poured syrup on my pancakes.

"Lance. He said that's what you did. You took an oaf."

Mom and I laughed. "I took an oa*th*," I corrected her, enunciating the *th*. "And part of my oath was to protect us from enemies foreign and *domestic*. Do you know what that means?"

She shook her head as she shoved pancakes into her mouth.

"*Foreign* means people from other countries, and *domestic* means people here." Should I even explain to her that we had enemies here in our own country? Would that scare her? I had no clue what to tell kids and what not to.

"Oh." She looked past me for a beat, like she was deep in thought. Then she shrugged. "Okay. That makes more sense than what James told me and Madeline."

"What did James tell you?" asked mom.

"He said that domestic was like stray dogs and cats. They got dangerous so we had to have people make sure they didn't hurt anyone."

I chuckled. "What?" Wow, this conversation was off the rails. I had to change the subject. "Okay, well, Mom," I said, turning to her, "what are the plans today?"

"Uncle Rowan, I want to hang out with you today. We can go somewhere fun, go out for lunch, then you can come to my house and see my daddy."

"You're sick," I told her. "You shouldn't go out when you can't go to school."

She whispered and put her hand to her mouth, "I'm not really sick. I just have a bad cough and contesten."

I narrowed my eyes and glanced at my mother for translation.

"Congestion, honey," Mom corrected her. "She didn't sleep well because of her cough. She's been on antibiotics for twenty-four hours, so she technically isn't contagious anymore. Your call."

"Yay. A day of fun with Uncle Rowan."

"I'd say your day's planned," my mother said to me with a cackle.

I chuckled and took a sip of my orange juice. "Okay, as long as you don't get me in trouble. Where do you want to go that's fun?" I asked.

"To Shear Perfection and get our nails done."

I choked on my orange juice and my mother's cackle rang out. That damn laugh.

"Sweety, your uncle doesn't get his nails done."

"Why not? It'll make his hands look nice and we can talk with Summer. Daddy said you and Summer are friends from high school."

Summer. It wouldn't be so bad getting to see her. I finished the pancake that was on my plate before I said, "How about I take you to get your nails done, and we see if Summer wants to go to lunch with us?"

"Yes." Her eyes got wide, and her face lit up. "Summer is so much fun, and I bet she can tell me a lot about you, Uncle Rowan."

I bet she can.

"Well, I'm going to go see what Ruth's up to. We have our book club meeting tonight." My mom gave us both kisses on the head. "You two have fun, but make sure to rest, little girl." She had almost left the room when she turned around again. "Oh, before you leave, Rowan, please clean the kitchen. See you later!"

I watched my mother leave, then glanced around the kitchen. There were bowls and pans everywhere. "What did you two do when you made breakfast?"

Darcie shrugged. "I did all the mixing. Grandma did the cooking."

Yeah, I could see that. "Help me clear off the table, princess, and I'll get this cleaned while you find your shoes. Is that good?"

"Yep." She hopped up, helped me clear the table, and skipped off through the house while I cleaned up the mess.

It was a short drive to Shear Perfection Salon, which kept me from thinking too hard about my first meeting with Summer since our rocking night together.

From how she acted this morning, I was sure she going to blow things off. Act like it was just sex and put her shields in place, which were more like iron-clad curtains erected to keep out the enemy—the enemy being me, a man who has feelings for her.

Unfortunately for her, I knew her too well and was familiar with how she shuts and locks tight that gate to her heart.

"Uncle Rowan, are you listening to me?" Darcie asked from the back seat.

I glanced in the rearview mirror and had to chuckle. The look she gave was a *try-me* glare. So much like Jamison's. I'd seen that look many times growing up. "Of course I was listening, princess."

"Then do you?"

I guess I should have listened. Shit. Do I what?—or more importantly, what would I be agreeing to if I said yes? I pulled into the parking lot of Shear Perfection and parked next to my mother. Of course she was here. Where else would she be? And she made me clean her kitchen because she had somewhere "important" to get to. Ha! Luckily, I could use her as the scapegoat. "I don't know, Darce. Why don't you wait and ask Grandma?"

I heard a *click*, and then she forced her way between the seats and onto my center console. "Umm, are you allowed up front?"

"The car's not moving, Uncle Rowan," she said with a shake of her head. "It's safe. Duh." She rolled her eyes and held her hands out, palms up, like the sassy five-year-old she was. "But you really want me to ask Grandma?"

My hands got sweaty. Why was this miniature grown-up making me sweat? I was the adult here, so I needed to put my foot down. "Yes, Darcie, that's exactly what I want you to do."

I held the door open, and she jumped out and huffed out a breath. "Fine." She stalked toward the door with her nose high in the air.

"What the hell did I agree to?" I asked under my breath as I closed the door and jogged to catch up with the little fireball of a niece I had.

"Grandma!" Darcie swung her arms dramatically as she walked toward my mother, who was sitting in Kaye's chair. Kaye leaned on her station, an amused expression on her face.

"Hello again, my favorite granddaughter."

Darcie held up her hand and my mom sat tall and pinched her lips together.

Diane and Kaye giggled.

Mrs. Ledbetter, who had been one of my teachers in high school, sat in Summer's chair. "Rowan, welcome home," she said.

"Thank you, Mrs. Ledbetter. It's great to be home." I smiled at her, then at Summer, who suddenly became uber-focused on doing her client's hair and ignored me totally.

"Hey, Summer," I said, refusing to be ignored. Besides, it would be weird if I didn't acknowledge her.

"I'm working," she replied, not looking up. "I talked with you this morning."

"Grandma, I asked Uncle Rowan a question in the car, and he said I needed to ask you." Darcie crossed her arms over her chest. "I just think he wasn't listening to me and needed someone to pass the buck."

Laughter filled the room. "Baby girl, where do you get these words?" my mother asked.

"It doesn't matter." Darcie said, swiping her hand through the air.

Damn. Is she really only five?

"I said to Uncle Rowan that my dad and Lilly were talking and said that they thought Uncle Rowan came home because he finally wants to admit he has feelings for Summer. Do you think that's true?"

"What the fuck?" I asked as I choked on the water I'd gotten from the water cooler. I glanced at Summer. Her eyes were huge and her hands frozen over Mrs. Ledbetter's hair.

Mrs. Ledbetter pinched her lips together, and when I glanced at the other women in the salon, they all had the same expression and gazes were fixed on me.

Wonderful. Just what I needed, to be in Orlinda Valley for only a few days and already be on the town's gossip loop.

Kaye said, "Well there, little one, that's something you should have asked your uncle."

"I did." Darcie said her arms flapping up and down. "See, he wasn't listening to me and so I did what I was told and asked Grandma. Oh," she turned toward me and raised her brow with her hands on her hips, "you owe me a dollar."

I had to gain control of this situation. Every woman over forty in the shop was staring at me, wearing silly, uninterpretable looks on their faces—except my mother, who was, I think, in shock. Summer stomped into the kitchen, since Mrs. Ledbetter was one of the over-forty women who were staring at us, laughter and questions in their eyes.

"Yeah, no." I looked at Darcie. "This is none of your business, and you're not getting a dollar."

"Well, my dad said you've liked Summer since high school, but were just too into yourself to realize it and you owe me a dollar because you said a bad word. That's the rules."

The women in the room could no longer contain their laughter, and the entire salon rang with it. I'm glad I came home to be the laughingstock of the hair salon.

It probably wasn't the first time, but still. "Fuck." I couldn't think of anything else to say.

Darcie stuck out her hand and wiggled her fingers. "You owe me two dollars."

"I . . . what? Why the hell would I owe you two dollars? For what?"

"Three now." Her brows were again raised as she craned her neck looking up at me.

"There's no way to get around this Rowan." my mother said, finally gaining control of herself. "We all are held to the same rule. We cuss, she gets paid. Her father pays her a dollar for every cuss-word he utters."

I glanced at her. "I'm not her father. I'm not paying up."

"Doesn't matter, Uncle Rowan. And I only said what I heard. You don't have to be so rude." She walked to my mom and hopped on her lap.

Kaye said, "Well, Darcie, sometimes adults get rude when something is true, and they're embarrassed."

"Good Lord, Kaye." I raised my hands in question. Why did she have to get involved? "You're not helping."

"Summer left. Maybe there's something to this?" My mother said.

"Mom . . ." I stopped myself, then glanced toward the door to the kitchen that Summer had disappeared through. Well, better to clear the air now than never. I sighed and stalked heavily into the kitchen.

CHAPTER 16

SUMMER

What the hell was that about? Jamison and Lilly were talking about us? I leaned on the sink and stared through the window onto the parking lot at the back of the salon. A robin perched on the branch of a nearby Bradford Pear tree, and I watched him for a while to give my mind something else to think about. But then he flew off, and my mind was back on the gossip. Fucking hell. There was no *us* as far as Rowan and I were concerned—or there shouldn't be an *us*. An *us* would destroy the friendship we've always had, not that we could go back to that if we wanted to. Not after last night.

Warmth spread through my body and my nipples got hard just thinking of the things Rowan did to me. His lips, his fingers, his . . .

"Hey," Rowan was right behind me, thankfully interrupting my thoughts. I felt his presence hovering close, and my body went rigid. I stood tall and pushed back my shoulders. *Keep your thoughts and feelings in, Summer. It's what you do best. Don't get soft now.*

"Summer, you okay?"

I tried hard to keep my feelings in check, yet even as my stomach started to churn with anxiety, my body was still reacting pleasantly to the memories and Rowan being right here in the room with me. *Shit.* I leaned back onto the sink.

"Summer, don't be upset or angry. Darcie was just repeating what she heard."

I shook my head. I wasn't good at relationships and sure as hell didn't want to get hurt by Rowan—or hurt him, myself. My family's history with relationships sucked, to say the least. And, most of all, he shouldn't be with me. I was not a good choice.

He touched my arm and the *zing* that went straight to my heart was impossible to ignore—but I sure as hell had to try. I pulled away from his grasp.

But in typical Rowan style, he couldn't read the room—or wouldn't—and he touched my arm again. "Summer! Look. At. Me." His voice took on an I'm-in-charge tone I was used to hearing from him. "I'm sorry. I know how much that must have bothered you, but don't shut me out."

"Who all knew you liked me?" I asked, my voice thick with emotion. And I hated that too—I don't do *emotion*. I grabbed a cup from the sink, filled it with water, and took a long drink before I continued. "You told me it was only Trevor." I turned to face him and leaned back against the sink. His eyes were shrouded in hurt, concern—and something else—but I ignored it. I had to.

He raked his hands through his hair and breathed out heavily before he answered me. "Just Trevor, I swear! Jamison was guessing and teasing. It's no different than when Darlene and Kora have teased you about us all these years. My brothers have done the same with me. That's all. He had no clue."

I searched his face for any hint of a lie. "Fine." I knew Rowan better than he knew himself, and one thing he could never do was lie. Even after all these years, he still couldn't. I let my anger deflate, and a smile ticked at the corner of my mouth. "I believe you."

He returned my smile with his own.

That damn sexy smile—well it wasn't that sexy until two days ago. *Fuck*. Who was I kidding? It made me tingle all over, go weak in the knees. He stepped forward, and before I could stop him, he kissed me—sweet, soft, no tongue—and I returned it willingly.

Wait, what the hell? I came to my senses and pushed him away, my eyes wide and my heart stuttering in my chest. "Rowan, someone might see. You know the book club is nosy as hell."

He put up his hand. "Sorry."

I stepped away. "It's okay. I've got to get back to work." I grabbed a can of Diet Coke and strolled out of the kitchen as casually as I could, despite the feelings deep in my gut. I needed to get my mind back on work and off Rowan. I'd have plenty of time to think about him tonight.

"Summer, Uncle Rowan and I came here so I could get my nails done."

I looked down at Darcie, her hands on her hips and her red curls in her face. Tonya stood right behind her, her eyes studying me. "Okay, Darcie. I think I have enough time before my next client." I then glared at Tonya. "Problem?"

She glanced at me, then over to Rowan, then back at me, and *tsked* her tongue.

Damn, that sound annoyed me, grating deep into my chest—and she did it *so much*. I braced myself for a comment from her. I'm sure that the comments from the onlookers about me potentially hooking up with her baby boy ate away at that small, somewhat cold heart that hid in her chest.

She opened her mouth to speak.

"Mom," Rowan broke in, placing his arm around Tonya's shoulders. "Don't start. That was just talk." He glanced at me, winked, and turned his mother around. "Let's go for a walk. Summer has to work. I'm sure there's plenty of people who you would love to show me off to."

Rowan mouthed "Later" to me and led his mother to the door, saying bye to Diane and Kaye as he went.

"My nails aren't going to paint themselves," Darcie reminded me in a sing-song voice, wiggling her fingers in the air.

I almost forgot she was there. But it was Darcie. She made sure no one ever forgot her. "You're correct, school-skipper. What does the princess want done today?"

"I'm not skipping school. I've been sick. I can go back tomorrow, and I'll have pretty nails to match Madeline and Lena." She walked to the wall of nail colors and tapped one finger to her lips, placed her other hand on her waist and popped out her hip.

I shook my head and held in a chuckle. Jamison was going to have his hands full.

"Well, Madeline and Lena already got a pink on their nails." She said as she stared at the line of pink polishes and pursed her lips in concentration. "But I forget what color they said it was." She looked at me, her hazel eyes wide. "I need to match them, you know."

Yes, I knew that quite clearly. The three "Orlinda Valley Princesses" needed to do everything together. "Why don't you go ask Kaye. I'm pretty sure she painted their nails."

Darcie held up her finger. "Be right back. Don't go anywhere."

My eyes darted to the ceiling, and I planted my feet dramatically for her, demonstrating my inability to move. She nodded once and walked away toward Kaye. *For fuck's sake, this girl is bossy,* I thought. *There's no doubt she's Tonya's granddaughter. Bossiness must be genetic.*

"It's flamingo pink, Summer," Kaye hollered from across the salon.

I gave her a thumbs up, picked up the flamingo pink nail color, and sat at my station to do my weekly pampering of Princess Darcie McKendry.

It didn't take long to color ten tiny fingers and ten tiny toes flamingo pink. I sat her under the drying lights and turned the television on to a channel with silly pet videos. She was laughing heartily while I cleaned the station and waited for my next customer.

"Hey, Summer," Lilly greeted me as she sat in my seat. Lilly—just who I needed to see, and she was my next customer. We were going to give her hair a trim and play with different styles to decide how she wanted it for the wedding. Right now, I wanted to cut it all off out of spite and call it a day. Instead, I nodded, put my cape around her shoulders, and said, "Hey. Do you want me to grab you a drink? Sweet tea or water?"

"A water would be great," she answered.

"I'll take a juice box, please," Darcie chimed from the drying station.

I wasn't asking Darcie, but it was only a juice box. When I came back, Darcie had her ass perched on my station. "Can I ask what you think you're doing up there, missy?"

"My name's Darcie, not Missy. Missy's a mean girl in my class. But Lilly said I could watch you. You know I'm going to be the flower girl. I'm going to wear a tiara, and I have to look pretty too, so I want to see how well you do Lilly's hair to see if I want you to do mine also."

Lilly snickered at me in the mirror while I silently willed glue to stick Darcie's mouth together. "What will you do if you don't like how I do Lilly's hair?"

She shrugged. "Then Miss Kaye or Miss Diane will do mine. They cut my hair all the time, anyway. Red curly hair takes a special touch, that's what my grandma says. And I don't know if you have it."

"Okay," Lilly placed her hands on Darcie's legs just as the bells on the door tinkled that someone came in. "Why don't you run over and help your uncle and grandma bring in the boxes they have. It looks like they brought food for lunch."

Darcie jumped from the counter. "Yay, pizza." She skipped behind Tonya and Rowan. I made sure to look busy and ignored Rowan's gaze.

"Kaye, Diane, I have pizza for all." Rowan looked at the older women in Diane and Kaye's chairs. "And you two don't need to leave without grabbing a slice of pizza or a cookie I picked up from Cakes and More."

"That bakery next door is my favorite," said Mrs. Clowder, the eye doctor's wife. "Rowan, honey how is it you're still single? Such a good-looking young man, and such good manners!"

"I don't know, Mrs. Clowder. I guess the right girl hasn't taken notice of me."

"Well then, girls your age must be blind."

"Thank you, Mrs. Clowder. But none of the women my age are as sweet and as beautiful as you."

Damn, he was so charming. Why couldn't he be a jerk and unlikeable?

"Thank you for taking control of Darcie," I said to Lilly. "I love that girl, but she's a lot to deal with, and today it's been almost too much."

Lilly laughed. "You know, Summer, you've always been so good with Darcie, Madeline, and Lena. They love coming here and having spa days and getting their nails done by you. You know, you might make a good girl-mom one day."

I puffed out a breath and stood straight before I pulled the brush extra-hard through her hair. "Bite your tongue, woman, and watch what you say. Remember your hair is at my mercy. You've already created enough chaos for one day."

"Oww." Lilly jerked her head out of my reach. "Can we not be abusive? And what do you mean I've created chaos?"

I yanked her head back in a straight line. "Don't move your head and you need to be extra good. You've already pissed me off."

"Yeah," Lilly winced. "You've made that clear, but I don't know what you're talking about."

I held her eyes in the mirror. "You and Jamison had a conversation about me and Rowan in front of some nosy little girls, and one of them came in and told everyone in the salon about that discussion."

Lilly pinched her lips together and raised her brows. "Actually, it wasn't me talking about it. It was Jamison, so you don't need to take it out on my scalp."

"Technicalities." I said, anger receding. I *would* take it up with Jamison, but for now I got to work. After her trim we played with different styles. She had shoulder length hair, so I pulled all of it into a French twist with some wisps framing her face, then tried an updo with some curls on top and ringlets on each side.

"Lilly, that's perfect," Kaye said. "You look stunning."

Tonya, Kaye, Diane, and the other two ladies in the salon came to gawk at the finished look.

"You sure do," Diane agreed. "Jamison is going to be speechless when he sets his eyes on you, and wish he was the one getting married."

"Summer, you always pull off miracles," Tonya said. "It still amazes me you're so good at hair."

My hands dropped to Lilly's shoulders, and I glared at Tonya. "Tonya, you know what? I don't know if that's a jab at my styling skills, or at Lilly."

"Why would I be saying anything about Lilly? She's beautiful and will make me a perfect daughter-in-law, hopefully soon."

"So, then you're saying . . ."

"Both of you, just stop." Rowan stepped between us. "Mom, Summer's been doing hair here since she was nineteen, and you know she's good at what she does. She's good at anything she does."

"Oh yeah, Rowan? What else is she good at?" Lilly asked with a laugh.

All the women looked between each other, then Rowan, and me, eyes wide with speculation.

"Is there something going on here?" Kaye asked, pointing between us.

"No, Kaye. Rowan and Summer? That's not possible." Tonya's eyes bulged in the brief silence. "Is it?"

"What the fuck?" I said.

"Ooh, bad word," Darcie piped up. "Summer owes me a dollar."

"Hit up your grandma. She's the one who caused it."

"Everyone, enough," Rowan said. "Come get some pizza before it gets cold." He grabbed Darcie's hand and led her away. "And you need to stop being in everyone's business."

We followed them into the kitchen. I took a slice of pizza and leaned against the counter.

Lilly looked up from her phone. "Summer, are you busy tomorrow? Kora needs something picked up."

"Why me? Isn't there anyone else?" I asked. "I have things to do tomorrow."

"Darlene and Kora are working, and I have classes all day. So, no. There isn't anyone else. Can't you reschedule your appointments? She needs you."

Lilly suddenly puffed out her lower lip and pouted.

"What are you doing?" I asked.

"Do you want Kora's wedding to be a complete disaster?"

That sounded like something Kora would say. "Did Kora tell you to pout if you thought I wouldn't do it?"

Lilly shrugged. "Maybe. Will you do it, for Kora? Please? Will you?"

"Summer," Tonya said. "I'll go with you. Someone has to make sure you don't forget anything."

"Great. Just what I need. You to bug the shit out of me the entire day."

"Someone's gotta keep you focused."

"And the best person for that job is you?"

Tonya shrugged and raised her brow.

"Well, I think it would do you two good," Lilly said.

"How sweet. My two favorite women hanging out all day," Rowan said as he pushed lightly into me.

I slowly turned my head toward him and rolled my eyes.

"It is sweet," Lilly said, "and Rowan can go with you, to keep you both from killing each other." She stood and pushed herself between the two of us and draped her arms over our shoulders. "My boyfriend's favorite brother can use his military skills to keep you two, Kora's favorite aunt—"

"I'm her only aunt," Tonya snapped.

Lilly ignored her. "And her best friend—"

"I've always been good with Darlene holding that position," I muttered, now annoyed with Kora.

Lilly rolled her eyes. "From killing each other."

"Seriously? You think that's possible?" Rowan asked her. "You know that's a full-time job. I don't know if I have enough skills to keep that from happening." He glanced between us. "And what am I supposed to go with them to do, other than keep them from killing each other?"

"Kora wants me to be her errand bitch for the day," I replied.

"Yeah, and I said I'd go to make sure she doesn't mess it up. I mean, I have better things to do with my day, but this is important." Tonya said.

"Mom, as far as I can tell, you never have anything better to do."

"Exactly, Rowan," Lilly said. "And that's why you would be perfect to go with them. As far as I can tell, you don't have anything better to do either."

"So, you want me to go so I can be a witness to them killing each other?"

"Well, you are trained in self-defense and protection of your countrymen. I don't know who else would be a better candidate."

Rowan's gaze caught mine and he raised a brow—and *dammit* if I didn't feel the heat go up a couple degrees. My eyes roamed over his features, already forgetting what we were talking about. That face, perfect and chiseled . . . those brown eyes, deep as chocolate . . . those lips, warm, tasty, and so talented . . .

I shook my head to clear all those naughty thoughts before I started drooling—or worse, jumped his bones right here in front of everyone, secrets be damned.

I focused on the conversation. Rowan *was* going with us. Well, it could be worse. I could be going with Tonya by myself.

"Fine, I'll reschedule my appointments," I reluctantly agreed. "It was going to be a quiet day, anyway." I wiped my fingers on a napkin. "I guess Rowan will help make the afternoon a little less dreary and depressing."

"Yep, spending time with Summer will be a little less mind-numbing if my youngest is around," Tonya jabbed.

"Wow. I feel the love." Rowan's gaze passed between both of us. "Mom, I'll see you tomorrow." Rowan gave Tonya a hug. "I've got to go. I promised Jamison I'd take Darcie home, and I'm staying there for dinner. So, Lilly, I'll let him know you'll be there soon. And Summer," he paused until I looked at him, and even without touching me he set my heart to pounding. "I'll see you later."

Hell yeah, he would.

CHAPTER 17

ROWAN

It was almost nine when I pulled into the driveway of my temporary home. After dropping off Darcie, I hung out at Jamison's the rest of the afternoon and stayed for dinner. It was good seeing him and Lilly together. They made a perfect couple. And their girls—wow! I thought Darcie was a lot to handle, but, damn, Darcie and Madelyn together were exhausting. If Jamison and Lilly got married, which I was sure they would, they would have no peace and quiet until the two girls moved out for college.

I was still shaking my head at the fun, yet chaotic, night I had just endured at Jamison's as I parked next to Summer's car.

I glanced at it, and then at the house. Despite all our fun last night, my stomach seemed to curl into a scared little ball as I thought about what I might encounter once I ventured inside.

Summer's attitude had been all over the place today. One minute she ignored me, next she was irritated with me, then she responded positively to my kiss for a brief second before she pulled back and became frosty toward me again.

I scrubbed my hands over my face and blew out a breath.

Opening up to Summer and telling her the truth had always scared me. Hell, if I was honest, *Summer* scared me. God help the one who was ever on the receiving end of her wrath. But ignoring my feelings hadn't worked. I'd tried that for over a decade, and every time we hung up after talking on the phone, I missed home even more than the last time we'd talked—and she was the main reason. If I could only get her to see how good a relationship between us could be.

I sighed deeply and walked through the door of the small house.

Summer sat on the couch, watching television. When she turned to look at me, her expression was blank, void of anything—excitement, emotion, feeling.

"Hey Summertime. Whatchya watching?" I sat on the couch and lifted her feet into my lap.

"Nothing much," she said as she sat up and curled her legs under her.

Fine. I sunk back into the couch and placed my feet on the coffee table. "You want some popcorn? A Diet Coke?"

She shook her head without saying anything or taking her eyes from the screen. She seemed totally entrenched in whatever show she was watching—rich plastic women stomping around all dramatic and yelling about something. It was so ridiculous, I couldn't keep up. "Who the hell wears heals and those clothes hanging around their house?" I griped. "What the hell are you watching?"

The glare she gave me was hot as a five-alarm fire—and not "hot" like *let's go to the room and get it on again*, but "hot" as in *shut the hell up and leave me the fuck alone.* "Do you mind? I'm watching this."

"Sorry," I turned back to the television and tried to watch the train wreck that held Summer's attention.

The tension in the room grew so thick you could cut it with a knife. When I couldn't take the silence anymore, I jumped up and slapped my hands on my thighs. "All right, I can't handle this. I'm taking a shower and getting ready for bed. I'm sure Mom will be here early in the morning."

"No, we're leaving at noon. Your mom and I talked before she left the salon."

I stopped on my trek to the bathroom. "So, you do speak."

"Just answering your question. Don't get your dick all hard."

Fuck. Just hearing her say *dick* made my dick do just that. "If it was, would you take care of it?"

She flipped me the finger and added, "Fuck you."

"Promise?" I chuckled. Maybe I was a bit crazy, but her attitude turned me on. I winked and turned toward the bathroom. "I'll leave the door unlocked just in case you decide to join me."

I walked in the bathroom, laughing to myself as I pictured her pissed and seething. She hated to be taunted, and I knew for a fact that *she* knew I was completely aware of that, and still did it to piss her off more.

Once the water was hot, I stripped down and stepped into the shower. I grabbed the soap and washed, rinsed off, then put shampoo in my hair. I stood under the spray and let the pounding of the water against my body take the thoughts of Summer and what we could be doing from my mind.

Suddenly, the curtain pulled to the side and my eyes popped open.

"Thought I'd take you up on the offer," Summer said as she stepped into the tub.

My eyes rested on her breasts, nipples hard as the water cascaded down her cleavage, over her tight stomach and shapely hips, and down her long legs to pool between those perfect toes.

"Are you done gawking?" she asked.

I couldn't take my eyes off her, and words had fled my mind. "I'm not gawking. Just in shock." Maybe I *was* in shock. Does that cause you to freeze, unable to move?

"Why? You invited me. No need to waste water on two showers. But if you don't want me in here with you, I can leave."

She pulled open the curtain and that's all it took to yank me out of my trance. "No." I reached for the curtain and closed it. "Stay. Please." I placed my hand on her arm. It was slippery from the water, or maybe it was the shampoo still on my hand.

"Okay," she said, voice all sultry and seductive. "You just had to ask." She stepped closer and reached up to slide her hands through my hair. "You still have some suds," she said, leaning my head back to rinse it.

She scrubbed slowly and massaged my head with her skilled hands. I closed my eyes and relaxed. Her fingers lingered at my temples, sending a slow, rush of desire deep in my gut. Who knew hands rinsing shampoo could be this sexy, this erotic.

Suddenly her lips were on mine and her hands laced behind my neck. I groaned partly with surprise, but mostly with pure primal desire. I pulled her under the shower with me and we devoured each other's mouths, our tongues touched and curled around each other. I couldn't get enough of her. Her taste, her touch, how she felt against my body.

My hands moved to cup her breasts, which filled my hands with more to spare. I played with her nipples until I could free my mouth from our frantic kissing and suck them in till they filled me. The moans that escaped her made the desire that was churning in my gut release itself and filled my entire being with need.

Suddenly, she pulled away and her hands brushed down my neck, caressed my chest, and slowly made their way down to the area I needed them to touch the most. As she cupped my hardness in her soft hands, I sucked in a deep breath and breathed out, "Summertime."

Then she was on her knees in front of me, licking from the base of my dick to the head. I glanced down, and the wicked smile she sent me made me harder, if that was even possible. When her mouth surrounded me, my hands went into her hair and guided her as she sucked and licked and drove me wild. "God, Summer." My insides became warm, then hot as an inferno. My dick throbbed, and the shock that went through my body caught me off guard.

Summer pulled away and kissed a trail up my body while her hand finished me off.

An earth-shattering orgasm shook my core as her mouth finally found mine. The kiss was intense, deep, needy.

I rinsed off and reached behind me to turn off the shower. My body was hot for her, but a part of me was concerned that she might overthink things and pull away again—or worse, shut me out. No way in hell did I want that to happen.

I held her hand as we stepped out of the shower, then grabbed a towel and started drying her off—first her shoulders and arms, then her chest and stomach, and finally her breasts, which I lavished with my lips and tongue.

"You're beautiful Summer. Perfect."

She combed her fingers in my hair, and I lifted her onto the counter. "My turn." I kissed her mouth briefly before I traveled down her body, stopping here and there along the way to nip at her skin and enjoy the taste of her. She leaned back against the wall as I kneaded her breasts, moaning in the sexiest way.

Finally, I separated her thighs and found what I searched for. My thumb moved over her most sensitive spot as my tongue tasted her. She was delicious—everything about her tasted so sweet. Her breathing quickened as I picked up my pace. "Come for me, Summer," I said.

Her breathing became rapid. "Rowan, yes." She convulsed and moaned her pleasure. I stayed there a little longer to make sure she was finished, then kissed my way back up her body, enjoying the sound of her panting, the rise and fall of her breasts, and the flush in her cheeks. She looked even more beautiful than ever.

My mouth found hers again. I lifted her and carried her the short distance to the room, our lips locked together. I laid her down gently and reached for the condoms, hard as a rock again and ready for more. "I want you now, Summer."

"Yes, Rowan. Take me."

I rolled on a condom and slid inside her. She was wet, slick, warm—heaven.

I thrust into her as she wrapped her legs around my waist and pushed me deeper, her hands on my ass. I tried to go slow, enjoy the feeling of Summer beneath me. Our eyes met and we held each other's gaze.

She pulled me to her and kissed me. Her hips found a rhythm to match mine and she pushed me deeper. "Rowan," she whispered.

I felt her release and she cried out in my ear.

"Rowan, yes," she said as she pushed me harder into her and I let go of all control.

Pulse after pulse, I came until my body was taken over by tremors. Finally, I slowed my movement and peered down at her. We both breathed heavily, and she looked at me through her eyelashes, lips parted as she basked in her own feelings.

She was stunning, and I was speechless.

She leaned up and again her lips met mine. It was a tender, affectionate kiss that I didn't want to end, but it had to. "Hold that thought," I whispered, "I'll be right back." I lifted myself away from her and went into the bathroom to dispose of the condom. Then I crawled under the sheets and pulled her to me.

She laid her head on my chest and her hands traced circles on my abs. My breathing became even, relaxed. This was exactly what I hoped it would be. "Thank you, Summertime."

She looked up. Her eyes were bright, happy, full of life. Not something I saw in her often. "Thank you for what?"

I shook my head and brushed hair from her face. "For not blocking me out, not pushing me away. But most of all for that fucking amazing blow job in the shower."

That got a loud, hearty laugh from her. "You challenged me."

"You're right. But I sure as hell didn't think you'd take me up on it."

"Why not? When was the last time you knew me to back away from a challenge?" Again, she leaned up.

I thought about that, and didn't have an answer. "Don't know, but you were all over the place with your emotions today." I shrugged. "I didn't know what to expect when I got home tonight."

"Yeah, well, as usual, I spent my day overthinking things. Stressing over why I should make sure to not do anything rash. Why this isn't a good choice. But as soon as you sat down on the couch, my body reacted, and my brain put all my overthinking on hold and finally listened to what I wanted."

"Well, your brain made a good decision." We held each other's gaze for a long beat.

"Yeah, it did." Summer closed the space between us with a long, deep kiss—which once again made me hard, and we took no time going for round two. This time, though, when I crawled back in bed, Summer kissed me and rolled over. She pulled my arms around her and cuddled into me. I fell asleep with the warmth and softness of her skin against my chest, and the smell of her filling my senses.

I closed my eyes and pulled her even closer. I didn't know how long this Summer would last before she doubted herself—and us—again. Hell, I didn't know if she'd even acknowledge any of this in the morning. But I was determined to keep all those negative thoughts at bay and enjoy whatever I could get from Summer, for as long as I could.

After all, tomorrow I would be spending it with her and my mother together, and I was sure something would go wrong enough to make tonight seem like a dream—like a fantasy that never really happened.

Chapter 18

ROWAN

"What is that?" I mumbled into the pillow as a rooster crow, just outside the bedroom window, woke me from the most restful sleep I've had in a long time. The sun streamed in through the curtains. I considered rolling over and throwing the pillow over my head, but Summer's leg lay across mine and I didn't want to move.

I turned and looked at her. Her eyes were closed, her breathing even. Her hand was tucked under her pillow. I lightly brushed my finger along her cheek and tucked hair behind her ear, then kissed her softly on her angelic forehead.

Another loud crow came from outside.

"I'm going to fucking murder that damn rooster," Summer mumbled as she rolled over.

"Oh, no you don't." I pulled her back toward me and cuddled into her, placing a kiss on her neck. "Ignore the rooster."

"We've got to get up, Rowan." She reached for her phone on the end table. "Damn, it's ten thirty. We slept in."

"Did we really? Oh well. That's what happens when you keep me up all night."

She shot me one of her looks, then cuddled closer.

I took that as a positive sign and continue to tease her. "Last I knew it was after two. So, see, we didn't sleep that late." I kissed her shoulder and pinched her nipple.

The tired moan that came from her made this day already a great one, but getting lost in Summer for a little while more would make waking up next to her so much better. The fact that she hadn't pushed me away, and was kissing my chest was just the motivation I needed. Our lips met. Maybe today would be different. Maybe . . .

A door slammed, and I could hear footsteps in the house. Summer froze mid-kiss.

"Summer, Rowan? I know you're here. Your cars are in the driveway."

"Fuck." Summer whispered then sat upright in bed. "It's your mother." She jumped out of bed and threw a shirt over her naked body, eyes wide. "You need to get out of here." She hissed in a whisper as she opened the window.

I walked over to her. "What are you doing?" I asked as she yanked the screen from the frame and leaned it against the wall.

"I'm helping you," she hissed.

I looked at Summer and then at the open window. She pushed me toward it, and it became clear what she expected me to do. "Oh, hell no," I said, my voice rising.

She shushed me with her hand over my mouth. "She'll hear you," she whispered as she pushed me closer to the window.

My chest tensed and I shot her a harsh look. "I'm not climbing out that damn window," I hissed at her. This was ridiculous.

"Summer, are you here?" my mom asked, her voice moving closer to the door.

She threw my clothes out the window. "Climb out, get dressed, and come around to the front door. Act like you've been out running or something."

Was she serious? I stood there in all my naked glory, my hands out to my sides helplessly, watching her bounce around the room like a pinball, gathering up clothing.

She hissed at me through gritted teeth, "Get out that fucking window. NOW." Her eyes were wild, like she'd gone mad.

"Goddammit, Summer," I said as I looked out the window. My clothes were strewn all over the ground. It wasn't a far drop. I could easily climb out. But still. "I'm naked."

"Get dressed when you get out there. It's not like anyone can see you from the road."

There was a knock on the door.

"Give me a fucking second, Tonya," Summer yelled. "Damn. You woke me up. Make me a cup of coffee, please."

"Fine," my mom said just outside the bedroom door. "But if we're leaving at noon, you really shouldn't be sleeping in so late." She paused, and I thought maybe she was going back to the kitchen, but then she asked, "Do you know where Rowan is?"

"Go." Summer mouthed the word and shoed me away.

I shook my head and sighed deeply as I folded myself out the window and jumped to the ground. My feet barely hit when the window slammed shut. I picked up my boxers and sweatpants from the grass. "This is so damned stupid."

I bent to put my leg in my boxer, but froze when Big Red crowed again, loud. I looked up and there he was, behind a nearby bush and strutting toward me, his wings out to his side. "Go away, damn bird."

He danced to the side then took off toward me. "Fucking *seriously*?" I ran and tried to step into my boxers at the same time. I fell on my face and pulled them up as he leaped on top of me and did a chicken kick-thing.

I kicked, cussed under my breath, and flailed my arms. "Damn bird! Get the fuck off me."

I finally got a decent enough contact with him that he flew a couple feet away, which gave me time and space to get up and run around the house, my sweatpants in my hand.

I froze. Jamison was there.

"What are you doing, Rowan, and why are you outside with your boxers partially pulled up?" The laughter in his voice was unmistakable.

Could this morning get any worse? I adjusted my hastily thrown-on boxers and stepped into my sweatpants. "Don't ask. Trust me, it's not worth it." I noticed blood on my chest. "Shit." There were a few scratches, but it looked like nothing serious.

"Hey, Rowan." Lilly said as she climbed out of Jamison's truck. "What are you doing outside stepping into your pants?"

Yep. There was my answer. This day *could* get worse, and now more humiliating.

"Both of you, just don't." I put up my hand as I adjusted my sweats. A harsh crowing sounded behind me. I jerked around. Big Red stood there, staring at me.

"Get away from me, you fucking cock, or I will catch you and roast you for dinner." I could have sworn he winked at me before he strutted off in the opposite direction. "I hate that damn rooster. It makes for a shitty day when I get chased by him before I've even had my first cup of coffee."

"First cup of coffee? How about before you even got dressed?" Jamison's laughter reverberated across the back field. God, I hated brothers.

Lilly hid a laugh behind her hand. "Sorry, Rowan," she said, "but how come you came outside undressed?"

"The rooster's fault," I said as I stormed past them toward the house.

"What, he undressed you?" Jamison chuckled. "You can't tell me that rooster pulled your sweats and boxers off."

"Shut up, asshole." There was no way I could ever talk about this. How the hell could I make this make any sense to anyone? *Well, I had sex with Summer, and—even though we're consenting adults—when my mother walked into the house, Summer made me jump out the window naked so no one would know we spent the night together. Then, as I was dressing in the grass in the front of the house, the crazy rooster chased me down and tried to impale me.* Yeah, fat chance of that story ever seeing the light of day.

Damn, I needed a stiff drink, but coffee would have to do. Hopefully Summer had a pot brewing and had already dealt with my mother. "Why are you two here so early, anyway?"

"It's not early. It's almost eleven," Lilly said with laughter in her voice.

I shot her a narrowed gaze.

She bit her lips and grabbed Jamison's hand.

"I had to give something to Mom," Jamison said. "When I called, she said she was coming over and I should meet her here." There was no mistaking the laughter in his voice. "Did she surprise you, and you had to make a quick escape from the house naked?" He opened the door, and I stepped past him. No way in hell was I going to answer him. I really needed a fucking cup of coffee.

Chapter 19

Summer

Tonya was at the Keurig when I finally composed myself to enter the kitchen. Facing her was a challenge on a good day, but this morning . . . I took a deep breath and brushed my hands through my hair. "Hey, Tonya, what the hell are you doing here so early?"

"Girl, it's not early. It's almost eleven. Here." She handed me a cup of coffee. "Drink it and relax. I made it how you like it."

"Thank you," I said as I sat on a stool at the counter. I sipped the coffee. It was velvety smooth and rich. I could feel the caffeine work its magic immediately—and with how this morning started, I needed a good, caffeinated kick in the ass.

Rowan and I hadn't slept much last night—not that I was complaining at all. His expression of anger mixed with shock as I forced him out the window filled my mind. Okay, maybe I overreacted a bit. We could have played off the shared bedroom thing a little better. Well, I could have, anyway. I took another sip of coffee. Luckily, Rowan was a good sport and never held a grudge.

"You need to drink that and wake up so we can leave in a bit. By the way, you never answered me. Where's Rowan? His car's here, but he's not."

"I'm not sure," I said. "He said he was going out for a run this morning, so I guess that's what he did."

"Hmmm." Tonya eyed the room. "He must have folded up his bed clothes, because I don't see that he slept here on the couch. There's no pillow or blanket."

Shit. Could she not stop being such a nosy busybody? "Yeah, well, you know he still has that military in him. He always puts everything away as soon as he's up." I laid my face in my hand. I was going to have to act like she was invisible and ignore her. Maybe if I kept my mouth shut and drank my coffee, she would disappear.

Just then, the back door opened. "Good morning, everyone," Jamison said as he and Lilly walked in.

I felt my body deflate. Fuck. Maybe I could fold up into myself and hide away until Christmas. We might be able to get one past Tonya, but Jamison and Lilly would be a bit harder.

"Look who I found outside hanging with a rooster," Jamison said with laughter in his voice.

I sat up straight when I saw Rowan behind Jamison, looking like he'd seen better days. His hair had that sexy, just-out-of-bed look, but his shirtless torso had some patches of dirt, like he'd rolled around on the ground. And were those scratches on his chest? Did I do that to him last night? I checked my nails. I didn't think so.

My eyes traveled down to his sweatpants. They had what looked to be grass stains here and there, but how they hung low on his hips. Damn. I did a once over up and down his body again, and yeah,

I wanted to be back in that bed with him. Why didn't I think of throwing a T-shirt out the window? I didn't need his mother and brother around to see me gawk at him.

Our eyes met, I had to hide my face in my mug of coffee, because the look he gave me could have boiled water it was so steaming hot—with rage. Sure as hell, not desire.

"Good morning, Rowan." Tonya said in a sappy sweet voice that made me want to vomit. She went over to him and wrapped him in a hug. "Umm," she said, holding him at arm's length and glancing down. "How did you go running? You don't have any shoes on."

He looked at her quizzically.

I interrupted. "Yeah, running, Rowan. You told me you were going running this morning, but that's not what you usually wear."

His eyes held mine. He was pissed, all right.

"Yeah, well, I decided running wasn't what I wanted to do. I thought I would just go outside, enjoy the fresh morning air, and bond with that fucking rooster. I didn't figure I'd be outside for long, so I didn't take my shoes. I enjoyed the morning dew and soft grass in between my toes as I got chased by a rabid devil-chicken."

Oh *shit*. I'd wondered what the commotion was outside the window after I'd shut it, but I'd been too consumed with trying to find my underwear. It was clear I hadn't put him in the best mood by forcing him naked out of a window first thing in the morning. Being forced naked out of a window and landing face-to-face with the devil-rooster would have pissed me off too. Damn. I fucked up.

"Yeah," he continued, with biting sarcasm oozing off his words, "as I was enjoying a stroll, thinking I'd make a friend, I got attacked by that damn rooster and stuck with one of those spears he wears on the back of his feet."

"Oh, my God." Tonya said as she held him at arm's length. "That looks bad." She rushed to the sink and wet a paper towel, then took it back to Rowan and started to wipe the blood off.

He grabbed the towel from her grasp. "Thanks for your help, Mom, but trust me, I don't need it." He wiped away the blood and chucked the paper towel into the garbage can with a swish.

I stood from the stool with trepidation as guilt tore through me. He was injured because I forced him out a window. I needed to do something.

I retrieved the first aid kit from the cabinet under the sink and took out a bandage and antiseptic spray. "Here. You should probably put this on. Roosters aren't the cleanest animals." I held the spray bottle out. "Can I?" I asked. His gaze hadn't cooled down from the rage I saw in them earlier. I raised my brow in question.

"Go for it," he said, his voice flat.

I sprayed the antiseptic, and he hissed in response as his abs contracted at the cold. "Sorry." I whispered. "It doesn't look too bad," I said as I covered it with a bandage. "There. I think you'll be fine."

His gaze caught mine. "Thanks." He picked my hand off his abdomen, which I hadn't realized I was still touching. "Next time, though, I'll be more careful when I. Go outside. To Enjoy. The Morning." He enunciated his words in clipped phrases, his gaze burned so hot I backed away from him and stood against the counter.

He needed some time to cool off, and I couldn't blame him.

Tonya glanced between us with her lips pursed in thought. "I guess I have no choice but to believe you, Rowan, honey. But you being outside with only sweatpants on makes no sense. You don't even have a cup of coffee."

Jamison grabbed a cup from the cabinet. "Yeah, it doesn't make any sense Mom," he said. "I found him running from a rooster, pulling up his—"

Rowan interrupted him. "It doesn't matter how you found me, asshole. I'm here and I had a run-in with the rooster, that's all. I tripped as I was running and fell to the ground. The insane rooster jumped on top of me, and I had to fight him off."

"Rowan," Tonya said in a motherly voice, "Jamison did nothing to warrant using that language."

"Exactly," Jamison agreed as he handed Rowan a fresh cup of coffee, a goofy grin plastered on his face.

Rowan drank deeply as a giggle escaped from Lilly.

"Aren't you being a little overdramatic, Rowan?" I said trying to lighten the mood and tension that had filled the small kitchen.

His eyes blazed.

I backed away slowly. My attempt didn't work.

"Okay, well," Lilly spoke up. "Tonya, Jamison, why don't we deal with whatever it is we came over to do and leave these two to . . . well . . . yeah. Come on."

Tonya's gaze lingered for a split second between Rowan and me, but Rowan's gaze stayed locked on mine. The intensity reminded me of a storm cloud rolling in—Dark. Wild. Impossible to outrun.

I turned from him and forced a smile at Tonya. "Once we're ready to go, we'll come get you," I said, my voice probably a little too chipper.

Lilly, smirked like she knew exactly what was going on, led Tonya toward the door and yanked on Jamison's arm as she passed him. He finally pushed himself off the sink and gave me a thumbs up sign, then followed.

Once the door closed, I turned back to Rowan. He was *seething*. His breaths came quick and sharp. His chest rising and falling in a steady rhythm, abs tightening with every breath.

Damn. Pissed-off Rowan was fucking hot.

He took a slow, measured step toward me, his eyes dark and narrowed. "You think *I'm* being a little overdramatic, Summer? Seriously?"

Heat radiated off him, sank through my tank top, and sent a delicious shiver down my spine. My spine was far too interested in this version of him. And as much as I loved to poke at him, even I had to admit that maybe—just maybe—I'd taken things a little too far.

But, damn, he was sexy when he looked like he wanted to impale me. And there was one thing I wouldn't mind being impaled with—though now was not the time for that thought. *Get your mind focused, Summer!* I exhaled sharply and brushed past him. I needed space before I did something reckless.

He wasn't finished. "If I'm being a little overdramatic, sweetheart, I must have learned it from you." His voice dripped with heat and irritation. "You seem to hold the real estate in that department."

I spun back to face him, my pulse skittering. I needed to put even more space between us before I actually did become overdramatic—like let my hands roam all over that frustratingly perfect chest. "You know what? I'm going to go clean up in the bathroom and leave you to enjoy your coffee." I nodded awkwardly, turned quickly, and almost fled to the bathroom.

As soon as I shut the door, I sagged against it, dragging in a shaky breath. I could have handled this entire morning completely different. Shoving him out the window—naked? *What were you thinking, Summer?*

Suddenly there was a banging on the door. "Summer, it's me," Rowan demanded. "Open the damn door."

I opened the door a crack and Rowan pushed his way in.

"Never again, Summer," he said as he approached me, venom in his gaze.

Every step he took forward, forced me back until I was up against the wall.

He planted his hands on either side of me, caging me in. I could feel his hot breath on my face.

"Don't you *ever* push me out a fucking window again," he said, his face inches from mine. I couldn't tear my eyes from him.

"Do you understand me, Summer?" He lowered his voice until it was quiet and controlled. "Last night was amazing and I don't care if any of them know that we spent the night in the same bed. Hell, I don't care if they know the things we did to each other."

I was breathing hard. Not out of fear—I was turned on. Rowan, this pissed off, was as hot as molten lava.

Suddenly his thumb caressed my cheek, and my pulse picked up its pace. I closed my eyes, and my mouth went dry.

"Are you turned on by this, Summer?" he said, voice now seductive and sexy.

I opened my eyes. "Yes, Rowan." I said, my voice a strained whisper. I licked my lips and brushed my hands up his hard abs. "Very much."

He leaned closer and our lips almost touched. God, I wanted to taste him so badly. I don't know what it was, but something about him in this state—this agitated, this ready . . . God, I just wanted him right here, right now. My hands reached his neck and brushed against the stubble on his face.

"You want this don't you?" he said. "You want me."

I swallowed hard as my body reacted to him. I nodded and met his gaze. I couldn't talk. I couldn't find my voice.

He pushed away from the wall and stood tall. "Sorry, sweetheart, this ain't happening right now. I gotta get dressed. We have stuff to do." He turned away and left me alone in the bathroom.

I melted against the wall and took in several deep breaths. That didn't go well at all.

CHAPTER 20

ROWAN

"I don't think I've ever seen you two act this harshly with each other." My mom looked between Summer and me like she was watching a tennis match. "You've been biting each other's heads off all afternoon. Is living together finally straining your friendship, or am I missing something?" She raised her brow.

I huffed and stalked ahead, away. I needed space.

We were at The Landing, a one-stop outdoor shopping area featuring high-end shops, restaurants, a big-chain bookstore, and small boutiques, all anchored by a movie theater. I was tired of walking and shopping. We had already picked up Kai's gifts, a personalized hand-crafted leather tool belt—which was fucking cool—and the blueprints of their house in a custom frame. I had to admit, Kora knew how to make a lasting impression.

Since then, Summer and my mother had been strolling through every fucking store. The candle store, the jewelry store, a shoe store—at least that one was useful. I needed a new pair of sneakers. Now we were in one filled with lotions and shower gels. There were so many smells I was getting a headache.

Summer tried her best to act like this morning didn't happen by being friendly and sweet. I was so over it. Even as she picked up the lotion and shower gel that made me hard because it was her signature scent that I memorized years ago, I was pissed and told her maybe she should grow up and find something new. But, damn, that was the last thing I wanted her to do.

Finally, she'd filled her basket and got into the checkout line, and I trudged outside to get fresh air, my mother tight on my heels.

"Is there something going on between you and Summer?" She took me by the arm and turned me toward her. "You've both been acting weird since I showed up this morning."

I yanked from her grasp.

"Don't ignore me. I'm still your mother."

I rolled my eyes. "Trust me, it's nothing you need to worry yourself about, Mom."

Just then Summer strolled out of the store swinging a pink bag from her arm. Her hair blew in her face, and she flipped it over her shoulder like she didn't have a care in the world.

She looked like a damn goddess. My body lit up. Hot and reckless Fuck.

I tore my gaze away and headed toward the car at a quick pace. I was pissed at her. That needed to stay front and center in my mind.

"There you are, finally," Mom said to Summer. I heard their footsteps behind me, and my mom continued. "I was trying to get Rowan to explain to me why you two have been so irritated with each other. I've never seen you argue this much. Is living together finally getting to you?"

"Well, you could say that, or you could just say your son's a slob."

My steps faltered. Did she really just call me a slob? My chest tightened and heated. Ignore her. Get to the car.

Summer's voice again met my ears. "All was fine in my little dwelling the week before he moved in and then shit went downhill. Did you know he leaves his underwear on the bathroom floor, he doesn't know how to wipe out the sink after brushing his teeth, and his nasty toothpaste gets stuck to the side?"

"But just this morning you said that he was super organized from being in the Army," Mom said.

I froze. This was ridiculous. I turned toward them, squared my shoulders, stared down at Summer, and countered, "Summer never puts her coffee cup in the dishwasher and is an absolute bitch in the morning."

"Just the morning?" Mom asked.

"Tonya, I thought you'd be on my side," Summer snapped.

"I'm not on either side," my mother said, hands on her hips. "I'm just trying to make sense of this and something's not adding up."

I put my hand up. "Stop. The both of you. I don't have time for either of y'all." This was more of a nightmare than I thought it could be, and staying here longer than I needed to was not going to happen. I turned and continued toward the car. "This shopping trip is done. We're leaving."

The short car ride home was painfully quiet, and the tension between me and Summer was thick enough to cut with a knife. Summer kept her arms crossed the entire way, glaring out the window as if she could shoot laser beams into the world, while my mom hummed softly from the back seat.

I glanced over at Summer. Her eyes caught mine and she raised her brows. I turned from her quickly and focused on the drive. I wouldn't let her off that easily. Hell, she threw me out a fucking window just hours ago. If whatever this was between us was going to work, we had to admit our feelings and let others know like consenting adults, not sneak around and act like immature teenagers.

By the time I pulled into my mother's driveway, I was practically vibrating with the need to escape. Summer grabbed her bag from the back seat and muttered something about needing a nap and she'd take the path home.

My mom gave me a knowing look as she shut the passenger door and said, "You could use a little time by yourself. Maybe go for a run, or something." She turned toward her house.

"Yeah," I muttered. "Or something."

As soon as Summer disappeared from view, I threw the jeep into reverse and peeled out of the driveway. I didn't have a destination in mind, but I couldn't go to the house.

Jamison's wasn't far, and I figured he'd let me crash for a bit, but it was a workday and he was probably still on the clock. So, instead, I made the turn toward town and Jerry's Pub. Trevor would be available. Even if he was at work, his job forced him to listen to people's problems, being a bartender and all.

As I parked in the lot, I felt like a balloon on the verge of popping. I pulled open the door. There were a few tables filled with customers enjoying a late lunch, but luckily the bar area was empty. I parked my ass on a stool and grabbed a menu.

Trevor's voice came from the kitchen. "Hey, man. Be right with you."

He finally emerged from the kitchen and placed a basket of pretzel bites in front of me. "Here you go. Nico made some soft pretzels and beer cheese for us to snack on. Want a drink?"

"Just a Coke," I said as I dipped a pretzel in the cheese.

He raised an eyebrow at me. "You look like you just survived a war."

"Close enough," I muttered.

"What happened? Summer finally kill you with her sarcasm, or did your mom start digging through your embarrassing childhood stories again?"

I scrubbed a hand over my face. "I came here because I need to be distracted with some mindless conversation which isn't at a bitch-decibel."

Trevor chuckled. "Welcome to the sanctuary of the fed-up and exhausted. Stay as long as you want. A bar is a great place to let your negative feelings out."

For the first time all day, I relaxed. Maybe I could survive Summer and my mother driving me batshit crazy after all—at least for now.

"She's impossible, and I'm done. There's a week until the wedding, and I don't know if I'm going to be able to make it."

"I take it things you're talking about Summer, and things between y'all aren't going well? Does that surprise you? Isn't that why you never told her how you felt, and part of why you ran away and into the military?"

I narrowed my eyes. "I didn't run away."

He raised his brow and leaned against the counter; his arms crossed over his chest. "Really? That's how it looked from where I stood."

Fuck. He was right. I did run away but hoped no one would ever figure it out. I had been over trying to make my life happen here in small-town USA. I needed to get away—away from Bryson and his all-knowing attitude, and away from Summer and her need to stay independent when I wanted to be with her. Instead of talking with her, I ran.

"It doesn't matter. I'm home now. Do you know of anywhere I can rent a place until I decide what to build on my property? Hell, maybe I'll keep things simple and offer to buy Kora's. Then I'll already have a house and be able to kick Summer out on her ass."

Trevor chuckled. "Like that would ever happen."

I shrugged. "It could."

Trevor shook his head. "Not likely, but I'll ask around."

"Thanks," I said. "Now I need to get a job, then I'll be set. You're going to the party Saturday, aren't you?" Since Kora and Kai had been living together for a while, the book club ladies decided to have more of a housewarming for them than a wedding shower, and everyone was invited.

"Possibly, but I'm not sure yet."

"Well, make sure to have someone cover the bar. I need you there to have my back. Oh, do you mind if I crash at your place tonight—again?"

"As long as you don't mind the couch—again."

"Nope. Grab me the key. I want to go now."

"What, you're not going to be here tonight?"

"Nope. It's been a long and busy week, ending with this shitty day. I want to veg in front of the television and relax."

CHAPTER 21

SUMMER

On Saturday, I parked in Kora and Kai's driveway next to Darlene's Nissan. We were helping to prepare for their housewarming party that evening.

"Hey, Summer," Darlene greeted me as I walked into the backyard.

"Hey, Dar," I hugged her and looked around. "I thought Kora asked us to get here at noon to help set up. It looks like you're about finished." The yard and patio were lined with lights and torches. The trees, which bordered the back of the yard and hid the Red River, were decorated also.

"You know how Kora is. She and Kai did a lot of this last night. I'm just touching things up. Help me get the tables and chairs around."

"Where's the happy couple, anyway?" I asked. It wasn't like Kora to not be bossing us around, making sure we did exactly as she expected.

"They went to the airport to pick up Kai's sister. They should be on their way back. Her plane got in at eleven."

We put up tables and chairs in different areas of the yard.

"Looks like you two have everything under control," Tonya's voice made me turn. The book club had arrived.

"Yeah it does. I guess we can go break into the wine and relax until the food gets here," Kaye said as she walked into the house.

Tonya hugged Darlene. "How's my favorite daughter-in-law?" she asked.

"She's amazing, Tonya," Darlene said.

"Taking care of my newest grandbaby, I hope."

"Of course. You have nothing to worry about."

"You and Bryson having another baby," Tonya said and turned to Diane. "Adler and Leila are adding to their family, Jamison has Lilly, Kora has Kai. Just about everyone is happy. Now, if my Rowan would settle down . . ."

"And Lance," Kaye added as she joined everyone with wine in one hand and a stack of clear plastic cups in another, "Of course, he needs to grow up a bit first." She poured everyone a cup and passed them around.

"Kaye," said Diane after she took a sip of her wine, "one day at a time. He's been seeing that girl for a while now. What's her name?"

"Jayla," Ruth said as she unfolded a table cover. "She seems sweet."

"That's right," Diane said as she snapped her fingers.

I blocked out the women as they continued to talk about Lance and Jayla. My mind went back to what Tonya said about Rowan settling down. I wish I could say that he was with me, but after how I treated him, I couldn't be sure. Forcing him out the window naked, right into the path of Big Red, then me acting like nothing happened

. . . What was I thinking? I acted like an immature teenager, not a grown woman.

He's made it clear what he wants. But me? What did *I* want? Or the better question, what could I really give him?

"Summer, those are a little fragile," Tonya said.

I was plopping vases on the center of the tables harder than necessary, and Tonya took one from my hand. "What's up with you?" she asked.

I shook my head. "Nothing. Was just thinking."

Tonya fixed the flower arrangement that I messed up when I placed the vase on the table and looked at me through narrowed eyes. "What's going on, Summer?"

Kaye looked at me and raised her brow.

I shrugged.

"I feel like I'm missing something here," Kaye said as she pointed between Tonya and me.

"Oh, yeah, you're missing something," Tonya answered her. "We're all missing something."

"Why, what did you witness?" Kaye asked.

"I'm not sure," Tonya said as she stepped back and eyed me suspiciously. "But there was something weird going on between Rowan and Summer yesterday, and if I didn't know better, I'd think they were having a post-coital temper tantrum."

"T!" Kaye said with a gasp of shock, as Diane about spit out her wine.

"Wouldn't be a surprise," Ruth said as she continued her straightening of tablecloths on the last few tables. "Honestly, I'd say it's about time."

I stood there and stared at the women. Tonya and Kaye spoke wordlessly through their gaze like they seemed to always do, Ruth continued to straighten things and fix tables like she didn't just make an announcement that embarrassed me, and Diane and Darlene's shoulders shook with laughter.

"Who's having a temper tantrum?" Kora asked as she, Kai, and a pretty girl with dark hair like Kai's entered the back yard. "What's going on?"

I sent a glare in Kora's direction. "Nothing." I said to her, then shot daggers at the women laughing. "They're all being bitches."

"Okay, let's not go there," Darlene said as she tried to rein in her laughter. "I didn't say a word."

"Me either," said Diane. "It was all Ruth."

"Me?" Ruth said. "Tonya made a comment, and I agreed." She brushed her hands together, grabbed her wine, and sat down. "That's it."

"And from what I witnessed Friday, it's the truth," Tonya said as she walked toward Kora and the dark-haired girl, a smile on her face. "But it doesn't matter. You must be Susie."

"I am."

Tonya wrapped her arms around her. "Welcome to Orlinda Valley. Was your flight okay?"

"It was, thank you. A little long, but fine."

"Well, good. Come and meet everyone. These two are Darlene and Summer, Kora's best friends."

Darlene hugged her and I gave her a small, slightly awkward hug also. "Nice to meet you," I said.

Susie's eyes were as silver as Kai's, her skin a perfect ivory. She was adorable.

"Well," Kaye chimed in, "aren't you a spitting image of your brother. Are you sure you two aren't twins?"

"We hear that all the time," Susie said with a shy smile. "Honestly, my twin, Sebastian, looks more like Kai than I do."

"It's too bad he wasn't able to make it to the wedding," Ruth said as she gave Susie a hug and introduced herself.

"We would have loved to have met him," Diane agreed.

"Yeah, but he'll hopefully be able to visit soon," Kai replied. "Come on, Susie. Let's get you settled and leave these women to finish up."

Susie gestured to the yard. "Maybe I should help."

"No," Darlene said as she shooed them toward the house. "Go get settled and we'll let you help later."

Kora straightened a tablecloth and looked around the yard. "Looks great, everyone. Thank you so much for doing all this." She put her hands on her hips. "Now, what did I miss?" Her eyes landed on me, and she lifted her brow in question.

I shook my head. No way in hell was I going to bring this up.

"Kora, dear, it was nothing," Tonya replied, waving her hands in the air dismissively.

Of course I don't have to say a thing, I thought as I rolled my eyes toward the sky. *Not with all these nosy-ass women around.*

"I just voiced my observation that something weird was going on between Rowan and Summer yesterday, and if I didn't know better, I'd've thought they were having a post-coital temper tantrum."

"What?" Kora's eyes were wide, and she tried to hide a laugh, but failed miserably.

My heart slammed against my chest. "Y'all," I said, my voice rising with irritation. I didn't want to have this discussion.

"Summer, relax," Tonya said.

"Relax?" I asked her, my composure cracking. "Just so you know, I haven't seen your son since he dropped us off at the house yesterday." I turned toward Kora with venom dripping from my words. "So, unless he starts talking to me again, nothing matters." I spun back toward Tonya. "*And*, we weren't having a 'post-coital temper tantrum'," I shouted as I stomped my foot. "Who the hell says that anymore, anyway?"

"Ummm, what did we miss?" Rowan's voice cut through air

Fuck I said under my breath as my heart did this annoying leap thing. I turned around. Rowan, Bryson, and Lance were standing in the yard with boxes and metal containers.

He glanced at me, then his mom, then the rest of the women. My stomach flipped at the sight of him in jeans and a T-shirt, looking fine.

"We come bearing food?" Bryson said, his tone raising in question.

"Thank God." Darlene hurried forward. "Something to do."

"Yeah, let us help you," Kaye answered as she took the containers from Lance's arms. "I'm sure y'all have more in the truck."

Darlene, and Kaye hurried into the house with their arms full, and Diane and Ruth rushed after them.

Bryson and Lance said nothing, but got more food containers from the truck as Rowan watched me. I avoided his gaze and followed the women inside.

Once everything was unloaded, the book club got to work with the food, and I had a chance to sneak away. I needed air and space.

I walked out of the house and followed the gravel path down to the bank of the river. As soon as I got there, I picked up some rocks and hurled them into the water. The light splash they made was not satisfying. I needed something to make a sound. A loud crash would be much better. I threw a rock against a nearby tree. There. Better.

What was I doing? Why did I let Tonya's words get to me? She wasn't being mean, just posing the obvious. Then Ruth. What she said hit me in the gut. Did everyone think the same thing in this god-forsaken town?

Hell. It wasn't like I hadn't thought it. I mean, sure Rowan said he'd always had feelings for me, but if that was true why had he always dated girls so different than me? Girly girls, cheerleaders, bubbly annoying bitches who I couldn't stand and were no more like me than that squirrel climbing the tree across the river.

"You okay?"

Rowan. My shoulders slumped. Of course he followed me. He could always tell when I was irritated, and could never leave me alone with my thoughts. My irritation deflated a bit at the sound of his voice, just as much as my stomach fluttered. "I'm good," I said as I let another rock fly through the air. I felt immense satisfaction when it, again, smacked against a trunk of a tree.

"What did we walk in on back there?" His voice was soft and laced with concern.

I let out a chuckle. "Nothing. Nothing that matters, anyway, not as long as you and I don't talk."

Splash. A rock hit the water.

I could feel Rowan's presence, but he didn't say anything. I needed to apologize or we would never be able to move on. I sighed and turned toward him. My eyes raked over his body. Every bit of him handsome and perfect. I finally met his eyes, and my heart cracked. I was selfish and immature. I let out a light sigh and said, "I'm sorry,

Rowan. I've messed this up." I gestured between us. "I shouldn't have forced you out a window." The realization of what I did hit me. "What the hell was I thinking? Fuck."

I spun back toward the river. *Splash.* Another rock

He grabbed my arm as I was ready to let another one fly and turned me around.

I stared at him and chewed on my bottom lip. His brown eyes were wide and questioning.

My vision blurred.

I blinked rapidly and looked away from him and his perfect features—his sweet, handsome face. He could have anyone. So why was he choosing me? Why now? What if I wasn't enough? "I'm sorry," I whispered. "I've been acting so stupid. Immature. Irrational."

His gaze softened as he lowered his head, and a smile crept up the corners of his mouth. Damn he was handsome.

His grip on my arm became tender and he pulled me toward him slightly. His voice gentle. "You have been a bit of all those things, but I would expect nothing less." He lifted my face until my eyes met his. "I accept your apology," he said as he closed the space between us. "But promise me one thing."

I raised my brow. "Anything."

"No more windows."

I released my breath and laughed gently. "Of course. I promise." I gently licked my lips, as his lips closed on mine. The kiss was soft and so sweet, and I got lost in it. I forgot where we were and what I had been thinking. I placed my hand on his cheek as our tongues met.

Maybe this was real. Maybe we could be good for each other. Maybe I had to trust that everything would work out. That I was enough.

"Hey, y'all—" Kai's voice stopped mid-sentence, and I broke the kiss.

Rowan whispered. "Really, Kai?"

Chapter 22

ROWAN

After Kai interrupted us, the rest of Saturday was a blur of activity. Kai and I won a cornhole tournament, with Bryson and Lance giving us tight competition, while the women opened the gifts. It amazed me how much more stuff Kora and Kai received. Who knew you needed all that crap when you got married.

When I left Summer behind Saturday night—the girls had their bachelorette party in Nashville and would be getting home to-day—things were good between us, but it still felt like something was off with her, like there was more she wanted to say.

I spent Sunday working around my temporary home and my mom's house—cutting grass and getting to know Big Red. I fixed up the chicken coop and placed his food and water inside the large shed. He watched me most of the day, perched just outside the double doors on a single fence post I dug into the ground. By the time I was done, I think he and I had finally called a truce.

The guys came over for a cookout Sunday evening, and I spent another night alone.

Now, here it was Monday morning, and I needed to start my day. I put a coffee pod in the Keurig, spread cream cheese on a toasted bagel, then slipped on my Hey Dudes and headed outside.

I breathed in deep, filling my lungs with the crisp morning air and stretching tall. I took in a few more deep breaths—then was interrupted by a loud crow. Big Red had greeted me once again.

"Hey there, dipshit. Did you sleep in your new house?" I pulled off a piece of my bagel and squatted. I held out the bread and stayed perfectly still, waiting to see how he would react. The large red rooster slowly strutted toward me and plucked the bread from my grasp, just as Summer's car came up the driveway. He clucked and strutted away quickly, bread still held in his beak.

My eyes followed her car as she pulled beside the Jeep. I stood, wiped my hands on my pants, and tried to calm my heart.

She turned off the car, got out, and finally made eye contact with me. "Hey," she said, a bit more chipper than I expected. The smile she gave me filled her face and took my breath away. She looked put-together, like she'd already showered and was ready to start her day. She didn't look worried at all. Maybe I was reading too much into things.

"Hey," I answered. "Did you have fun?"

"Yep," she replied, greeting me with a quick kiss before walking toward the house. I followed behind, leaning against the counter as she got a drink from the refrigerator and opened it. *Be patient*, I told myself. *See if she brings anything up.*

"Rowan, I've been thinking. About us." She sat at the counter with her back ramrod straight.

My brows raised. Whatever she had to say seemed damned important.

"You can have it your way," she said.

I leaned back against the sink, crossed my arms over my chest, and tilted my head. "I can have *what* my way? We haven't talked since Saturday." I motioned with my hands. "I have no clue what you mean."

"We can be a couple, because I've got feelings for you." Her eyes softened and her voice calmed. "I spent two days thinking about us and how you feel."

I was in shock. She said this so nonchalantly. Did I hear her correctly?

"But we've got to do somethings my way too," she said.

I walked to the counter and leaned across from her. I wanted to say something, yet at the same time, the thought of stopping her from saying more scared me. I wasn't sure where this was going, but if I understood at least one thing from her revelation, it was that she had feelings for me. That was a start. A pretty damn good one. "I'm all ears," I said.

She hopped off her stool and started pacing, gesturing almost as much as she spoke.

It was fun to watch.

"We need to keep this under wraps. We can't go around all lovey-dovey and hang all over each other. No handholding in public either. We can't be kissing when people are around. No one wants to see that or know what we do behind closed doors. Do you understand?" She finished her speech with her hands on her hips and a saucy head-tilt.

Damn, she looked hot. *This* was a version of Summer I could get used to.

I chuckled, even though I knew it would piss her off. But how the hell could I help it? She just admitted to me she had feelings for me. She admitted to me she *wanted* me. Being incognito so no one else knew was something I sure as hell could deal with—for now, anyway. My grin felt like it might split my face.

"No stupid grins," she said.

I shrugged, "Thought you liked my grin. You said it was sexy." I walked around the counter toward her.

"Did you not hear me?" she asked as I rubbed my hand up her thigh.

"Oh, yeah, I heard you. I heard you say you had feelings for me, and we could be a couple. Compared to what I thought you were going to say, this is amazing. If I need to keep it all incognito, I'll take it—for now." I placed my hands on her ass and stood close. "You and me? I like it." I leaned in to kiss her, bringing my hands up to the sides of her face and holding her while I took the kiss deeper. She wrapped her arms around me, and I felt her shiver. I moaned and pulled her closer until we came up for breath moments later.

This Summer was so much better than the one who pushed me out the window into a rooster. She felt more confident and ready to face the world.

"Are you good with no PDA?" she asked as she leaned back.

My eyes passed over her beautiful face and porcelain skin. I combed through a lock of her chestnut brown hair. "Summertime, I'll do anything it takes to have you. I'd go incognito, undercover, stay behind closed doors, and keep you my secret as long as you need. Fuck. See how hot all those things sound?" Yeah, my dick thought so too. "Trust me, it's hotter than if everyone saw us in public holding hands and doing whatever else. You and me behind closed doors is my favorite."

I kissed her again hard, demanding more. Our tongues danced together. My fingers grasped her hair and held on tight until she broke the kiss and let out a heavy puff of breath.

"I'm so glad I got that off my chest," Summer said. "and I'd like nothing more than to strip you naked. Drag you to the bedroom. Suck that delicious cock of yours. But I've got to get to work. It's a busy week. We have a wedding to prepare for." She pushed me away gently. "I'll see you later," she said with a wicked grin.

She walked out the door and I adjusted my pants. She wasn't the only one who had somewhere to go. I had a meeting with the bride, groom, and Susie. I was now running late, but sure as hell needed to hop in a cold shower first.

CHAPTER 23

ROWAN

I pulled to the side lot of Orlinda Valley Pharmacy and flew through the door. The pharmacy was a cozy little corner store that had been around since the start of Orlinda Valley, with what used to be called a soda fountain— but was now a small restaurant—in the rear. It had seen its share of history, growth, and face-lifts, but the owners still kept it going.

Over the years, they'd increased the food they offered. For breakfast, you could get the basic Southern comfort foods: eggs, sausage, biscuits, and bacon. They also had the best lunches around. Their hot dogs were to die for, served with milkshakes and fries.

When Kai saw me coming, he glanced pointedly at his wrist—even though he did not wear a watch. "Better late than never."

"Yeah," added Kora. "What held you up? It's not like you to be late."

Kai chuckled. "Or, better yet, *who* held you up?"

I glared at them both, refused to acknowledge their comments, and grabbed a menu as Mrs. Johnson, the owner of the pharmacy, approached the table.

"Well, Rowan, honey," Mrs. Johnson said in her deep Southern drawl. "I heard you were home. How are you?"

I knew I should have come by to say hi to Nancy and Pat Johnson before this, but it had been a busy week and I'd been preoccupied.

I'd dated the Johnsons' daughter, Melinda, briefly in high school. She was one of those cheerleaders that went really well with the captain of the football team. In a small-town like ours, people thought that type of couple was destined to get married right out of high school, but things didn't work out that way for us. She was now happily married to Robby, an old teammate of mine, and they had two children. They'd started dating right after I broke up with her. It was funny how life turned out sometimes.

"Hi, Mrs. Johnson," I answered. "I'm doing great and I'm glad to be home. Not sure if I'll be staying, because I have to head back to Texas soon for a job interview, but for now it's all about the wedding."

"I'm glad you made it. This is going to be a whole-town event—everyone's going. Even Melinda and Robby are going to be there. I'm sure they'd love to talk with you."

I smiled wide and opened the menu I still clasped in my hands. Maybe she would take the hint and back off a little. "Of course, Mrs. Johnson. It would be great catching up with them, and I'm glad you're doing well." She finally took my order and left us.

"How sweet," Kora teased. "You get to see your old flame *and* your teammate. I'm sure they will love to talk with you." Kora laughed and I shot her a glare.

"Your old flame?" Kai asked. "I'd love to hear about this."

Why couldn't Kai drop it?

Kora jumped in with the explanation. "Mrs. Johnson's daughter, Melinda, was the captain of the cheerleading squad and had it bad for Rowan."

"From what I hear, everyone had it bad for the stud," Kai said with a huge grin.

"Fuck you," I muttered through gritted teeth.

"Anyway, they ended up dating, but he broke up with her, and she started dating Robby Hendrix, who was also on the team." Kora continued her explanation of my high school love life until Mrs. Johnson finally arrived with the food.

"Here you go," Mrs. Johnson said. More customers sat down then and needed her attention, so she couldn't stay and chat with us and prolong my suffering. Thank God.

"I'm honored y'all feel it necessary to make me the topic of conversation," I said, picking up my fork, "but it's been a long morning and I'm starving. Can we please eat and get this meeting over with?"

They finally agreed and we ate in silence.

Once Kora was finished eating, she pushed her plate away and got out her notebook and a stack of manila folders. "Okay. Let's do this." She passed a folder to each of us, keeping one for herself.

"What do *I* need this for?" Kai asked holding it up.

Kora held her hand palm-out in front of Kai. "Don't ask questions. Just listen and follow directions."

He put one hand up in surrender and opened the file on the table.

"Like I was saying. These are the schedules for this week, what needs to happen when. Rowan, your list has all the things I expect the guys to accomplish, especially their tuxedo fittings. You need to make sure they actually *try them on* and that they fit well."

"Wait, you want me to go with each of them?" I asked as I looked at the schedule.

"Absolutely," she agreed. "They're all going on Wednesday, so there shouldn't be any problems. It's your brothers, and Kai, of course. They'll all be fine. The only one who might give you any problems is Lance, but you know how to handle him."

"Seriously? Are we going here again?" Kai asked.

"Sorry, honey, but if you knew him as long as we have, you'd know plans tend to be all about Lance. I mean, come on. He's thirty-six and still very single."

"It doesn't matter," I cut in. "I can handle him. He's like another brother. He won't be a problem." I read over the list. "So, it looks like I need to focus on the tuxes and that they try them on before they bring them home. It says here that there's a bachelor party Thursday night and I'm planning that." I glance at Kai. "Shouldn't I have been told this?"

"Consider yourself told," he said with a smile.

I rolled my eyes.

"And Friday night," Susie said, taking over for Kora, "is the rehearsal at the Warfield ranch, and everyone needs to be there by four. Practice is first, with dinner following at five thirty."

"Yep," answered Kora leaning back with her coffee in her hand.

Susie continued. "Rowan, starting Friday, I'll make sure everything runs smoothly. You just need to be by my side, and make sure to do whatever I tell you during the wedding. But beforehand you'll be with the guys, making sure they have everything they need."

I chuckled. "Absolutely, ma'am." I gave her a military salute.

She nodded. "Good." Then she turned to Kora. "See, he listens well."

"Sis, you make him sound like a dog," Kai said.

"It's okay. Seems like he's as loyal as one, and we can see he's just as cute." Her quip made Kora laugh, at least. I couldn't decide if she was being funny or rude. But I did know that she was coming out of the quiet shell she had been in when I saw her at the housewarming. She turned and talked with Kora about other wedding details I couldn't—and honestly didn't—want to keep up with.

As they talked, I checked Susie out. Not that I was interested in her—not in the least. Sure, she was sweet, but her looks reminded me of one of the cheerleaders I dated once or twice in high school—and she was nothing compared to Summer. Summer's quick-wittedness and sassy attitude were fucking hot, not to mention kept me on my feet and in check.

"How long are you staying, Susie?" I asked when they took a break in their conversation.

"I have school Monday morning, so I leave early Sunday. I should be home by late afternoon. I'll be back in the summer. Hopefully, by then I'll have a niece or nephew to love on."

"No pressure, sis, thanks," Kai responded.

"Just letting you know what I'm expecting. It's been nice visiting. I wasn't sure about seeing dad, but he's cleaned himself up. Things were a little awkward at first, but I can tell he's really trying to make amends for all the years we missed having a father. Kai, that's all your doing."

"What do you mean?" Kai asked.

"You could have kicked him out and ignored him. You know me or Sebastian probably would have, but that's never who you were. It's just like you to give everyone the benefit of the doubt."

Kai shrugged. "I guess. But everyone here was so welcoming to me, I had no choice but to return the favor. I've told him that even though he wasn't much of a father, we could figure something out. He's stepped up since, so it's all been pretty good."

They talked more about Terry and how well he'd done in the Alcoholics Anonymous group he attended. It was good to learn about Kai's family, and it made me appreciate how lucky my brothers and I were. We had two parents who loved us and each other.

Kai, Susie, and Summer weren't that lucky. Kai, though, came out pretty good on the other end, and eventually learned to believe in love.

That gave me hope for Summer.

CHAPTER 24

SUMMER

Wedding week was off to a great start. Wednesday, the princesses came in for their nail appointments. Those three girls were already a handful, and they weren't even out of kindergarten, but the salon lit up when they visited. At times they remind me so much of me, Darlene, and Kora when we were in middle school—except they were always happy, they didn't have blue, black, or red hair like I did, and they weren't rude or ignorant like I was. Thank God.

I was in such a good mood that day that Tonya's comments all afternoon didn't even irritate me. I couldn't figure out if it was because she was actually less irritating, or if my naughty thoughts about her son—his warm lips as they kissed all over my body, his arms as he held me tight, sleeping next to him every night without her knowing—gave me a joy that her irritation couldn't penetrate.

Now it was Thursday, and I was at Jerry's Pub with Kora, Darlene, Susie, and Lilly. We were meeting for one last wedding plan review. I swear, if we did any more wedding reviews, I was going to strangle Kora. It was a small wedding at a ranch, not a royal ball. What else could we possibly learn? I didn't know, but I was there, once again, and ready to receive last-minute information. So annoying.

They were all there when I entered—just a little late. Rowan and I had another fun night, and tearing myself away from him was a little difficult. He was going back to Texas for his interview in a week, and I didn't know whether he'd be coming back or staying there, so I was trying to get my fill of him for as long as I could.

"Hey, Summer," Kora chimed as I walked up to the table. She stood and gave me a hug.

"Good morning," I said.

"It's a little late for morning," Darlene said. "It's about noon.

I sat, took a sip of the mimosa waiting for me, and shrugged. She was right, and I had no reason to argue.

"So," Darlene said, cocking her head and narrowing her eyes at me, "you showed up late *and* you're awfully chipper. What's up with that?"

I held her gaze and said, "Well, it's been a great week, and my best friend's marrying an amazing guy. Maybe it's giving me a little hope in humanity."

Lilly leaned forward. "I seriously doubt that. Who are you and what did you do with Summer?"

I wasn't going to let these women get to me or ruin my mood. I took another drink of my mimosa and, suddenly starving, dug into the breakfast burrito bites on the table. Damn they were good, and there weren't nearly enough. I cleaned the plate and finished my mimosa.

"Maybe some hot times in the hay with my cousin is creating this new happier Summer," Kora added, eyeing me as I licked my fingers. "Though it *is* a little creepy."

I glanced around the table. They all had ridiculous grins on their faces and watched me expectantly. I had to change the subject. "You asked us here. It's lunch. The mimosas are gone. Are you going to feed us now and maybe spring for some margs?" I stopped. Their grins were now annoying. "What? I missed dinner last night."

"I bet you did," Darlene said.

Kora, Susie, and Lilly laughed.

Trevor showed up to save the day. He dropped off nachos, the mini tacos we loved, and a pitcher of margaritas. Thank God.

"Here you go, ladies," he said. "Good afternoon, Summer. Good to see you finally made it outside before dark with the long hours you're keeping with my best friend."

I shot Trevor an eat-shit-and-die glare, but I couldn't deny it, which only served to prove all their suspicions correct.

"So, it *is* true," Darlene said as she sat up straighter and moved to the edge of her seat.

Dammit. These nosy-ass friends. "He doesn't know what he's talking about," I said.

"Oh, I call bullshit," Kora said. "Rowan tells Trevor things he doesn't tell me, and he's been here a lot. Maybe he's venting and getting everything off his chest? Give up the goods, Trev."

Trevor put up his hand and took a step back. He was a smart guy at times. "I don't know. I just walked into something, and now I've gotta get out of it." He backed away like he was walking out of pasture full of cow shit in Crocs—which was a pretty true comparison at this point.

I took another sip of my margarita, then clasped my hands on the table. Here goes nothing. "We like each other more than 'just friends'."

Kora laughed. "No kidding!"

"We've known that for ages," Darlene added. "There's got to be something going on."

"Fine," I said. Rowan had kept his promise, time for me to step things up. "We're an item."

I held up my hands and shook my head to ward off all the ear-splitting squeals and hollers that erupted around the table. It did nothing.

Trevor appeared out of nowhere, pulled up a chair, and sat backward on the seat. "About damn time," he said.

"I knew it," Kora yelled.

"Good for you," Lilly chimed in.

Darlene leaned forward. "Give us more!" she demanded.

"Okay, whatever," I said. "But I told him it's a go. I'm all for it, but I didn't want to do any public displays of affection—not even handholding—because I didn't want it to be a big deal."

Terry brought a platter of chicken fingers and fries to the table. "Here you go, ladies," he said as he placed it on the table. "I feel a little wrong interrupting the fun."

I looked at Kai's father. "Trust me, Terry. You're doing us a service. Thank you." Then I turned on Trevor. "You can leave. You've done enough damage for one day."

"Yep," he said. "I'm going to call Rowan. Tell him congratulations."

I rolled my eyes as he walked away. "Now that my secret's out, and y'all have torn me away from a day filled with my body being ravaged by Rowan, we can get back to our purpose of being here and focus on Kora and Kai."

CHAPTER 25

ROWAN

Trevor and I were getting last minute things together at Jerry's Pub for the rehearsal dinner, which we would have to leave for in less than an hour.

"Nico," Trevor said, "Carter will be here soon to man the bar, and Shannon and Barb are working the front. We're heading to the rehearsal."

"Got it," Nico answered, giving us a thumbs up before getting back to his work.

We got the van loaded with the food and drinks, then hopped into the front seat. It was about a thirty-minute drive to the Warfield property, so I got comfortable and found some decent music on the radio.

After we'd been on the road for a while and I had relaxed and was enjoying the music, Trevor interrupted the vibe. "So, dude, I've been keeping out of it for a while, but what exactly is going on between you and Summer? She admitted to the girls yesterday that you two were an item, but she told you she wanted to keep things quiet."

A wicked grin filled my face. The things going on between me and Summer were hotter than I'd ever fantasized, and damn, my fantasies were awesome. If I had any future say in our relationship, the quiet, incognito shit she'd been forcing on us was going to change—and soon. I couldn't keep hiding us from the world forever. I'd wanted her for ages, and now I wanted to show her off.

I watched the countryside pass by before I spoke. "Well, we're a couple, but you know Summer. She's too insecure to take it out in the open right now."

"Maybe it's better that way. Aren't you leaving next week to go back to Texas for that interview? What if they offer you that job?"

I shook my head. "I'm going to the interview, but if they offer me a job in Texas, I'm not taking it. They have an office in Nashville, so I'm going to ask if they have any openings there. I don't want to leave this place. This is home, man. I was gone for too long. I want to stay."

Trevor glanced quickly at me before putting his eyes back on the road. "And?" he asked.

I chuckled under my breath. He knew me too well. "And, I don't want to leave her again. Being away from her never worked for me."

Trevor eyed me for a few seconds longer this time. "Have you told her that yet? When she was talking about it yesterday, she acted like it wasn't a big deal."

"Shit. You know Summer. She can't admit her feelings to anybody, and she acts like nothing bothers her. But I think she feels more for me than she's willing to admit. She should be happy that I don't want to go."

"If you're sure."

I glanced at him through narrowed eyes. "Why wouldn't I be sure? Don't hold back, man. What do you want to say?"

Trevor took a right turn and shook his head. "Like you said, I know Summer. I've also been here while you haven't. She has a way of ensuring she's never happy. It's like her superpower."

"Keeping herself miserable is a superpower?"

"Every relationship she's been in has turned toxic. She has the ability to make the good things rotten."

Fire erupted in my gut. I knew what he was talking about, and yes, she did seem to always turn things into a hot mess. "Maybe she hasn't met the right guy for her. Once she does, her superpower will change. Trust me. She has some superpowers that are made for good."

Our discussion finally ended as we pulled up in front of a big metal gate with a W on it. We pushed the intercom button, and the gates opened.

I'd never been here before, but damn it must have been nice to grow up on a gated property. We wound our way up the driveway lined on one side with rose bushes and a tree line on the other. The main house soon came into view—and what a view it was. "Fuck," I said. "No wonder Diane's granddaughter goes to a private school."

"No shit. I knew they had money, but damn," Trevor agreed.

We made our way to the back of the property where the Warfields had a pavilion and barn specifically for outdoor events. This was where the wedding was going to be.

Trevor pulled up and we climbed out of the van. Wow. I did a three-sixty, and the gorgeous views of hills, houses, barns, and fields of horses and cattle went on forever in every direction.

The wedding coordinators met us, and we helped them unload the food and kegs. After that, I had to go find Susie, so I left Trevor with them and headed to the pavilion, which was already set up with tables in long lines and a dance floor in the center.

Susie was on the other end of the pavilion, talking with an older lady. I walked in their direction. "Hey, the food's been delivered. Is there anything else you need help with?"

"Hi Rowan," Susie greeted me. "This is Annette. She's the head coordinator and will be our go-to person if we need anything or have any questions."

I shook Annette's hand. She was a pretty woman, with blonde hair cut just below her shoulders. She wore a black skirt with a white button up blouse, and crazy-high heels. How the hell could women walk in those things? "Nice to meet you," I said. "I hope I don't become too big of a pain tomorrow. I have no clue how I'm going to help them with anything."

She laughed. "Don't worry about bothering me. That's what I get paid for. Making sure everything goes off perfectly is my job, and with y'all being friends of the Warfields, things need to be even more perfect than usual." She inclined her head toward the other end of the pavilion. "The rehearsal must be over. Excuse me."

My gaze went automatically to the group that was coming through the opening. They were led by Kora and Kai, but I fixed immediately on Summer. I couldn't tell what she said, but with her body language and attitude that emanated from her, I was sure Jamison and Lance said something to piss her off. That was my girl. All sass and sarcasm. My blood warmed and pooled in areas it didn't need to be—well, not now, at least. Finally, her eyes caught mine and I winked. She answered it with a soft smile.

That smile meant more to me here amongst our friends than anything else.

"Why don't you go say hi instead of gawking at her," Susie said.

"I'm not gawking," I said.

Susie laughed. "Okay, keep on believing that." She walked away as the wedding party assembled at the head of the line for dinner. They went through the buffet line first, followed by the family, which included me, Kora's dad and my mom, Susie, and Terry. Everyone else followed.

I sat at an empty seat next to Summer. Susie, Trevor, Bryson, Darlene, Kora, and Kai sat with us.

As we ate, we laughed over high school memories, making sure Kai knew he wasn't marrying the perfect Orlinda Valley princess the town made Kora out to be. She, Summer, and Darlene had been into all sorts of mischief when they were younger, but got away with almost everything.

During the meal and discussion, my hand was never far from Summer's thigh. Every now and then she would cover it with hers and give it a squeeze. That simple touch sent sparks shooting throughout my body. I held her gaze for a brief second, and the desire to kiss her lips burned deep.

"Rowan," Trevor said, pulling my attention from Summer—for the moment, at least. "Do you remember that one time when we were at the river, tubing? You were dating some girl, I don't remember who. I could never keep them straight." He swiped his hand through the air at me when I glared at him. "Anyway, you had this huge fight, and she started screaming and went ballistic?"

"I remember that," Darlene said. "She was Sara. She didn't like how little attention she was getting."

"Oh yeah," Kora added, her eyes wide. "She was pissed because Rowan and Summer were off in their own little world, alone. I guess we'll never know what they were doing." She smirked at us impishly.

Summer looked at Kora, her eyes narrowed. "We weren't doing anything. He was teaching me how to skip rocks. Trying to help me finally figure it out."

"Yeah," I agreed. "It didn't work."

She shrugged and her hand left mine to pick up her drink. "I've gotten better over the years."

"You've gotten better at a lot of things over the years," I said. Our eyes locked, and I couldn't help it. I reached over and dragged my fingers across her cheek. "We both have," I added.

Her gaze seared into me and my heart skipped a beat. Then she leaned in, and our lips met. My eyes bulged wide, caught off-guard by her sudden willingness to show affection in public, but I quickly regained my composure and kissed her back eagerly.

It was a soft kiss, an amazing kiss, and it broke all her rules.

I slid my hand behind her head and twined my fingers in her hair, holding her there, not wanting this to end. The noise in the pavilion ceased to exist. I don't know if it was because everyone was stunned into silence at what they were witnessing, or if the world fell away in that moment.

It didn't matter. She'd kissed me in front of our friends here at the table.

Finally, she broke away and held my gaze for a brief second, then winked. "There," she whispered. "Are you happy now? Everyone knows."

My heart slammed in my chest and a smile crept across my face. I said the first thing that came to mind: "Hell yeah! That's all I wanted that day at the river. That's all I've wanted for years. Thank you."

"Okay, stop." Bryson sounded shell-shocked. "What the hell is going on here?"

"Come, on Bryson," Darlene said. "How could you not know?"

"You knew?" he asked.

She threw her hands in the air. "Who didn't?" She looked around and everyone nodded.

"So," Bryson asked, "y'all knew there was something going on between them?"

"No, we weren't sure," Kora answered, "but it was obvious they've liked each other forever."

Bryson turned to me. "Dude, if you wanted her this entire time, why did you give me such crap when I started dating Darlene?"

And here it was. Better late than never. "Bryson, I didn't give you crap because you were dating Darlene. The issue was that she was my friend, and you were constantly inserting yourself into my business. I needed space away from you, but since you were dating Darlene, you were always there. It was so annoying."

Bryson thought about that for a moment, then nodded. "I can see that. I think we both needed space."

"And maybe we both needed to grow up," I added.

"Definitely," Bryson agreed. "We've been total dicks to each other our entire lives and messed so much up."

"You could say that," I agreed.

"I'm glad you're home, Row," Bryson said.

"Thanks. I'm glad to be home."

Darelene sniffed. "You two are so sweet," she said between sobs. "I'm so glad you finally made up."

"Babe," Bryson put his arms around her, and she turned her head into him.

What the hell was going on? "Dar, you okay?" I asked.

"Pregnancy hormones," Kora answered. "She's an emotional mess."

"No shit," Summer added. "Always blubbering about something."

Darlene sniffed and took the napkin Kora handed her. "Just wait till tomorrow, Summer. I'm going to need you to lean on."

"Thrills," Summer deadpanned. "Just what I love to be—a human tissue."

Kai chuckled. "You have a heartfelt woman there, Rowan."

"Trust me, she's all bark and not much bite."

"Hmm, I might have to prove that wrong later." The grin Summer gave me made my pulse pick up.

"Damn, back up, you two," Bryson said. "Keep things PG. There are kids present." He took a sip of his drink, raised his brows, and leaned back in his chair. "Don't mean to bring up anything negative, but you two seem to have something good going on. Aren't you going back to Texas for a job interview?" he asked me.

"Yeah, about that." I took a sip of my beer. "They have an office here in Nashville and it's possible I could work there. If I'm offered the job, I could stay home if I wanted to. It's a good company to climb the ladder, even remotely. I'm going out for my interview next Thursday, but we're going to talk about the job in Nashville."

The excitement around the table became real as the possibility that I could stay and not go back to Texas sunk in.

The rest of the night was a whirlwind of activity—talking, toasts, and drinking. Finally, it was eleven o'clock and time to go. The ladies were staying here at the guest house, and we were all staying at Kai's.

As everyone got ready to leave, I grabbed Summer and led her down a path and to a small pier where we could look out over the pond and into the dark expanse of the rolling hills and the sky filled with stars. It was a perfect night. "You good?" I asked as we leaned on the railing and I slipped my arm around her waist. She'd become quiet suddenly during dinner. "Seems like something's bothering you."

She stared out over the fields, saying nothing. It was okay—I could wait. I pulled her closer to my side and she finally rested her head on my shoulder. I leaned my cheek against her hair and sighed. This was relaxing. It was what I'd needed—hell, it was what I'd always wanted.

"It's so pretty and quiet here," she said.

"No kidding." We stayed like that, both lost in our thoughts, but I couldn't shake the feeling that there was something wrong—something she wasn't telling me. I kissed her head, and the smell of honeysuckle and coconut filled my nose.

She lifted her head from my shoulder. "I've got to go."

"Hey, are we good?" I asked.

She puffed out a breath and glanced at me. "Don't start being weird, Rowan. I don't do weird, and this"—she motioned between us with one hand— "I can't do this if you get weird. So please think before you act."

I laughed, even though I knew laughing at her pissed her off and she would storm away from me, just as she was doing now. I ran to catch up and grabbed her hand, pulling her back. "Don't walk away from me, and stop letting everything get to you."

She squeezed my hand, gave me a smile, and said, "Don't be one of those overbearing boyfriends who thinks every time their girlfriend is quiet something's wrong."

We walked hand-in-hand back to the pavilion. "That would be fine if I thought that was the case. Do me a favor, Summer." I pulled her to a stop, and she turned to me. "Don't block me out. If something's bothering you, we need to talk about it."

"Fine. We'll talk about it when something bothers me. Now, though, I have to go."

I pulled her in and gave her a quick, yet heated kiss. "I'm going to miss you tonight," I whispered.

"Me too," she answered.

"Can't wait to see you in that sexy dress tomorrow."

"Can't wait to see you cleaned up and in that tux."

"There you two are," my mother said as she walked up. She glanced between us, her forehead creased in thought. "This isn't a surprise. It's about time you two acted on the sexual tension between you. There's no way a man and woman could be . . ." she brushed her hands through the air. "Anyway, the bridegroom has to go. It's almost midnight and he can't see Kora until tomorrow." She grabbed my arm and pulled me away. "You boys need to leave. Now."

"Until tomorrow night, Summertime. Save me a dance." I winked and let my mom pull me away.

Chapter 26

Summer

"I've got to tell him." It was early Saturday morning. I'd woken at five, made coffee, and was outside watching the breathtaking sunrise over the hills at the ranch as I sat at a stone table just outside the pool area.

It was going to be a busy day, and I needed time to think. I'd hardly slept last night, despite the comfiness of the bed. The secret I'd kept to myself for so many years was eating away at me. Why had I never said a word to Darlene and Kora? Hell, why hadn't I ever said anything to Rowan? They should all know. But, as always, I chose to bear this cross alone, without the support of my amazing friend group.

"Hey, I thought I'd find you out here when I saw the coffee pot already on." Darlene sat at the table next to me. "What's going on, Summer? You were really quiet last night. Were you missing Rowan?"

I shot her a look that I hoped she'd take as *shut up, I'm enjoying the quiet*, but I couldn't be that lucky.

"Sorry," she added. "Just making an observation. You did get up early."

I shook my head. "Just couldn't sleep. Your snoring kept me awake."

She nudged into me. "I don't snore."

"How do you know?" I tilted my head up at her. "You were asleep."

"True."

She finally stopped talking, and we both sat and enjoyed the view.

"Hey, y'all." Kora joined us and wrapped her arms around our shoulders. "Can you believe it's my wedding day?"

I knew it was her special day and all, but her voice was annoyingly bubbly. "Kor, it's too early for your happiness," I muttered. "Please bring it down a notch." I pulled away from the weight of her arm on my shoulder.

She joined us at the table. "I guess you having daily orgasms isn't helping with your attitude, Summer," Kora said.

"Nope. It's not helping at all," Darlene agreed. "Maybe Rowan's not good in bed."

I chuckled. "Trust me, he's just fine."

"Fine? You think he'd like to be considered 'just fine'?" Darlene asked. "His brother's amazing." Darlene glanced over her shoulder. "What do you have to say about *your* McKendry brother, Lilly? Summer says Rowan's sexual knowledge is 'just fine'." She made air quotes with her fingers.

"Oh, Jamison is a god," Lilly said with laughter in her voice. "Trust me."

"Enough." I had to stop this. "I don't give a shit how good your men are. But if you must know, Rowan knows exactly what he's doing in the bedroom, in the shower, on the kitchen counter . . ."

"Woah." Kora had her hands up. "My kitchen?"

"Your countertop is a perfect height."

"God, I'll never be able to cook in there again."

"Like you were ever planning on it?" Lilly asked.

"Nope, guess not," Kora agreed. "So have at it, Summer. As long as Rowan makes you happy and can satisfy your stubborn ass, I guess it's okay."

"Thanks for your vote of confidence." I turned to leave. "Y'all interrupted my quiet morning. I'm taking a shower."

Once I was showered and dressed in yoga pants and a button up shirt, I settled at the kitchen table with the others and ate breakfast. There was an entire spread made and delivered by the Warfield's cooking staff. I was finishing my coffee when there was a knock on the door. "Hey, it's me." Leila walked in the house with Skylar not far behind.

"Good morning, Leila. Morning, Skylar." Kora greeted them with hugs.

"Can I have a bagel?" Skylar asked as she sat at the table.

"Of course," Darlene said. "Which one?"

"Cinnamon raisin with cream cheese, please."

Are y'all doing okay?" Leila asked. "Kaye and Diane will be here soon to start your hair. They just called."

"Yep," said Skylar. "And the girls will be here also. Summer, my fingernail messed up." She showed me her middle finger.

"Skylar!" Leila chided her.

I grabbed Skylar's hand. "It's just a finger. Not a big deal." I looked at her nail. "Sweety, that's an easy fix. Once you're finished eating, we'll go in my room and fix it up, good as new."

"Thanks, Summer. You're the best."

I smiled at her. I don't know about being the best, but I was pretty damn good.

It didn't take long before the book club ladies joined us, along with Madeline, Darcie, and Susie. Ruth said hi, then took Skylar and Lena to Leila's house.

Makeup, nails, and the girls' hair were all my jobs. I got lost in the precision and technicality of it all. That, and talking with Darcie and Madelyn kept me occupied and helped to tick away the morning until it was afternoon. We ate a quick lunch, then Darlene, Lilly, and I got dressed while Kaye, Tonya, and Diane fussed over Kora.

My hair was up in a French braid with wisps around my face. I had natural makeup, yet my eyes were lined in dramatic fashion. I finished my look with red lipstick—my favorite color when it came to dressing up. With my porcelain skin, hazel eyes, and dark hair, bright red lips always made me feel beautiful. I hoped Rowan liked what he saw.

We all wore formal black gowns, as black and white were Kora's wedding colors. She loved dark purple, but none of us wanted to wear that, so we all agreed on black, with lilac bouquets wrapped in white ribbons.

I smoothed my dress down my body and along my hips, as I admired myself in the mirror. I glanced at Darlene. She struggled to get her growing stomach into her dress.

"Look at me. I can barely breathe." Darlene came up next to me, arms contorted behind her back, fighting with her zipper. "Summer, I can't get the zipper up all the way. Can you help?"

She stood tall and sucked in her belly.

"Dar, is that safe? You know that belly is holding another being."

"It's fine. But between my belly and my boobs, which have filled out even more since trying this dress on, I don't know if I'll be able to get it closed."

"Hold still." I wiggled her dress around and pulled it up a little higher, and then it zipped just fine. "There." I brushed out the wrinkles. "Perfect."

She stood and checked herself in the mirror. First her front, then her profile. She brushed her hands lightly over her small baby bump.

"You look beautiful, Darlene," Lilly said.

"You do, Dar," I said.

She beamed. "Thanks, y'all. So do you two."

"I can't believe you only have four more months," Lilly said. "And then there will be another baby in the family."

"Maybe you and Jamison will add a baby soon also."

Lilly shrugged. "You never know, though getting married first would be a good start."

I turned from the mirror and their talk of babies. "Let's go see Kora. It's almost time for pictures."

We walked across the house to Kora's room. I knocked softly and opened the door. The three of us froze.

Kora stood in front of the bay windows, the sunlight streaming in wrapping her in a glow. Not that she needed any help glowing today.

She and her father, Nigel, were finishing up their pictures. As soon as they were done, Darlene and Lilly rushed to her side and gushed all over her.

I held back.

Nigel came over to me. He'd just arrived from Florida, where he'd retired to, and looked tanned and handsome in his tux. I noticed there was more gray in his dark hair since the last time I'd seen him. "Hello, Summer."

"Hi, Nigel." He never liked me calling him Mr. Mitchell. We hugged in greeting. "Kora looks beautiful," I said.

"Yeah, she does." He sighed deeply.

"Are you going to be all emotional today too?" I asked him.

He chuckled. "Unfortunately. I can't help but wish her mother were here to see her. She'd be so proud."

Kora's mother died a long time ago. I was surprised Nigel hadn't found someone else by now. He had always been a handsome and hardworking man with a big heart. He loved his daughter, was an amazing father, and had never questioned me when I spent the night during the school week back when my parents split up. He was like the father I never had, parenting me when I needed it and allowing me under his roof like his own daughter.

"Summer, come here," Kora waved me over.

"Gotta go." I smiled at him and walked to my friends. Kora made a beautiful bride. I hugged her tightly. "Kor, you look . . ."

"Don't be getting all serious, Summer. I need you to keep things focused and reined in. I'm counting on you for your lack of emotions and ability to tell it like it is."

Darlene and Lilly wiped their eyes.

I took a deep breath and did what I was told. I reined it in. "You got it, Kor." I gave her a hug. "I promise I'm not bullshitting you when I say you look absolutely stunning. If Kai doesn't want to throw you over his shoulder, run you down the aisle, and fuck you against the first wall he comes to, I'll have to make sure he gets his head examined."

That got the reaction I expected. All three laughed and wiped their eyes. "Good," I said. "Now we can do this and not worry about the makeup I spent hours working on getting smeared. It's time for pictures."

Chapter 27

Rowan

This "helping with the wedding" as a runner thing was such a joke. The guys were already dressed and hanging out at the small groom's cabin behind the wedding pavilion. The cabin was a newer building, built for the wedding venue just last year. It contained a dressing area, two bathrooms, a small kitchenette, and a game room which contained a dart board, television, and pool table for killing time before an event.

I sat on the oversized couch in the game room with my feet up and a beer in my hand, waiting. I had nothing else to do. Susie was with the women, and, according to her texts, she'd been pretty busy. Meanwhile, not much had been going on here except for a lot of trash-talking, alcohol consumption, and dart-throwing.

"Hey, bro." Bryson fell into the cushion next to me and threw his arm over my shoulders, Jamison falling into place on the other side. "What're you doing by yourself?"

Jamison smacked me on my thigh. "Here, brother pic." He held up his camera and we all squished together. They smiled, I lifted my brows, and he snapped the picture. "Yeah. You're quiet," he said as he tapped away at his phone and sent the picture.

"Texting Lilly?" I asked.

"Yep. I promised Darcie I'd send her a picture of us. But let's get back to you. Why you so quiet?"

"Quiet? Hell, what do you expect of me? Y'all have been drinking and acting the fools you are. I have to stay focused and get you where you need to be on time." Just then my phone pinged. I read the message. "And it's time for the first look. Kai, you ready? The girls are on their way, and you need to go into your room until you're told to come out."

He blew out a breath. "Looks like we're doing this." He clapped his hands and rubbed them together. His smile filled his face and his silver eyes gleamed.

"You're not crying, are you?" Lance asked.

"Shut up, Lance," Jamison said. "Maybe one day you'll fall in love and understand how important this day is."

"What girl would be dumb enough to deal with his standards—or lack thereof?" I asked. Lance was not the type to focus on just one girl. Though their mom, Kaye, is a sweet woman, Lance and Lilly's father was an asshole—and, unfortunately, Lance might have inherited that trait. He was someone I could barely tolerate on a normal day, but somehow he remained Jamison's best friend. I'd never understood that.

"Whatever, dick. I don't see you with anyone draped over your arm."

"You didn't see him last night with Summer?" Bryson elbowed me. "I think Summer has finally opened her eyes to what's always been right in front of her."

"Yeah, well we all know what kind of person she is. Her standards are pretty low. Hell, *I* wouldn't even go there, and if Rowan thinks *I* don't have standards, what does that say for him?" Lance laughed at his own stupid joke, but I saw red-hot fire behind my eyes. I jumped up from the couch.

I'd be damned if I'd let someone talk about Summer with disrespect—and Lance, of all people, sure as hell wasn't going to get away with it. "What did you say, asshole?" I asked, nose-to-nose with him. We were about the same height, so his bulky size didn't intimidate me.

"Rowan, back off," Jamison said as he came up beside me and placed his hand on my arm.

I pulled out of his grasp, keeping my gaze on Lance. "Leave it, Jamison. Let me take this asshole. He's always irritated me. I never understood why you kept him around."

"What, Rowan?" Lance taunted. "You're the small-town god and military hero. Was it so hard to find a beautiful piece of ass anywhere else to shack up with on your trips around the globe, that you had to come home and settle for Summer?"

That was it. I didn't think, I just reacted. *Crack!* My fist made contact with Lance's nose, and the spurt of blood that ran down his face and splattered on his tux was in high contrast to the white shirt he wore.

"Fucking-a, you piece of shit!" Lance bellowed as he covered his nose with his hands.

"What the hell are you two doing?" Kai hollered. He glanced between me and Lance, his eyes bulging when he saw Lance's face. "Shit! Jamison, get your brother out of here. Bryson, get me a towel and some ice. Kora's going to be pissed." He led Lance to the kitchen. "And you need to get your shit straight. You're walking Summer down the aisle."

I didn't hear what else was said, because Jamison pulled me outside just as Susie came around the corner of the house.

"Hey, guys," she said, her voice upbeat and oozing with excitement. Then she froze when she saw me shaking out the pain that shot through my hand, and her eyes trailed over me. "What happened?"

I cradled my hand in my arm and paced in tight, angry circles. I needed to get a grip before my anger took over completely.

"Oh, nothing much," Jamison spat, directing his sarcasm at me. "Just Lance and Rowan having some words. Lance getting his nose broken. Rowan bruising his knuckles."

"Why does Rowan have bruised knuckles?" Kora came around the bend along with her dad. Nigel came over to me and put his hands on my arms to stop my pacing and checked out my hand.

"Uncle Nigel, good to see you," I said through gritted teeth.

"You too, Rowan." He grabbed my hand then caught my gaze. "It's swollen, but I don't think anything's broken. You need to ice it."

"It's fine," I seethed.

"What happened, Row?" Kora asked

His gaze wandered across my face and a smirk ticked at the corners of his mouth. "Good luck dealing with her." He jerked his head toward Kora and smacked my arms, just as Kora walked up.

"Yeah, Rowan?" my mother echoed. Great, she and all the women were there too. Summer's eyes were huge.

"Rowan?" Summer said as she rushed to my side and grabbed my hand. "Who did you punch?"

I shook my head and closed my eyes.

"He punched Lance," Susie said as she came out from the house with Bryson right behind her. "And Lance has a broken nose."

"What?" chorused every female voice in the vicinity.

Bryson came to my defense, his hands in the air. "Lance deserved it. He was speaking shit and Rowan shut him up. Sorry, Kaye."

"Speaking shit about what?" Kaye asked.

"Or better yet, who?" my mother added.

I shook my head at Bryson. Hopefully he got the message that he better keep it quiet.

"Great," Kora fumed. "You dumbassess can't keep your testosterone in check for a day? This is my wedding!"

I turned toward Kora and froze. She was beautiful—angelic.

Guilt filled my gut. "Damn, Kor. You look amazing. I'm sorry, but if you knew what he said—trust me, you'd support me."

"I'll find out later. Right now, I want my first look. I'm dying to see my future husband, so everyone go away and let us do this."

We all filed into the house. I pulled Summer off to the side. There was no way in hell I was going to let her anywhere near Lance, and *I* sure as hell didn't want to be in arm's reach of him. I'd only punch him again for good measure.

Every place in the cabin had a good view of Kora and Kai's first look, since the wall along the back was basically one long window. Summer and I stood off to the side, left alone while everyone was getting ready to gush over the bride and groom.

"What could Lance have said to piss you off enough that you punched him?" Summer asked. "I know he's not your favorite person, but, Rowan, seriously? Fighting isn't your style unless you're . . ." She stopped and looked at me.

Damn. I turned away from her. She really knew me. Too well.

She turned me back to face her. "Who were you sticking up for?"

I looked away. "Shouldn't you be watching this?" Kai was already outside, waiting with his back to the bride's entrance, and Summer reluctantly turned her attention away from me as Kora walked around the corner and stood close to him. He turned around, and the expressions on their faces were priceless. They both cried and wrapped each other in a hug. Everyone in the cabin did the same. I admit, even I got a little misty watching my cousin wrapped in the arms of the man she loved.

I heard a sniff and turned to Summer. When she looked at me, she smiled and gave a small shrug. I wiped a lone tear from her cheek. "Look at you. Getting sappy in your old age?"

"Fuck you," she said with a laugh.

"I'd like that," I said with a wink.

She laughed again and rolled her eyes.

I wrapped my arm around her waist and pulled her close. "You look amazing," I whispered. She did. The dress she wore hugged all her curves and showed just enough cleavage that it was sexy, yet not overdone. Spaghetti straps showed off her shoulders, and the back dipped low toward her hips. I held her away from me and gave her a once-over. Her chestnut hair and brown eyes popped against the bright red of her lipstick. I leaned in to kiss her.

She put her hands on my chest. "You'll mess up the lipstick. We have pictures in a minute. But you also look pretty damn handsome, at least for someone who's just the help."

"Yeah, well," a voice said nearby, "that's a good thing, as he's no longer the help."

I turned to see Kai and Kora standing next to us.

"Seems that Lance has to take care of an injury," Kai said, "so it's a good thing you have on a tux. Looks like you're in the wedding."

"Think you can handle taking Lance's spot and escorting Summer?" Kora added.

"I think I can handle it," I said as I turned to Summer and my blood pulsed through my veins. "Looks like it's you and me, Summertime."

She smiled. "I guess so."

"Good. Stay close. We'll need you both for pictures." Kora pulled Kai away to continue their circuit around the room.

Summer closed the small gap between us and placed her hands on my chest. "So, did you hit him so you'd get in the wedding, finally? That's pretty desperate of you."

I placed my hands on her arms, feeling the need to tell her the truth. "Lance was being his typical jackass self and needed to be put straight."

"That's what I figured," Summer said. "You never answered me. Who were you sticking up for? And tell me the truth. If it was me, I can take it."

"What makes you think it was you?"

"If it was anyone else, one of the other guys would have punched him. He said something to get to you, so I'm figuring it was about me."

"Beautiful and smart." I nodded. "Yeah, it was, but don't make me repeat it."

"I won't, because I don't care what he thinks of me. Never have. He's too much like his old man, and I don't have time for that kind of shit in my life." She wrapped her arms through mine, stood on her toes, and kissed my lips. "Thank you for still being my knight in shining armor—or, I guess, my knight in one hot tux."

She kissed me again, soft and sweet. I hovered there a moment, enjoying her scent and warmth. Then I smirked and said, "Thought we couldn't mess up your lipstick."

"It's long-lasting. It won't wear off that easily." She winked and smiled. "Even if it did, I can reapply."

"Okay everyone," Susie announced. "It's time for pictures, then we need to get a couple married."

"We'll continue this later," I said to Summer as we joined everyone outside.

CHAPTER 28

SUMMER

The wedding was perfect, and having Rowan across from me made it even better. His tight-cut hair, the scruff that covered his face, his brown eyes, and the perfectly fitted tux made him look like a billionaire businessman—yet more handsome and hot than any billionaire businessman I could imagine.

We sat at the head table and watched as Kora and Kai took their first dance as husband and wife. Then Kora danced with her father, and Kai surprised everyone when he asked Tonya to dance with him, since he didn't have a mother. She was shocked speechless and beamed. She might be a pain most of the time, but she loved her people big, and she deserved to be in the spotlight.

"Now the bride and groom want the wedding party to join them on the dance floor," the DJ announced.

The couples walked hand-in-hand onto the dance floor, and as soon as Rowan wrapped one arm around my waist and pulled me close, my heart fluttered, and my knees went weak—but the look he gave me made my insides liquify. I couldn't pull my eyes from his. How could he look at me like that and still have composure on this floor? Or expect me to? Shoot, I was having a hard time not ravaging his lips on the spot or pulling him from the dance floor and finding a storage closet—or better yet, a large tree or stable stall—to take advantage of him. He was too delectable to ignore.

"What's going through that mind of yours?" Rowan asked as we spun slowly to the beat of the music.

"If you really want to know," I snickered, "I was wondering where I could take you to let you have your way with me. You in that tux is . . . mmm, mmm, mmm." I skimmed my tongue over my lips and got the exact reaction I was hoping for: his mouth on mine.

I could tell how much he wanted what I wanted. I could feel it in his kiss. The need, the desire, the want. I pulled away just enough to say, "People are watching."

"Good," he said. "Let them watch."

My eyes trailed over his face as we swayed in each other's arms. This seemed all too familiar. "Do you remember prom?" I asked.

"How could I forget it," he said. "I'd just broken up with Melinda and your boyfriend had dumped you, so you wore the dress you'd already bought, I wore the tux I'd already rented, and we went together."

"Yeah, we did. We danced the entire night. It was so much fun, as far as a high school dance went. It didn't feel like this, though."

Rowan's eyes held mine. "Maybe for you, but I was at prom with my dream girl."

I was his dream girl. My heart swooned, yet it didn't seem possible. "Why didn't you ever say anything?"

He pulled away more. "I was afraid I'd scare you off, and then I would have also lost my best friend."

He was probably right. My headspace sucked senior year, well all through my teen years. I didn't think I was worthy of anything and was lost in my depressed world.

But now, I had to know something, "Why tell me now?"

I didn't get an answer.

"Okay, lovebirds," the DJ interrupted, "let's get this party started and open up the dance floor." He turned up a fast tune and the floor filled quickly.

Rowan gestured to the tables and I gladly obliged. "I need to use the lady's room and grab a drink. Want me to grab you anything?"

"A beer, please." He kissed me. "Hurry back."

I was beaming and floating on a cloud. Who knew being with an amazing man could make a woman fell like this. My eyes caught Kora and Kai, and Darlene and Bryson on the dance floor. Okay, Kora and Darlene. That's who.

There was a spring in my step when I got out of the restroom and stopped at the bar to order our drinks. I doubted anything could bring me down to earth, and I wasn't going to complain.

Lance joined me as I waited for my drinks. I glanced at his face. It was swollen and bruising. "I'm surprised you're still here," I said, wincing. "Thought you'd need to go lay down. It looks like it hurts."

"Just a bit." He asked the bartender for a beer. "Can't miss this wedding, though." Lance leaned against the bar. "Don't know what you did to get Rowan to bow at your feet, but he's pretty smitten with you."

"Smitten?" I asked, and thanked the bartender as he placed our drinks on the counter.

"Yeah. He must be, with how quickly he was willing to stand up for you."

I shrugged. "Yeah, well he shouldn't have to stand up for me." I narrowed my eyes. "What did you say that got him so pissed off?"

"Doesn't matter. Just trying to rile him up, you know—pick on him like the good ol' days."

"Yeah, well looks like that was a piss-poor idea."

"Nice language."

"No worse than the trash you date."

"You would know."

Yeah, that dig hit home, but there was no way I'd ever let Lance know how much his words hurt. "What you think of me has never bothered me. Too bad you can't have some of your mother in you. I guess Lilly took all the good DNA."

Lance took a deep sip of his beer, and I walked back to the table, which had been filled in at one end with James, Lena, Madelyne, Darcie, and Skylar. I sat next to Skylar and gave Rowan his beer.

"Well, if it isn't the most beautiful princesses of Orlinda Valley—and James, of course," I said.

"Hi Summer," Darcie said. "We saw you kissing my Uncle Rowan."

"Yeah," James said, his voice suspicious. "Why were you kissing him? You aren't married."

I glanced at Rowan, and he hid his face in his beer, a sexy smirk plastered on it.

"Duh," Madelyne said as she rolled her eyes dramatically. "You don't have to be married to kiss."

"Yeah," Skylar agreed. "Don't you know anything?"

"Boys are so stupid," Darcie said.

"I'm not stupid. Kissing is gross, and you shouldn't kiss anyone until you're ready to have babies," James insisted.

"Uh, who told you that?" I asked.

"My grammy, and she knows everything."

"I love Grammy," Madelyne said, "but she said that Summer had a bad attitude, and that's not true." She turned to me. "You don't, Summer."

"Attitude? What's that?" James asked.

"OMG, James. You really don't know anything, do you?" Darcie teased.

"Y'all . . ." I tried to calm them down as Rowan shook with laughter. I gave him a side-eyed glance. He was no help.

James leaned toward Darcie. "Not true!" He yelled. "You're just a mean old little witch."

"Kids." I put my hands on each of them. "We can't talk to each other like this. Especially on Aunt Kora and Uncle Kai's wedding day. That's not nice. If you want to talk things out, you should do that, but yelling isn't the answer."

"So, we should fight and break each other's noses like Uncle Rowan did to Lance?" asked James.

"What?" Darlene bellowed, suddenly paying attention to the kids' conversation. "No, James. Not acceptable."

I laughed and some of the concern oozed from my chest. "James, your mom's right. You should never fight. Your uncle was sticking up for a friend."

"Oh, so when someone picks on one of the girls at school, then I can punch them in the nose?" James asked.

"Good God, James," I said, and glanced at Bryson or Rowan for help. They still were useless. "No, you can't. Now, why don't you each see if your grandmas will get you a piece of cake?"

"Yay, we can have cake!" they cried as they bounded away toward the grandmothers.

I watched the kids run across the pavilion, then took a big swig of my drink. Damn, they were a handful.

"You're so good with those kiddos," Darlene said. "I can't wait till you get to meet our baby. You'll have to babysit."

I laughed. "Of course! You know I loved sitting for James and Darcie."

Darlene took a sip of water and spoke over the top of her glass. "You'd make a great mother one day, Summer. I've always known that."

I shrugged. "Maybe, but no time soon."

"Watch out, Rowan," Bryson quipped, "or she'll have you getting ready for a child soon. Even without marriage."

"I don't think we need to talk about that," Rowan said as he choked on his drink.

"Why, don't you want to be a dad?" Jamison asked.

"Of course I do. More than anything. Someday. But . . ."

And that's all I heard. Rowan wanted to be a parent more than anything. My heart, which was still floating from Rowan's closeness just minutes ago, plummeted in my chest so hard it was like a plane crashed in my gut. I didn't even feel this upset when Lance was putting me down at the bar. I glanced around at everyone, wondering if they'd seen my shift in mood, and then tried my best to keep up with the conversations around me, but failed miserably. Lilly sat close to Jamison, his arm draped over the back of her chair, and Bryson leaned his elbows on the table, head of the conversation as usual.

Couples were everywhere. I glanced around the room, and my eyes fell on Leila and Adler, who sat with the book club ladies, deep in conversations as the kids ate their cake. Leila was also pregnant, due in February. Then, of course, there were Kora and Kai, snapping pictures with guests, both of them glowing. I would guarantee she'd be pregnant by Christmas. I knew they didn't want to wait.

Everyone happy. Everyone a family.

Darlene was talking to Rowan, and I caught part of their conversation. "I'm glad you'll be here to be a part of this one's life from birth. She'll need her uncle around to keep her grounded and keep her daddy from going ballistic. You're the focused and calm one of the three, Rowan," Darlene said as she rubbed her small belly. "Well, usually." She winked.

Jamison agreed. "You're like Dad that way. He had so much patience and was always so even-keeled."

"He had to be," Bryson said. "Look at Mom. Talk about opposites attracting."

The music picked up tempo and the DJ announced it was time to do some line dancing. Lilly and Darlene pulled me on the floor, soon followed by the guys, and all talk of children was forgotten.

CHAPTER 29

ROWAN

Damn, I needed water, or a beer. We'd been dancing forever, but Summer was my permanent partner, so I was not complaining. Dancing with her was always a party. Shy, she was not—her craziness came out on the dance floor. She started a line dance and pulled me down the center with her at one point.

I leaned into her ear as one song ended and another began. "What do you say we get a drink?"

"Sure."

Thank God. I pulled her from the floor and wove our way around tables to the bar. I ordered two waters—hydrating was more important now than alcohol. We found a quiet table and sat, relaxed. Kora and Kai were both still on the dance floor, surrounded by our friends and family. "I don't know how they're going to have much of a wedding night. They've got to be ready to collapse."

Summer's gaze followed mine. Kai leaned toward Kora, and she leaned her head back in laughter. He kissed her on the cheek as a slow song started and he wrapped her in his arms.

"I'm sure they'll be fine," she said. "They've been planning this for a long time. You haven't been here to hear the disgusting stories of what they want to do to each other on their wedding night. Way too many nights at Jerry's Pub have been spent talking about it." She glanced at me. "I can tell you condoms are not in their travel bags. Baby making is part of their honeymoon plans."

"Already?" I asked. I couldn't imagine having a baby as soon as I got married.

"They've been together a year, and, as Kai said, he's in his mid-thirties. He's not getting any younger. His sperm count gets smaller every day."

"Summer!" I chuckled. "You've always had a way with words." My eyes raked across her face and down her chest. A need clawed at me deep in my gut—a need to be with her—in private. "What do you say we get some fresh air?"

She looked around. "We're in an open-sided pavilion. I think we have as much fresh air as we can get on a cattle farm."

I shook my head. "Fine, let's get out of here. I have a need only your lips can fill."

"You want me to . . ." She stuck her tongue in her cheek and wiggled her brows suggestively.

I choked on my water and pounded my chest. "No, Summer. At least not here, not now. Later, absolutely." I grabbed her hand and gestured with my head. "Come on."

I pulled her out the back of the pavilion and down a path. We walked in silence, hand-in-hand past the pier we stopped at last night. I wanted to be far away from wondering eyes.

The path had small solar lamps lining it, giving off just enough light so we could see where we were going. The moon was almost full, bathing the hills in a silvery glow. Up ahead was a covered bridge, and we walked to the middle of it and leaned on the railing. The view was amazing. The path continued ahead of us and stretched out into the rolling hills, where a few cows grazed. It was a clear and peaceful night, and a few stars from the early night sky twinkled above.

I reached out and intertwined our fingers. Summer glanced at me and gave me a small smile, which I willingly returned. No words were said—none were needed—and she laid her head on my shoulder.

This was what I had been missing while I was in the Army. Being back in Orlinda Valley and around my family and friends again, and being with Summer, filled a vacancy I'd carried around for a long while.

This night had been perfect—with the exception of Lance's comments and my reaction. My heart hammered against my chest. I wondered if Summer could feel it. I breathed in deep and let it out. That got her attention, and she lifted her head.

"What's up?" she asked.

My eyes searched her gorgeous face, slid across her cheeks, down to her chest. Back up to her face, because I could not think about her chest right now.

"Rowan? What the hell's wrong with you?" She backed away a bit. "You look weird."

"I'm just thinking."

"Well, stop. You're creeping me out."

Typical Summer. I shook my head. "Do you know why I came home? Why I got out of the Army?"

She shrugged. "You were tired of being gone and missed everyone. We've talked about it. I wasn't surprised like everyone else." She stopped and tipped her head to the side. "Well, I was a little surprised to see you standing in my kitchen when I got out of the shower, acting like a stalker, but it's turned out pretty good for the most part."

"For the most part?" I made a face, but then saw the laughter in her eyes, and the world slowed as I took her in.

I reached out and tugged on a strand of her hair that had fallen loose from her clip, then closed the space between us and grabbed her hands. "Summer, you're right. I needed to come home to be closer to everyone. To reconnect. To be a part of Kora's wedding. But those aren't the only reasons."

I let go of one of her hands and brushed my knuckles across her cheek. Her skin was so soft. I tucked a piece of hair behind her ear. "You were part of the reason I came home, Summer. I needed to see you, to talk with you face-to-face, not through a cell phone. Nothing filled the void being away from you had created."

I held her hands again, more so she wouldn't walk away than needing to hold them. I looked deep into her eyes—those beautiful, large, hazel eyes. I've watched them shine with laughter, glow with happiness, flare up with anger and vengeance. Now they were wide with questions.

Here goes nothing.

"Summer, you're the one person who truly understands me. You've known me for so long and have always been there for me. You make me who I am. You make me feel special."

I paused and took a breath, then glanced down at our hands and squeezed her tighter. "I need you to know this, because," I stopped and held her gaze, "I can't live without you anymore."

I felt her try to pull away, which I was expecting, but I held her tight and resisted her attempts to flee. I knew Summer better than she probably knew herself, and I knew her pattern of running away from relationships. But not this time. I held her tight and wouldn't let her go anywhere. "Don't pull away, Summer. This week has been amazing. It's been everything I always dreamed about."

She shook her head. "Rowan, I can't. You know I don't believe in marriage and long-term relationships. They never turn out. They always end badly. You're going back, anyway. Your job isn't here."

"Not true. Have you not been listening to me? I'm going back Thursday to interview, but they have a job available here. I can stay if I want to. And I want to. More than I've ever wanted anything. Home is where you are."

I brushed her hair from her face. I didn't want her to look away. I needed her to see me. "I know how hard relationships and love are for you, but you know what's possible. You just have to see that you're worth it. And, Summer, you are so worthy of respect, and you *can* be in a positive relationship. You *can* be loved." I held her face tight and looked hard into her eyes. "And I love you, Summer."

I felt her freeze. Her body went rigid. Those were the words she feared above all else. Words she put no stock in, ever.

"Breathe, Summertime," I begged.

She took in a breath and let it out but stood there still and quiet. I had a hold of her. She couldn't move, so she closed her eyes—her way of closing out reality.

I moved my hands to her shoulders and waited.

The world stopped.

The music from the reception faded away. The only things I focused on were me and Summer. The saying *silence is deafening* became my reality. There were no truer words.

"Say something," I whispered.

She shook her head. "I can't," she said, her voice soft. She opened her eyes. They looked lost, empty, and glistened with tears. "We have a good thing, Rowan. Why ruin it? I don't know how to love. And, anyway, there's so much more you don't—"

I placed my fingers lightly over her lips to stop the negative words from escaping. "Here's what I know about you. I know your family life sucked. I know your parents' relationship made you tough, independent, a little mixed up and confused during your goth years, and gave you the take-no-shit attitude that everyone who knows you loves about you. I know you deliberately chose assholes to date because you're afraid of putting your heart out there to get stomped on again. I know all those things and I *still* love you. I've always loved you but have been too stupid until recently to act on my feelings. And I know you feel something for me. I felt it in your kisses and your body when we've made love."

She squirmed beneath my hold, but I held on tighter and lowered my gaze to hers. "Summer, we made love, and I know that's uncomfortable for you, but you need to face it. You feel something for me. And it's good. It's real good. Hell, it's the best damn thing that's ever happened to me."

I waited. My heart beating so damn hard, it hurt. I don't know how I expected her to react, but if she ran now . . .

"Rowan. Stop." She jerked from my grasp, breaking our connection. "There's just so much more I . . ." she shook her head and took a step back. "I can't do this." She put her hand up between us as a single tear fell down her cheek.

I moved forward, but she shook her head. "Don't . . . I'm sorry." Her chest heaved, and she turned and walked quickly away.

"Summer!"

She ran faster up the walk toward the pavilion.

I watched her as long as I could before I needed to lean on something. "Fuck," I hissed, and leaned my elbows on the rail.

I tried. I gave it my all, but it was too little, too late. My heart grew heavy, and I combed my fingers through my hair. The words she left unfinished echoed in my ears. Just so much more *what*? Why did I feel like there was something left unsaid?

But most of all, what would it take to get her to realize love was worth it?

CHAPTER 30

SUMMER

I turned before going into the pavilion. At the sight of him leaning against the railing of the bridge in defeat, my heart shattered like a crystal chandelier falling on a tiled floor. What had I done? The most caring guy I knew was hurting because of me. Maybe I should go back. Explain things to him. Tell him why I can't promise him anything.

"There you are." Darlene's voice broke through the melancholy filling my soul. "Kora's going to the house to change and get ready to leave."

I nodded and gazed one last time toward Rowan. "Okay." I walked past Darlene, but she stopped me.

"Summer?" She pointed toward Rowan. "What's going on?"

I looked at her and felt my eyes fill with tears. I swallowed hard against the lump that formed in my throat. "Doesn't matter. Come on. Kora needs us."

She didn't say anything else. Instead, she followed me silently to the house that had been taken over by the bridal party.

Kora, Susie, and Lilly were already there, and Kora was stepping out of her dress.

"There y'all are," Kora said. "This has been the best night!" She gushed as she pulled on her white jumpsuit, her going-away outfit. When she turned, her face filled with emotion. "Thank you so much for being here and being a part of this day." She hugged Lilly and Susie.

"Of course," Lilly said. "Nothing could have kept me away."

She then turned to me and Darlene. "And you two."

She looked at us for a second, then the waterworks she had been holding in all day finally gushed forth. Darlene followed suit. I was already emotional because of my own shitty situation, but I wasn't going to let it out here.

Kora wrapped her arms around us both and said between sobs, "This was so much better than I ever imagined. I'm so glad you two were a part of this day."

Darlene's sobs matched Kora's.

"Good God, you two," I said, trying unsuccessfully to separate myself from them. "Come on! It's not like you haven't planned your wedding for a lifetime, or had a year to prepare your emotions." I sniffed as thoughts of what I would never have wracked my brain, and a picture of Rowan jumped into my head.

"Hey," Kora separated and wiped her eyes. "Are you crying, Summer?"

Fuck. "No." I turned away. "Of course not." I wiped at my cheeks quickly. Damn emotional bullshit.

"What's going on, Summer? I know you're not emotional about my wedding." Kora dabbed at her eyes with a tissue and Darlene did the same.

Then Darlene snitched on me and said, "When I left the reception, I found her outside watching Rowan, and though she won't admit it, there were tears in her eyes."

Kora turned to me in shock, and I glared daggers at Darlene.

Kora started to speak, but I stopped her. "Don't," I said. "Today is not about me. It's about you, and right now your husband's waiting to whisk you off somewhere romantic, where I'm sure you'll get pregnant so you and Darlene can raise your babies together like you've always dreamed of."

"Yeah, Summer, you're probably right," Kora said. "But he can wait a little longer. What's going on with you?"

I swiped at the air and tried my best to act like nothing was bothering me, but I was never good at acting and had to swallow down the lump that had grown in my throat. "Nothing's going on. I'm fine."

Yeah, I wouldn't make it in Hollywood. Kora didn't believe me.

"Stop, Summer," Kora insisted. "If there's' something going on, you can talk to us. Though I don't know what could have happened. I know how Rowan feels about you. I know he loves you."

I let out a sigh. Of course she did. "It doesn't matter. I told him I couldn't give him the relationship he wanted, and I don't believe in marriage. He's wasting his time if he thinks I'll change my mind." Frustration fueled my words, and I walked away, my hands on my hips. I stood tall and took in deep breaths to calm my aching heart as I stared through the windows into the darkness. *No one understands what's going on, because I never told them. If they knew, they'd understand why I can't be with Rowan.*

"Hey," Kora turned me toward her. Her determined face took me aback. "No, Summer," she said. "*You*'re wasting your time if you think you don't deserve him. You do. Your heart knows it. That's why you're so upset. Don't let your past dictate your future. Don't repeat your parents' mistakes. Make a new path for yourself. You've done so much already! You put yourself through beauty school *and* you're a successful stylist. You *can* love someone. Especially Rowan."

"Kora's right," Darlene agreed. "Summer, let yourself be happy."

Lilly jumped into the conversation. "Not that you care what I think, but I grew up watching you go head-to-head with people at every turn. No one ever intimidated you, and Rowan always stood by your side. You two have always been perfect together."

"I know I really don't have a say as I've only been here for a week," Susie said, "but I believe your upbringing isn't something that defines you unless you let it. Look at Kai. If anyone had a right to not believe in love and family, it's my brother. He never had anyone to take care of him or show him what it meant to truly love someone. He did all the caring. But he found Kora and let himself love her and be loved."

Well, that was the nail in the coffin of my excuses. Damn her and her relevant life experiences. How could I tell her to shut up, she's wrong?

I couldn't. She was new here. She was too sweet. Hell, she made a point I couldn't argue with. "Fine," I conceded. "I'll think about what y'all said. But now we need to get the glow sticks outside and let you start your honeymoon." I grabbed the boxes of glowsticks and passed them around to Lilly and Susie.

"Summer, wait. I want to talk with you." Kora took the glowsticks from me. "Darlene, can you go with them and hand these out?"

"Of course," she said and followed them out.

"Summer, talk to me. Just me."

Kora, the friend I could always count on . . . I looked at her and again my eyes filled with tears. "I know what you're going to say, Kor, but I don't know how to love him," my voice was a whisper. "He deserves more."

"You don't know how, or you're scared? I remember when your dad left you and how hurt you were. Then when your mom started drinking, you felt alone. Then your grandma died, and you felt deserted. But you always had us. My family. We always included you. No matter what you think, you know how to love—and you've always been different when Rowan's around, a better version of yourself. There's a glow about you, and even your sarcasm isn't as harsh."

Dammit. I hated when she was right, but she didn't know the entire story. She didn't know my secret. That was one thing I'd never even told her.

"I can't promise that you aren't going to hurt sometimes, but love is worth it," she continued. "If you can tell me you don't feel better just being around Rowan, I'll shut up. If you tell me you have no feelings for him, I'll never mention it again." She grabbed my hands. "But, Summer, if you can't say those things, you deserve to trust your heart and try. Rowan's one of the good ones, and he loves you."

Why did my best friend have to be so perfect, and so good at making speeches?

"I've got to go," she continued. "But I didn't want to leave without saying this to you. Promise me you'll think about what I said."

Like I could tell her no. I nodded. "Yes. I will."

She beamed at me. "Great," she said as she bounced on the balls of her feet. "Thank you." She pulled me in for a hug.

I laughed and hugged her back. "Okay, okay. Let's get you to Kai. You need to get out of here."

I watched with everyone else, cheering as the limo drove Kora and Kai down the winding driveway and out of view. I smiled. Couldn't help it. As I'd watched Kora walk toward Kai and seen his face light up with love at the sight of her, my heart filled with joy. Their embrace and kiss seemed different than it had all night. In normal clothes, they looked more in love, and it seemed more official.

Yep, marriage looked good on both of them. Not that I had any doubt.

"It's good to see you smiling." Darlene wrapped her arm around my shoulders.

"How could I not? Those two are finally married. They looked different just now. Like they were meant for each other."

"Yeah, marriage will do that to you."

"Maybe they'll stop being all disgusting all the time," I said.

"I doubt it. Do you think Bryson and I aren't disgusting anymore?"

I thought about it. They'd been married for almost six years, and yes, they were still quite disgusting. "Nope. I guess it takes decades to wear off."

"Whatever, Summer. You love us."

"No shit," I said, then laughed and pulled her in for a hug.

"I'm glad you're happier than you were a bit ago. Maybe you can go talk to Rowan? He really wants to talk with you."

My happiness evaporated instantly, and I pushed her gently away. "Did you come over here to bask in the happiness of our best friend, or to get me to talk to Rowan?"

Her shoulders met her ears. "He's one of our best friends."

"Such a bitch."

"No. I did come over here to bask in the joy of Kora going off on her honeymoon, but letting you know Rowan wanted to talk didn't seem like such a bad suggestion."

"I can't."

"Summer, why not? You're being ridiculous."

"Stay out of it, Darlene. Please. And tell him to stay somewhere else tonight." I walked quickly away, and in typical Darlene style, she followed behind me as I entered the house to clean up.

"Stop, Summer. There's more than you not being able to love Rowan, because I know that's bullshit. You love him, everyone can see that. So, what's really bothering you?" She grabbed my arm and turned me toward her. "Talk to me, Summer."

Her eyes, filled with concern, spoke volumes. She and Kora were the best. They were like the sisters I never had—and never needed, because I had them.

They were my friends who were always there when my life was falling apart after my parents' divorce, and when my first boyfriend broke my heart and walked away because Rowan scared him off.

Because they were always there, I should be able to confide in them. I sighed deep and a sudden feeling of exhaustion and defeat filled me. I sunk into the couch, "You're right. There's more," I said, and placed my head in my hands.

She sat next to me on the edge of the cushion and faced me.

Telling Darlene now might make it easier to tell Kora later. I took in a shuddering breath. I couldn't keep this to myself any longer—it was eating away at me. Once I got it out, they would understand.

I took a large cleansing breath and said, "Do you remember how bad my periods were when I was in high school? I missed a week of school and ended up at the doctor?"

She nodded. "Why?"

"I have something called endometriosis. It's when your uterus is messed up. I've had all types of tests and procedures done over the years." Tears poured down my face as my voice caught. "I can't get pregnant. I'll never have babies." There I said it.

"What?" Darlene's voice went up a few octaves and she sat up straighter. "How long have you known this?"

I took a deep breath. "I found out when I was eighteen. I've had procedures done over the years to try and reverse it, but they never succeeded."

"You've never said a word to any of us? Rowan doesn't even know?"

I avoided eye contact and shook my head.

"Summer!" She grabbed my hands. "Are you sure there's no way? I've heard—"

I stopped her. "There's a ninety-eight percent chance I will not be able to get pregnant."

"Ninety-eight isn't zero."

I laughed through the tears. Always Darlene finding the smallest ray of light in the darkest night. I shook my head. "Not gonna happen."

"So, you're using this as your reasoning to not love Rowan?"

"Yes." I finally met her gaze. "He needs to be a father—and before you say anything, I know we could adopt, but I want him to have a chance to be with someone who can give him a biological child. He deserves it."

"Shouldn't you tell him this and let him decide for himself?"

A pit opened deep in my chest, and I swore I was going to be sucked into it.

I looked at her and the tears in her eyes caused my own dam to break. I couldn't hold them in any longer.

She wrapped her arms around me and held me. "Summer, I wish you would have said something sooner."

My shoulders shook with sobs. Years of dealing with this on my own and holding in the anger and frustration came out on Darlene's shoulder.

Finally, my tears subsided, and I pulled away. She handed me a tissue and I dried my eyes.

"You need to tell him." Her voice was soft. "It seems only fair. He thinks you don't love him."

I didn't think my heart could break any more, but I was wrong. "I can't," I whispered. "I can't."

CHAPTER 31

SUMMER

Darlene took me home Saturday night and I begged her to make sure Rowan kept his distance for the weekend. She was the only person I texted Sunday, though Rowan tried his hardest to get me to answer him.

I ignored him. I wasn't ready to talk. I needed time, so I finally turned off my phone and hid it in my dresser drawer. Out of sight, out of mind.

By Monday morning, I was sinking in my depression, and ready to get out into the world. I grabbed my phone, which was now dead, plugged it in, and left it in my room for the day. My weekly Monday duties were calling, and without my phone I'd be able to focus on my work. I needed to place an order for product, and I wanted to talk with our salesperson to ask about the curling iron he showed me a few weeks ago.

I threw on my favorite gray sweats and black tank top and went to the only place that could give me peace and get me out of my own head—Shear Perfection.

No one was at the salon when I arrived, which was typical. Diane and Kaye didn't show up on Mondays until around lunch, and knowing I'd be here most of the morning, they always brought food. I locked the doors behind me, turned the music up on the Bluetooth speakers, and got to cleaning. The music was loud. I didn't want to hear the phone or anyone who might possibly come knocking or looking for me—especially not Rowan.

My heart clenched tight in my chest at the simple thought of his name. I was thankful he didn't follow me home after the wedding. I needed space and time to get my feelings under control.

I realized while I spent agonizing time away from him, that I was falling in love with him too. Fuck, who was I kidding? I wasn't *falling* in love. I'd *been* in love with Rowan for, God, I didn't know how long—and now he admits that he's loved me forever? I brushed my hands over my face. I couldn't hide my feelings much longer. Anyone who knew me would see right through me and my bullshit. But my being with Rowan would be such a bad choice for him. He was a great guy. He needed more than I could ever give him.

I threw myself into organizing the inventory, and, as always, it worked to calm me. I didn't know what it was about the hair salon—whether it was the smells of the products, or the hum of the dryers that always took me away from life, but that's how it had always been. There was something grounding about washing, styling, and running my fingers through someone's hair, helping them create the look they wanted. Helping them to feel beautiful. Even filing and painting nails could put me in a place where I could be me and get out of my own head.

I cleaned behind every chair and in every corner. It always amazed me where hair could hide, filling the little cracks and crevices of the salon. Always trying to stay just out of reach so they could lay around a little longer, never seen and maybe forgotten.

It was a lot like the lies I'd told myself for years, and the lies I'd made my friends believe. Lies about how I didn't need love. Lies about how love wasn't worth it. It wasn't important. Lies about how I was good by myself. I didn't need anyone. If I just told one small lie at a time, it wouldn't hurt anyone—yet over time they built up a wall around me, and letting anyone in who I could trust became difficult.

Great, Summer, I thought as I finished sweeping. *You're comparing your life to the cracks and corners in a salon. Great metaphor.* Kora and Darlene's teacher-hearts would be proud.

I chuckled and turned the music up louder. Soon, I lost track of time as I washed towels, organized shelves again—which I'd done last week and didn't really need to do this soon—and other small repetitive tasks that comforted me. I was on the phone with our sales rep ordering more stock when the back door opened.

"Hey, Summer. Are you here?" Kaye's voice carried through the kitchen into the office. I muted the phone. "We brought lunch."

"I'm placing our restock order, Kaye. Be out in a minute."

She poked her head in. "Did you see the note I left about the color I needed?"

I tapped my pad. "On my list."

"You're awesome, Summer. Tell Jasper hi."

I relayed the message, finished the order, and clicked off my phone. I laid my hands flat on the table and leaned back to take in a deep breath. I entered the new products I ordered on our inventory spreadsheet and walked into the kitchen. Kaye and her husband, Charles, and Diane and her husband, Tom, were sitting at the round table in the corner, bags of my favorite food on the counter—bar-becue.

"We knew you'd be here," Charles said, "so we brought lunch. Grab a sandwich and some macaroni and cheese and eat with us." He held his sandwich high in the air. It was overflowing with bar-becue and looked mouthwatering.

I fixed my sandwich, piled macaroni and cheese on my plate, and sat at the table. "Don't you guys work?"

Charles swallowed a bite of his sandwich. "Yes, but not today. I took some extra days because of the wedding."

"Yep, we had Skylar," Tom said. "And had to get her to kinder-garten this morning."

Charles winked at me. "You must have had a fun time Saturday. No one heard from you at all Sunday. We went by Tonya's to see Nigel before he went back to Florida, and you didn't answer when we came knocking."

They came knocking? I'd had no clue. It could have been when I was in the bathtub with my earbuds in to drown out the world. I took in a deep breath to calm the knots that started to pull tightly in my gut. "I was probably relaxing in the tub, or in bed. I had my earbuds in most the day and was enjoying a day to myself. It was an exhausting week."

I took a large bite of the sandwich. "Damn, this is delicious. I think I forgot to eat yesterday. I'm starving." I washed my bite down with Diet Coke. "Thanks." I made eye contact with the men and smiled.

"Anything for you, Summer. You know that," Charles said.

I continued eating and didn't miss the wordless conversation going on around the table. I narrowed my eyes. What the hell was going on? This wasn't just about bringing lunch by. I was missing something.

Tom stood and took some of the trash on the table to the trash can. "Why don't you women come by Charles and Kaye's house when you're done here?" He looked at Charles and lifted his brow.

Charles got up quickly. "Yep, you ladies do whatever you need to do here. We'll see you at the house. Have some stylist time, girl time, whatever you need. I'm sure there's some wine in the fridge. Enjoy a glass and we'll see you soon."

The men kissed their wives, gave me hugs, and left the hair salon. They were not as slick as they tried to be. Lunch was a cover for getting the women here to talk to me. About what, I didn't know. But I could probably guess.

I made another sandwich. I knew I was hungry, and this barbecue and the fried pickles were the best. They even put holes in the box of the fried pickles so the fried goodness wouldn't get soggy in its own steam. I popped one in my mouth. It was heavenly. I continued eating and ignored Diane and Kaye, which was difficult.

They kept glancing between each other, then back to me. "Kora made the most stunning bride," Kaye finally said, "and, Summer, you looked breathtaking in that dress."

Diane agreed. "Absolutely. It was the perfect wedding and a perfect setting. The Warfields sure know how to put on a party."

"It's got to be easy when you have that spread and endless money to make things happen. Leila struck it rich when she fell for Adler. And not just because he's loaded." Kaye sighed happily. "He's the entire package. Rich, sweet, and good looking. I can't wait to see that baby."

"I know," Diane beamed. "And the best part is, when the baby's born, I'm staying with them to help them out. Take care of Skylar and get her to school."

I listened to their conversation. It seemed strained and a bit forced. I wiped my fingers on my napkin, finished the last of my drink, and threw my trash in the can. Things became quiet as I cleaned. Eerily quiet. I felt eyes on my every move.

That's when it hit me. They knew about the conversation I had Saturday night.

Darlene and Lilly were close and I'm sure what I told Darlene was eating away at her. With Kora out of reach, she probably talked to Lilly, and I'd bet my left tit Lilly talked to Kaye and Jamison. I leaned on the counter, my back to them.

I took in a deep, cleansing breath. "Y'all didn't come here to feed me barbecue. Just come out with it. I know you're itching to ask me something. It's not like you to keep your noses out of my business—or anyone's business for that matter. That's not the book club's M.O. So, for fuck's sake, just ask."

"Language, girl," Diane said.

"You know the language you use proves that you're feeling bad about something," Kaye agreed.

I turned to them but stayed where I was. "Bullshit." I crossed my arms over my chest. They were being ridiculous. "That's not true. I always use bad language. Ask Darcie. I could fund her first year of college."

"Fine." Diane brushed my last comment away. "We'll get right to the point." She glanced over at Kaye.

Kaye sat up straighter in her seat and said, "Darlene talked to Lilly, Lilly talked to me, and I talked to Diane."

I glanced back and forth between them. My secret was out, and it seemed like the world knew all about it.

"And we need to give you our thoughts," Diane added as she pointed toward my empty place at the table. "Sit back down, please."

I threw my hands in the air. "Of *course* you want to get involved in something that is none of your damn business." I leveled my pointer finger at each of them in turn as I sat in my seat. "Remember, I'm not your family. You don't have to get involved in my life."

"That's where you're wrong, Summer," Kaye said, her voice firmer than I was used to from her. "You are our family. We've known you as long as you've been friends with Kora and Darlene."

Diane nodded in agreement. "Exactly. We were around while you hung out with them. We watched you grow up. We had you and your grandmother over for our weekly get-togethers."

Kaye picked up where Diane left off, her eyes commanding my attention. "We've also watched how Rowan accepted your friendship for over a decade just so he wouldn't irritate you, get beneath your skin, and lose whatever it was that was going on between you both."

My heart seemed to stop, then crash in my chest. I cleared my throat against the lump that formed, and my eyes dropped to the table. I fiddled with the napkin I used at lunch. "If you all noticed that back when we were in high school, that means Tonya did also. Why is she always such a bitch to me?" My eyes met theirs and courage coursed through my veins.

"She's not a bitch to you," Kaye said.

I sat up straight. My pulse raced and I was sure my blood pressure was going through the roof. "Seriously? She argues with me constantly."

"Because you're just like her. Your strong, take-no-shit attitude matches hers to a T," Kaye said. "You put her in her place. Trust me, she loves you. She knows you're exactly what Rowan needs. You keep him in check. You balance him out. You call him on his bullshit."

"Kaye's right," Diane agreed.

I rolled my eyes up to the ceiling. "Look, I love you two. You're as close to mothers as I've ever had, since my mom was useless. You both took me under your wings and helped me hone this crap I absolutely love." I swept my arm toward the salon. "But . . ." Dammit. If they knew what Darlene and I talked about, why didn't they come out with it?

Kaye reached over and grabbed my hand. "Summer, talk to us."

I looked back and forth between them and tears blurred my vision. "Darlene didn't tell you?"

"She told us that you don't want a relationship and don't know what love is, but what else is wrong?" Kaye asked in a soft voice. "What else is there that you haven't told us?"

The words sat on my tongue and begged to be said. To finally leave the secret box they've been locked in for decades. I bit my tongue to keep it quiet, but it was no use. "Rowan deserves more than I can ever give him," I blurted before I could change my mind and keep my secret in for another ten years. "There's more going on with me than you guys know, and I know he needs more."

My voice cracked. The caring, motherly looks on the women's faces gave me the courage I needed to tell someone else my secret.

I took a deep breath and let the word-vomit out. "Rowan needs to be a father. He needs to have kids. He's so wonderful and amazing and would make a perfect dad. But I can't give him that." I took in a shaky breath. "I can't have children."

There. I said for a second time in as many days what I had kept in for over a decade, and my heart cracked into a million pieces.

CHAPTER 32

ROWAN

"Hi, Uncle Rowan." James dropped his school bag on the floor, climbed in the chair next to me, and grabbed the cookies I had on the table. It was Wednesday, and this was our new after-school ritual. I loved it—quality time with my nephew.

"Hey, stinker." I slid my glass over to him and he dipped a chocolate chip cookie in the milk and took a bite. "How was school?"

He shrugged and popped the cookie in his mouth. "Boring," he said through a mouth full of cookie.

"James, don't talk with your mouth full," Darlene said. "It's bad manners." She fixed a cup of coffee and joined us at the table. "So, are you still leaving tonight? Couldn't you wait until morning?"

"I've gotta go. It's a twelve-hour drive, and my interview's tomorrow at two, so I'm going to be pushing it. I'll get in early in the morning and try to grab a little sleep."

"Where are you staying?" she asked.

"With a buddy and his wife. After the interview I'll figure something out."

"Come on, Row. Stay until morning."

I shook my head. "I'm packed and ready. As soon as Bryson gets home, I'll say bye and head out." I focused on dipping a cookie in milk and avoided Darlene's gaze.

"James, honey, why don't you take your backpack upstairs and go play until dinner."

"Okay, Mommy. Say bye to me before you leave, Uncle Rowan."

"Of course." I gave him a high five as he ran from the kitchen. I watched after him, not wanting to be left alone with Darlene. She was going to try and talk me out of this, maybe even call Summer, but that was not going to happen.

I'd spent the past few days at Trevor's, helping around his farm while he worked at the pub, which I avoided like the plague. I didn't want to see Summer right now. She had ignored my texts and I was done trying. There was nothing Darlene could say to change that. If Summer wanted to talk, she could find me. Hell, she could text me.

"Are you coming back?" Darlene asked.

That threw me off. "Why wouldn't I?"

She shrugged. "Just not sure. With Summer ghosting you, I didn't know if you'd take a job somewhere else."

It was my turn to shrug. "I don't want to be anywhere else. I've missed so much already, but if the job at their office in Nashville doesn't pan out and I'm offered a job in Texas . . ." I couldn't finish that thought. I didn't want to be in Texas anymore, but I didn't want to be here without Summer.

"Rowan, James would miss you if you stayed in Texas. He's just getting to know you, and you're his favorite person."

I rubbed my forehead and sighed. "I know, Darlene." I was drained, and it bled into my voice. "But I don't know if I could stand being here. Seeing her and not being with her? Maybe in a year or so, yes. But now?" I laid my hands on the table and sat up straight. "I've spent most of my life loving her. I need to move on, and I wouldn't be able to do that here."

"You don't have to live in Orlinda Valley. Settle somewhere else around Nashville. Your family's here."

"I know, and I could, but Tennessee is filled with memories, and Texas is new."

Darlene nodded. "It makes sense, but does she know any of this?"

"Know what?"

"That you might not come back because of her."

"Seriously?" Heat rose in my gut. "She hasn't even answered my texts. The only time I heard from her was when she sent me a message asking me to clear my things from the house while she was at work." I held my hands palms up. "I had to sneak over to the house to get the rest of my things. So, no. I haven't told her." My gut clenched and I raked my hands through my hair.

Darlene's gaze held mine. Her eyes were filled with love and concern. "I'm sorry, Row."

I swallowed hard and took a sip of the milk.

"What do you have to be sorry for?" Bryson entered the kitchen and glanced between us. "Shit's serious in here." He kissed Darlene and glanced at the full suitcase by the wall. "What's going on?"

"A possible one-way trip," Darlene said.

His brows shot up.

I sighed. "Only if they offer me a job in Texas, otherwise, I'll be back," I said.

"Did you even say bye to Mom, Jamison? Anyone?" Bryson asked. His voice rose in anger. Our eyes held and his narrowed. "Don't run again, Rowan. You've got to learn that sometimes life is shit and doesn't work out the way you hoped. Running won't do anything but keep you from those who love you. Your family and friends. It's not always going to be about you."

"I'm not running." My voice rose to match his. Shit. What if he was right? It would be so much easier to leave and not face the possibility of living in Tennessee without Summer.

"Well, at least say bye to my son. He hardly knows you, but has become your biggest fan in the short time you've been here."

"I know. Darlene said the same thing." I pushed away from the table as James ran back into the kitchen. I gave him a hug and promised to see him soon. That was one promise I hoped I could keep. Then I hugged Darlene and lugged my suitcase out to the garage. I had to get out of here—now.

Bryson leaned on the driver's door of my Jeep with his hands shoved in his pockets. I gestured for him to get out of the way.

"Go after her, Rowan."

"Can't. She made it clear. She doesn't love me." I felt the now-familiar lump form and cleared my throat for what felt like the billionth time this week trying to get it to disappear, but it was no use. It always returned. "Get out of the way, Bryson. I've *got* to leave."

"You can get another interview—hell, another job. Find her and talk to her."

I clamped my teeth together, dropped my suitcase on the ground, and balled my hands into fists. "Let's not do this again. I've got to go. Get the hell away from my Jeep."

Damn, stubborn-ass Bryson. I didn't want to leave after a fight again, but desperation ate at me. I needed to get out of here. I grabbed his arm and pushed him away. He pushed back, and before I knew it, our judo holds came back to the forefront and we were grappling in the garage. This wasn't for fun, though. Like the last time I left, I wanted to hurt him. He had to stop getting in my way.

"What the hell are you two doing?" Darlene bellowed.

We froze. I had him in a headlock. He had his arms around my chest ready to lift me and throw me on the ground.

"Step away from each other. *Now*." Darlene used her "get control of the room" teacher voice, which never failed to get our attention, and I was sure it worked on all her students. In a quieter voice, she said, "Don't do this again." She stood between us, glancing first at Bryson, then at me. "You two are the most stubborn men I know."

She turned to me and gripped my biceps. "Look, Rowan." She paused and let out a breath. "She swore me not to say anything, but I can't let this happen." She turned her face toward the ceiling and said, "You need to know."

Her attitude was making me uneasy. "What do I need to know?" I asked hesitantly.

Her gaze returned to mine. "Do you remember back in high school, when Summer missed a lot of school, but never really said why?"

I nodded. "Yeah."

"She has something called endometriosis. Because of it, she can't have children and doesn't think you should have to deal with that."

I took a step back and tilted my head to the side and glared at her. "What? I don't understand."

"She doesn't want to love you because she doesn't want you in a relationship where you won't be able to have any kids of your own."

A tangle of emotions twisted inside me, leaving me dazed. She doesn't want to love me...because she can't have kids? I turned away from Darlene, stunned. I shook my head and tried to make sense of what I heard. "She can't have children? Is she sure?"

"Pretty sure. She's talked to a lot of doctors over the years."

I clenched my fists together and gritted my teeth. I tried to talk but words froze on my tongue. What could I say? This didn't make sense.

"So, she's decided," I started slowly, the words forming as I spoke. "That we can't be together . . . because she can't have children." I paced in the confined space of the garage. "She thinks I deserve to be a father . . . she can't promise me that . . . so we can't be together?" I stopped pacing as anger tore through my chest, my voice rising with irritation. "She's making that choice for me?"

Darlene's shoulders met her ears in a resigned shrug.

"That's my choice to make." My insides seethed as my pulse quickened.

"That's what I told her," Darlene said, her voice almost a whisper.

I paced again. This garage seemed big enough until I needed more space to sort out my thoughts. Now it was constricting.

I raked my hands through my hair and clenched my fingers together at the back of my neck. When I'd gotten ahold of my thoughts, I said, "I'm not sure what the hell endometriosis is, but I don't give a shit about children now. I want to be with Summer and she's letting this get between us." I leaned my elbows on my knees and struggled to breathe in. I wasn't sure what a panic attack was, but I thought in that moment that I might be having one.

"Breathe, Rowan," Bryson said as he bent down next to me. "You look like you might pass out."

I finally got control of whatever the hell had just happened and stood. A realization hit me square in the gut. "I've got to go to her."

"Hell yeah, that's what I'm talking about," Bryson cheered as he smacked me on the back.

"She's at work," Darlene added as she opened the car door.

"Perfect. Then she can't run." I was frantic as I climbed behind the wheel. The short drive to Shear Perfection never felt so long.

CHAPTER 33

ROWAN

I pulled in front of Shear Perfection, slammed the gear shift to park and ran inside. "Summer?" I called as soon as I flew through the door. "Summer?" Dammit. She better be here. My heart beat frantically as I searched the salon.

Diane and Kaye stopped the work on their customers and Kaye said, "Rowan, she went to grab something to eat. What's wrong?"

"I thought you were leaving for your interview," Diane added.

I paced the salon. Damn, I'd been doing a lot of that today. "I'm not going. I need to talk to Summer."

Kaye put her hand on my arm. "Calm down and tell me what's wrong."

Kaye was my mom's oldest friend and was always calm in the midst of chaos. I guess she had to be, with a first husband like hers and a son as high-strung and energetic as Lance had always been.

I forced myself to stay calm. "I just found out something and couldn't go to Texas. Not without talking to her."

Kaye raised a brow. "Mrs. Ledbetter, do you mind if I take a minute before giving you your manicure? I've got to talk to Rowan."

"Of course not," Mrs. Ledbetter said. "Rowan dear, calm down. Summer's not going anywhere."

I gave Mrs. Ledbetter a smile, nodded to her and Diane, as I followed Kaye into the kitchen.

"Okay, Rowan, what did you find out and from whom?" Kaye asked.

I leaned heavily on the counter, my hands rested behind me. "Bryson and I got in a fight, and Darlene—"

"Bryson and you what?" My mother came in at that time.

I guess it *was* after four. She had finished work, and this was where she always ended up. "Mom, nothing happened. Darlene stopped us—"

"Damn, you two boys." My mother had her hands on her hips and was ready to give me the riot act. "I thought one day you'd grow out of your inability to get along—"

"T," Kaye interrupted her rampage. "Now isn't the time."

"Yeah, Mom. Now isn't the time."

"Boy, you may be almost a foot taller than me but I'm still your momma and I can—"

"Enough," Kaye snapped her fingers in front of my mother's face. "T, I need to talk with Rowan—in private. You can yell and go all momma-not-nice-person later." My mom opened her mouth to say something, but Kaye shook her head and wagged her finger. "Uh-uh. Not now. I'm talking to him." She eyed my mother and their gazes froze on each other.

My mom threw her hands up in the air. "Fine. Whatever." She turned to me and put her finger in the air. "We aren't done here. You, me, and Bryson are going to have a talk." She started to walk out of the kitchen then turned around abruptly. "Aren't you supposed to be heading for an interview?"

"I was. But something came up. Texas can wait."

She narrowed her gaze at me then turned her head slowly to Kaye.

Kaye raised her brows and cocked her head to the side.

Mom pursed her lips hard, turned, and stormed from the room.

We both watched her retreat in silence for a bit then Kaye said, "You and Bryson better be ready for her wrath later."

I nodded. "Yeah, I'm sure she'll have lots to say, but things are fine between us now. It was about Summer, anyway."

"What do you know?" Kaye asked as she grabbed two drinks from the fridge and handed me one.

I opened it and took a deep drink, then picked at the label. I didn't know how much I should say to Kaye. Did she know anything about Summer? If she didn't and I said something, I would be crossing a line. Knowing Summer as well as I did and how private she was, I knew I would have a difficult time getting back on Summer's good side if I let something slip that I shouldn't.

Kaye must have known why I hesitated, because she said, "She told me about what happened after the wedding, and she told me why she felt she needed to say that to you."

I glanced at her. My heart skipped a beat.

"She cares a lot for you, Rowan, but she doesn't want to make a decision that would keep you from being able to be a father."

I nodded. "Darlene told me everything and that's what she said also." Irritation flooded through my veins. "But Summer doesn't have the right to make that decision for me."

At that time Diane came into the kitchen. "Your mom and Mrs. Ledbetter went next door to the coffee shop," she said as she sat at the table and gestured for me to join her.

I glanced at Kaye, who nodded and sat at the adjacent chair to Diane. Not seeing another choice, I joined them.

Once I was seated, Diane continued. "Rowan, I know Summer's action hurt you, but I understand where Summer's coming from. When I met Tom, I was in the same headspace she's in. I never wanted a long-term relationship because I couldn't have children. I didn't want to put any man who was strong enough to love me in that position." She intertwined her fingers on the table and leaned toward me. "It's hard enough when you're faced with that kind of news. It's harder to have someone you care about have to live childless. I felt guilty, and, like Summer, fought my feelings for Tom. But he didn't care. He loved me more than he wanted another child. Now, of course, he had Leila, though we never saw her. I don't know if you know this—we kept it away from you kids—but we tried to adopt, tried IVF, but in the end, we loved each other enough to be just the two of us."

She sat up tall. "Rowan, you need to make sure you love Summer that much. If you can see yourself with just her and no children, go to her and see what can happen. But make sure. It's a long life to live without a child. Trust me, I lived it."

I always saw Diane and Tom as my extended family. Tom would go camping with my dad and us boys, and Lance, every summer. Then when Kaye met Charles, he became part of the group. Diane and Tom's childlessness never seemed strange to me. It was just who they were, and they treated all of us as their own. "Y'all, I don't know what I see in my future with Summer, but—" Just then the back door opened, and Summer came in with a drink in her hand. She froze when she saw me sitting there.

Kaye and Diane rose.

"I've got one more appointment coming in soon," Diane said.

"Me too," Kaye agreed as she followed behind Diane. And, just like that, I was alone with Summer.

She finally unfroze from her shock at seeing me and walked into the back office. I followed. "Rowan, what are you doing here? I thought you had an interview to get to."

"I did, but I came to find you. I couldn't leave without talking to you."

She placed her purse in a desk drawer and her drink on top, shook her head, and spoke without turning around. "I told you there was nothing to say." She paused. "I don't feel the same way about you."

Her voice was Summer-strong, yet I detected a slight waver to her words.

That waver gave me courage. "I don't believe you. I know why you're separating us. Darlene told me."

She whipped around. Anger flashed from her eyes.

The corners of my mouth ticked up. That was the Summer-attitude I loved.

"What the hell do you mean Darlene told you?" she asked. "What do you think you know?" Anger flashed across her face, and she threw her shoulders back. She was ready for a fight, so I backed off. I needed to give her enough space to not feel suffocated.

Instead, I held my hands up, palms out, and said, "I know you're making decisions for me because you care." I watched her face, and the anger subsided just a little. That increased my courage, so I took a slow, cautious step toward her. "I know you want me to have a life with children—but, Summer, I'm not thinking of that right now. I'm thinking of you and me."

"Exactly," she spat, her eyes wide. "You're thinking of me right now. But what happens if we start a relationship and things go well, we want more and we take that step, then one day you wake up and realize that's as far as we can go? You want kids, but *I . . . can't . . . give them . . . to you*." Her voice cracked, and she covered her mouth with her hands.

I took a step closer, but she stepped back and shook her head as a sob escaped from her throat.

She leaned against the desk and brushed her hands over her face, then lowered them when she'd regained her composure. Her voice was softer when she finally spoke again. "I couldn't live with the guilt of putting you through that, and if you decided to leave, then . . ." Her words trailed off and tears fell down her cheeks.

I closed the space between us before she could stop me, and pulled her to my chest. I held her tight and kissed the top of her head. She didn't cry hard, but I could tell tears fell. I closed my eyes tight and took in a deep breath, Summer's scent wafting through my nostrils. The scent that would always remind me of that summer's day at the river.

When she sniffed and lifted her head, I loosened my grip on her and pulled away enough that our eyes met. "Don't you ever decide how I live," I said with a soft voice. My eyes wandered around her face, now wet with tears. I rubbed my thumbs under her eyes and held my hands at the side of her face. "If I choose you, I choose you because I love you. I love you, Summer. And if we work out and get married and can't have children of our own, I don't care. Being with you is enough. It will always be enough."

She tried to wiggle free.

"Stop, Summer. Dammit." My voice rose as frustration sliced through me. "Do you really think I'd leave you because of that? Do you think I'm as low as your father? Really?" Anger fueled my words. I was tired of this. I was tired of her bringing everything back to that asshole—and then comparing me to him.

This was crazy.

This was downright stupid.

"This is bullshit, Summer. You've known me since middle school. We've been inseparable, even through relationships with other people and being on separate continents. If I haven't left you by now, you should know I never will."

I dropped my hands and trailed them slowly down her shoulders and arms to her hands and I squeezed her fingers. I needed a minute to calm my pulse. I took a deep breath before I spoke again. "If you think that little of me, tell me now, and I'll drive to that interview and forget about the possibility of us. I promise."

Our eyes held and I tried to read her expression. Damn, how I wish I could read minds and figure out what she was thinking.

Just then, Kaye yelled from the main area of the salon, "Rowan!"

The sound of her voice and commotion met my ears and fear sliced through me. Summer nodded, knowing something else was possibly more important right now, and I turned and ran.

My mother was sitting in a chair with her hands over her chest, pale as a ghost.

"I'm calling an ambulance," Diane said with her phone on her ear.

"Momma, what's going on?" I asked, my pulse racing so fast I had a hard time breathing.

She shook her head, and I turned to Mrs. Ledbetter whose face was almost as white as my mother's.

"We'd just gotten our coffee and Danish and sat down," the older woman said in a trembling voice. "Suddenly, she grasped her chest and turned white. She wanted to come back here and almost collapsed when we got to the door." Mrs. Ledbetter put her empty hands up to her cheeks, her expression filled with worry, just as the salon door opened and paramedics stormed in.

CHAPTER 34

SUMMER

I followed Rowan into the salon and froze at the sight before me.

Tonya sat in a chair, her eyes were closed, and she looked bad. Real bad. Her breathing seemed shallow, and her skin looked gray and ashy.

Everyone's attention was on Tonya, and the paramedics were asking all types of questions. The bell over the door rang and Trevor walked in. Our eyes met and he came toward me. "I heard the call. You okay?"

I nodded. "I don't know what's going on."

He squeezed my arm and walked to the paramedics. I couldn't hear what they were saying. I went to Kaye and placed my hand on her back. Her face was a mixture of worry and fear. I'm sure mine looked the same.

"Ms. Tonya," Trevor said, "you need to go to the hospital, and the ambulance would be the safest way. They could keep an eye on you."

"Not doing it. I'm fine. All this fuss is ridiculous for some heartburn. Y'all can just pack up and get the hell out of here. Go find someone else to bother." Her voice sounded tired, a little weaker than normal, though her attitude was still all Tonya.

Rowan stood over her, his face pale and etched with a combination of worry and concern. "Momma, come on. Don't be so stubborn."

As Tonya continued to object, Kaye squeezed my hand, let it go, then strode over to her friend. "T," she barked, "get your ass in that ambulance and let them do their job. You're white as a ghost, you sound like shit, and I'll be damned if I'm going to get yelled at by all your sons for not making you go with the professionals. You're going with them. Now. They will make sure you're okay and not having a damn heart attack in my salon."

Tonya, opened her mouth to protest further, but Diane jumped in. "No arguing, T. Just shut your mouth and listen."

"They're right, Ms. Tonya," Trevor said. "Symptoms of heart attacks are different for women. It would be best if we get you to the hospital as soon as possible."

Rowan nodded and squeezed his mother's hand. "Mom, I'll follow behind so I can take you home after they're done and say it's safe."

"Fine. Do whatever." Tonya leaned back in the chair and was soon bundled into the ambulance. Trevor left with Rowan, and Diane, Kaye, and I closed up the salon and followed behind, because no way were we staying here.

I talked with Darlene on the phone while Diane drove us to the hospital. Darlene and Leila were staying home with the kids. I promised I'd keep them informed of everything.

When we arrived at the hospital, Ruth was already waiting outside the Emergency Room entrance. We headed in together, finding

Jamison, Bryson, and Rowan deep in conversation, huddled close. Ruth, Diane, and Kaye stepped in to join them, but I hung back, feeling like an outsider.

I wrung my hands together. How was Tonya doing? How were the guys? My eyes were glued to Rowan, but his back was to me. If his face looked anything like Jamison and Bryson's though . . .

Finally, a doctor appeared. With a few hushed words, he led the boys through the double doors. Kaye and Diane found seats nearby, and I quietly sat beside them.

I grabbed Kaye's hand. "What did the doctor say?"

Diane shook her head. "Not much. They're still doing tests, but she's awake and alert."

"Poor doctors and nurses," I said.

Ruth laughed. "No kidding. It would be easier for them if she wasn't awake. T is an awful patient."

They told stories while we waited of when she was in the hospital after the birth of each of the boys. Taking orders from people wasn't a strength of hers on a good day.

The double doors opened, and the guys walked through. They were laughing about something, so that was a good sign.

The four of us stood, and Kaye, whose face was covered with worry asked, "So, how is she?"

Jamison hugged her. "She seems to be okay. They are keeping her here overnight for observation and will let us know more in the morning."

I was listening to Jamison, but I turned my gaze to Rowan. Our eyes locked for a brief second before he turned to his phone. He held it in the air. "It's Texas. I'm going to take this out in my Jeep."

His eyes stalled on mine briefly, and he gave a small smile before he walked away and answered his phone.

I watched as the automatic doors slid closed behind him, and couldn't help but wonder if this would be it. If he might accept the job in Texas.

My heart thumped wildly. It would have been easier if he'd never known my big secret. I could go on thinking I'd done the right thing, made the right choice. But now that he knew, and said it didn't matter, I had to admit I might have been wrong.

Shit. Why did Darlene talk to him? I wanted to go give her a piece of my mind. Tell her to stay out of my business. This secret was for *me* to tell, if I chose to, and she had no right to tell him anything.

Now, though, nothing mattered but Tonya. Yes, she might have been a royal pain in the ass, but she was still Tonya. She had so much energy and was the life of every picnic and get-together.

"Summer, she wants to see you too." Jamison's hand was on my arm, but I hadn't heard a word he said.

"Excuse me?" I asked.

"My mom wants to see you too." He gestured toward the door.

Diane grabbed my arm. "Come on in with us."

The smell of the ER as we went through the doors hit me like a punch in the face. This was the reason I avoided hospitals at all costs. The smell—a combination of antiseptic, a shit ton of disinfectant, and sickness—always gave me nightmares.

I followed Ruth, Kaye, and Diane into a room as a nurse held the door open for us on her way out. "Ms. McKendry's a pistol," the nurse said.

They laughed heartily, and Diane said, "You're not telling us anything we don't already know."

I nodded at the nurse, and she shut the door behind us.

Tonya had an IV in her arm and an oxygen probe on her finger. A machine beeped nearby, lines flashing across the screen.

"You look much better already," Kaye said.

"Yeah, you looked like death at the salon," Diane said.

Tonya huffed, irritated. "Well, I feel just fine, but they won't let me leave. Thanks to you two bitches and insisting on calling an ambulance, I'm a prisoner for the next twenty-four hours." She air-quoted "twenty-four hours" and rolled her eyes.

"Oh, you'll get over it," Ruth told her. "Maybe you'll have a hot doctor and can drive him crazy."

Diane chuckled. "Oh, she'll drive him crazy all right. That's one of her many talents."

They laughed and Tonya's gaze narrowed. "See, y'all are bitches."

That made me laugh.

Tonya's narrowed eyes turned to me. "Is something funny, Summer?"

"Listening to y'all bicker reminds me of how Kora, Darlene, and I argue. I swear we've said the same exact words sitting at Jerry's Pub. I know I've called them bitches at least a dozen times over the years."

"Wait till your friendship hits more than thirty years. A dozen will seem like a drop in a bucket," Tonya said, giving a weak smile.

"All joking aside, T," Diane said, her smile fading a bit, "you do look better. You scared us."

"Hell yeah, you did," Kaye agreed.

Ruth stepped forward and squeezed Tonya's hand. "You need to suck it up and be ready to do whatever they tell you to, and if it's staying overnight, then you stay overnight. We need you around a bunch more years."

Tonya let out a breath. "Fine, Ruthie. I'll try my best to be good. But it won't be fun."

"Of course it won't," Ruth agreed. "But do it, anyway."

Just then a nurse came in. "Gotta check your vitals."

"Didn't you just do that?" Tonya asked with an eyeroll.

Kaye, Diane, and Ruth laughed. Kaye patted Tonya's shoulder. "We'll let you be. We have phone calls to make."

"Yep," Ruth said. "We need to get the Orlinda Valley message line going with an update."

"They will all be happy to know you're here to annoy everyone for a while more," Diane added with a laugh.

I started to follow the other women out of the room, but Tonya said, "Summer, can you hang out a bit? I want to talk with you."

I raised a brow and waited against the wall while the nurse did whatever she was doing and typed notes into a computer. The nurse nodded and said, "I'll let you two be, and I'll see you again in a bit, Mrs. McKendry. Everything looks good, and they're waiting to get you a bed."

"Great. Just what I need."

"She means 'thank you'," I said to the nurse, since Tonya wasn't being cordial. As soon as the nurse was gone and the door had closed, Tonya gestured me closer.

"Summer." She pushed herself higher in the bed and patted the mattress next to her for me to sit—so I sat. "I know you and I don't always see eye-to-eye, but we've known each other a long time. You've always been important in the lives of Rowan and Kora, and it seems like you've become more important to Rowan than I realized."

I had no clue where she was going with this talk, but when she got to the part about me and Rowan, I stood. I didn't like her tone, which sounded increasingly rude and abrasive the more she spoke.

"Summer, stop. I'm sorry. My tone sounded harsh. Look, I know your mother wasn't worth a penny, and your dad was worth even less, so I tried to be there for you. I opened our door and invited you in as a part of my family. Hell, you even spent the night in Rowan's room on occasion."

I raised my brow.

"I've ignored his feelings for you over the years, and hoped he would find someone else eventually and move on."

"Where the hell is this going, Tonya?"

She put her hand up. "No, Summer, I'm sorry. It's coming out all wrong. Please hear me out."

I puffed out a breath and cocked my head to listen. I didn't know why the hell I gave her the time.

"I know he has feelings for you, and I don't know where you fall in a relationship, but I want you to know that I would love for you both to be together. It was a bit of a shock at first when I saw you at the wedding, but I also saw a light in Rowan that's been missing for so long. You make him happy, and that's all a mother wants for her sons—women who make them happy. Whatever's going on now, please figure it out. He's not going to stay here if he doesn't have you."

I sat straight. "What are you talking about?"

"That job in Texas. He might take it. He's not going to stay in Orlinda Valley, or even Tennessee, if you aren't in his life."

"How do you know that?" I asked.

She shrugged. "I just know my son."

My eyes roamed the room. Rowan might leave? Again? I shook my head. "If he leaves, then . . . But, I can't promise . . ." I sighed. My insides were knotted up. I stood and chewed my bottom lip.

"I know," Tonya said.

I looked at her, confused. "You know? What exactly do you know?" What was she talking about? My feelings for Rowan? Or had Kaye and Diane talked with her—told her about me?

"Summer, your grandmother talked to me years ago. I know about the endometriosis. I know you may not be able to have children. She told me how upset that made you."

My grandmother told Tonya? Meaning, someone other than my grandmother and I had known all this time? I sat heavily on the edge of her bed again. Emotions I didn't want to deal with here and now came to the surface, and the room blurred as tears welled in my eyes. "You've known all these years?" My voice was a whisper.

She nodded.

"Then you, of all people, know why I can't be with Rowan. He needs to be a dad. He'd be such an amazing father, and the world needs more amazing fathers. There aren't enough—I should know."

Tonya sighed, reached toward me, and grabbed my hands. She had only touched me like this one other time, in my junior year of high school. I'd showed up at their house, late at night, with tears and a small suitcase. My mother had been drinking and kicked me out, and I didn't want to pull my grandmother into it, so I went to Rowan's. Rowan was out with his girlfriend, and I only had Tonya to talk to.

"You're right," she said. "The world does need amazing fathers, and Rowan would be just that—but don't keep happiness from your life because of the cards you've been dealt."

I held her gaze for a beat. She squeezed my hands, then continued in a soft voice, "Rowan would be lucky to have you, and I would love for you to be with him." She shrugged. "You're strong, witty, hard-headed, and keep him in his place. People like that are pretty amazing individuals." She smiled and wagged her eyebrows.

I smiled back. "They are pretty amazing," I said with a soft laugh. I leaned in and gave her a hug. She wrapped her arms around my shoulders.

I pulled back and smiled. "Thanks, Tonya."

"You bet. Now, get your ass out of here and hunt down my son."

Tonya pushed the button as I stood, and the last thing I heard her say was, "What's it take to get a Diet Coke in this damn place?"

CHAPTER 35

ROWAN

By the time I got off my phone interview and back inside the hospital, everyone had gone, and my mother had just been moved to her room for the night. Jamison sent me a text and I took the elevator to the fifth floor.

It wasn't hard to find her room. I just followed the cackling laughter that reverberated through the halls. Mom was already making friends with the nurses. "Hey, Mom."

"Rowan, baby. You found me."

"Yeah, it wasn't hard. I just followed the laugh."

Bryson rolled his eyes while Jamison shook his head.

Tonya sighed dramatically. "Well, I got to make the most of my next twenty-four hours. There's no reason to be a stick-in-the-mud. When life gives you lemons . . ."

"Enough of the stupid sayings," Bryson said. "Look, you're just fine. If it's okay, I'm going home to check on my wife and your grandkids."

"Sure, baby. Go ahead. All three of you don't need to stay. It's getting late."

Bryson gave her a hug. "I'll be here tomorrow. Don't cause too much trouble, Mom."

He left and Jamison followed, since he also had a child to get to bed.

"I guess you've just got me, Mom," I said. "I don't have any kids to get home to." Hell, I didn't even have a *home* to get home to.

"Sit and tell me about your interview. How'd it go?" she asked.

I sat and told her the basics. It was a good interview, and a great company. "They offered me a position."

Her brow ticked up, but she didn't say anything—her way of letting me know she was listening, and I should continue.

"I have my choice of Dallas or Nashville. I've got to let them know by Tuesday."

We were quiet. She nodded and looked around, processing this new information.

I hated when she was deep in thought like this, because I wanted her to respond to what I'd told her. But Dad always said the best thing to do was to wait her out. This was her way of taking in news and digesting it, and she'd talk when she was ready. I'd learned the hard way that interrupting her could result in an eruption of epic proportions. So, I waited.

Her gaze finally met mine and she said, "Well?"

My shoulders slumped. I waited for that? That was the result of her deep thoughts? One word? "That's all you have to say?"

"I'm waiting to hear what you decided."

I shook my head. "I don't know. What do you think?"

She shrugged. "Not my rodeo."

Fucking seriously? Who was this woman, and what had she done with my mother, who'd always been in our business and had something to say about everything?

I covered my face with my hands and breathed deeply, then raked my fingers through my hair, linking them behind my head and leaning back to stare at the ceiling. "Why, when I need you to give me some amazing words of wisdom, you've got nothing? What do you know about rodeos, anyway?"

She cackled softly. "Look, Rowan, you've got to talk to Summer. Hell, I don't know why you're having issues with things. She'll eventually get over herself and realize she needs to be with you. You realized that a decade ago. Go make her see reason."

I dropped my chin to my chest. Maybe her heart scare made her crazy. Did she just tell me to go after Summer, and that she's known I've liked her for years? "Mom, are you sure you're not dying?"

"*Pfft*," she replied as she swiped her hand through the air. "Perfectly fine. I just don't understand why you're still here when you should be dealing with Summer."

I stood and digested what my mother had just said. She had no issues with me and Summer. That was a surprise.

I leaned on the small windowsill for a moment, contemplating, then opened the blinds so I could look somewhere farther than these white walls. The view overlooked the roof, which totally sucked, but the darkness outside kept me from focusing my brain on anything else.

Maybe I *should* stay. Go fight for her and not run away because she's pushing back on me. If Summer and I let this relationship between us grow, and it took off, would I be okay with the possibility of no biological children?

My mother's voice cut into my thoughts. "I know she probably can't have kids. Her grandmother confided in me a long time ago."

I turned and looked at her.

She tilted her head back and forth, looking as if she were mentally weighing her words. "I'd be lying to you if I said that played no part in why I fought your feelings for Summer. The thought of you spending your entire lifetime with someone who couldn't give you a family bothered me. You'd be such a great father." She sighed. "But then, tonight Summer said the exact words that I've always thought, and they sounded wrong out loud. Yes, children are wonderful and precious gifts, but so is true love."

She stopped and I waited. I thought she might have something else to say, but she laid her head back. "I'm tired. It's been a long day."

I pulled the blankets up over her chest and kissed her cheek. "Thanks, Mom. Love you."

She smiled a small, tired smile. "Love you bunches, baby."

I walked quietly to the door and pulled it closed behind me. I had to go find Summer and finish our discussion.

Chapter 36

Summer

I piddled around the kitchen, trying to find something—anything—to take away the quiet of this long night. I hated the
quiet. I was about to turn on some music when headlights lit up
the driveway. "Who the hell is this?" I walked toward the door with
heavy steps, and just as I got there, it flew open.

My heart skipped when I saw the wild look in Rowan's eyes. My
insides jumped in fear. "Is your mom all right?" I asked.

The wildness turned to confusion, then understanding. "Yes,
she's fine. When I left, she'd fallen asleep." He closed the door behind him and walked toward me. "We need to finish our conversation."

The way he was looking at me stirred something deep in my gut. I
walked away from him to the counter to put space between us. "It's
been a crazy night. Are you sure this is the best time? I bet you're
tired and would like to rest."

"No, I don't need rest. You said something before Kaye called me
that sounded like you thought I'd leave you. That tells me you think

I'm no better than your old man. I've thought a lot about us tonight, and I can assure you, leaving you is not what I plan to do."

I didn't think that little of him. Rowan was the sweetest man I knew, and nothing at all like my father. He put everyone first. He loved his family and friends in a big way—and he loved me. My heart no longer stuttered with that thought. It sped up and I filled my lungs with much-needed oxygen.

His eyes softened as he walked across the kitchen toward me. "Even if I have to wait forever for you to come to your senses and realize we're meant to be together, I will be waiting right here."

I searched his sweet brown eyes, then let my gaze wander over his perfectly chiseled features until they stalled for a brief moment on his lips. I met his eyes once again through lowered lashes. "What do you mean?"

"I took the job."

"You did?" I asked. My heart skipped a beat, and I swear I stopped breathing.

"I did. They gave me the choice: Dallas or Nashville."

He stood right in front of me, where I could feel the heat from his body and smell his cologne. My pulse raced. The seconds that ticked by as I waited to hear more seemed like a century. What if he chose Dallas? What if he left again? What if I lose him?

He gently held my hands in his. "I chose Nashville. Because I chose you. I always will, Summer. No matter what."

Fear coursed through my veins as his hands brushed up my arms on their way to cup my cheeks and tilt my head back to look at him.

"Summer, I want us together. I don't know what the future holds." He brushed his thumbs across my cheekbones. "Kids, or no kids—we'll face that when we get there." He dropped his hands and again clasped mine. Right now, I want us. I want you, Summer, because we've been apart for too long. And because I love you."

His big brown eyes held mine. I was speechless, unsure how to react to those words. I'd always backed away when they were casually flung around between friends.

But . . . Rowan.

My fingers fell from his hands. I wanted to promise him something, but I didn't know what. He's staying. For me. That's what I hoped to hear. That's what I wanted.

But fear gripped me and wouldn't let go.

I couldn't think with him looking at me with that much feeling blazing in his eyes, so I took a step back. I had to put space between us to separate myself from him so I could think. Process. But I couldn't get my brain to function.

"Summer . . ." He took a step toward me.

I took another step back, my pulse racing. I wanted to say something, anything, but I couldn't. It was like I was having an out of body experience. I wanted to tell him I loved him, but the part of me controlling my brain wouldn't have it. I couldn't say the words.

He shook his head, and the muscle in his jaw twitched. He held my eyes, but I couldn't move.

He pursed his lips and moved his gaze to the ceiling. "I . . ." He puffed out a breath. "I can't." And then he walked out.

My heart pounded in my chest, as if beating in his direction, and my stomach churned. What had I done? My brain finally took control and screamed at me to go after him, but my feet weren't listening. They were glued to the spot. Heavy as lead.

This is bullshit! Get control of yourself, Summer. You can't let him walk out. You can't lose him again.

My feet finally moved, and I sprinted the short distance to the door and out onto the driveway. There was no moon, so the only light came from the headlights of Rowan's Jeep.

I ran to the driver's door and opened it. "Rowan, stop!" I threw all my desperation into my voice. "*Please.*"

"What the hell, Summer?" He glared at me with one hand on the wheel and the other on the gear shift.

"I'm sorry," I sobbed. When had I started crying? I had never cried over a man before, but the thought of Rowan driving away and out of my life felt too final. "Don't go." My insides were in turmoil, and I thought I might throw up.

What if he decided he didn't want my chaos, or my stubbornness . . . or my infertility? But did I really want him to walk out of my life forever?

My voice came out soft, pleading. "I want you to stay. Please?"

He turned his face toward me, his eyes red-rimmed.

My stomach clenched. "Please get out. Please let me talk to you?"

He sighed and rolled his eyes. "Fine."

I stepped back and climbed out of the Jeep. His face was filled with irritation and anger.

I didn't blame him. I caused this—all of this. "I'm sorry. I know I should have told you about . . . Hell, I should have told you decades ago. I was alone and scared, and . . ." Shit. I looked down at my feet.

"And what, Summer?" he asked, his voice flat. Emotionless.

My eyes traveled up his body—the body that, until recently, I never let myself see as anything but "good-looking". But now I finally focused on the details: the tightness of his thighs, the contours of the muscles through his shirt, his loving heart. My eyes met his—those large brown pools that I'd looked into so many times over the years.

I reached for his hands—the hands that held me and consoled me throughout my lifetime, and recently touched me and sent me places I had never been before. A warmth oozed from my heart and a realization struck me like a bolt of lightning to the chest. The words I thought just now in the house were true.

I didn't want to live my life without Rowan. Not anymore. He knew my secret and he didn't care. He still wanted me.

A small part of me had not been surprised at all when he'd told me that—It was Rowan.

A single tear fell down my cheek and he brushed it gently away. I reached up, grabbed his hand, and held it against my cheek. "I'm sorry I screwed things up." I opened my mouth and closed it, unable to form all the words I wanted to say. My stomach rolled and my pulse picked up. "I want you to stay with me."

He tucked my hair behind my ear, pulled his gaze away from me, and breathed out one word. "Why?"

Why. Such a simple word, but a difficult question. I gave him the only answer I could. "Because you make me a better person. Because I need you, and I like who I am when we're together."

I took a deep breath. "But, most of all, because I love you."

His gaze caught mine and the corners of his mouth ticked up. "What did you say?"

My smile matched his and I breathed out a laugh. "I love you, Rowan. I probably always have but have been too stupid and insecure to realize it."

"Summer, you are anything but stupid. Insecure, ornery, stubborn, pig-headed—"

I punched him in the gut, and he doubled over with a laugh. "Okay, maybe I went too far with pig-headed." He stood and rubbed his stomach. "You've still got a mean jab."

"I had a good teacher."

He wrapped his arms around my waist and pulled me to him.

I wrapped mine around his neck.

"Yeah, you did," he said as his lips met mine. Our tongues danced and a moan escaped me. Kissing him made all my body parts wake up and come alive.

Chapter 37

Summer

Saturday afternoon found us at Kaye's. We were celebrating the homecoming of the newlyweds, which was supposed to have been held at Tonya's house, but since she'd just gotten out of the hospital and needed to take it easy, Kaye had everyone at her place.

Rowan and I showed up a little later than we should have. Making up took work, and we were making sure we were being *very* thorough.

"Well, it's about time you made it," Kora said as Rowan and I entered the yard holding hands.

They both looked suntanned, refreshed, and happy.

"Looks like everything worked out," Kai added as he pulled me in for a hug.

"Maybe," I said with a laugh.

"Definitely," Rowan added.

Kora pulled me away from Rowan and Kai. "I'm stealing her for a bit. We have to catch up. Seems like a lot can happen in a week."

Kora and I walked arm-in-arm to the food table, and I filled a plate with ribs, coleslaw, and green beans. "So," Kora said with a smile. "Everything between you two seems pretty good."

A smile tugged at the corner of my lips. "Yeah, it is." I turned and walked toward the table under the trees with the rest of the women.

Kora kept in step. "I'm glad. Love looks good on you, Summer."

I nodded with what I was sure was a goofy grin and admitted, "It feels good too."

She wrapped her free arm around my shoulders and gave me a gentle squeeze which I graciously accepted.

"Summer, you've got a glow about you," Tonya said as we approached the table.

I hugged her and took a seat next to her. "I don't know about a glow, but welcome home."

"I'm glad to be home. That place was a prison. Y'all wouldn't believe the rules."

Kaye laughed and said, "Just because they wouldn't give you ice cream, doesn't mean it was a prison. You were hardly there long enough to eat anything, anyway."

"Whatever. At least I'm eating good now."

"Well, you need to start taking care of yourself. I want my kiddos to have a grandma for a long time," Darlene said.

"Don't you worry. I started yoga right before my episode, so I'll be keeping up with that. Then, whenever it finally gets warm again, we're doing water aerobics in Kaye's pool."

"Yeah, we are," the other book club women chimed in.

"To book club," Tonya held her cup of water up with a cheer.

Kaye, Ruth, and Diane held up their cups of water—as they are all abstaining for wine for the time being to support Tonya—and cheered, "To book Club."

"Woo Hoo," answered Tonya.

I leaned back in my chair, and listened to the chatter and joking between everyone, and smiled. This is what family should be—joking, laughing, cutting up. I'd been a part of these cookouts and get-togethers as far back as I could remember. They'd always accepted me, even when my parents wouldn't.

My eyes traveled to the play yard where the girls and James ran around, lost in their own world of make-believe. Even if I couldn't have children of my own, I'd have these kiddos and all the ones still on the way. If that was all I could have, I'd take it and be thankful.

I looked to the other end of the yard, where the men were in a cut-throat cornhole match, and my eyes locked on Rowan's. The smile that had ticked at the corners of my mouth finally met my ears. He gestured to me, so I got up from my chair and met him in the middle of the yard.

"Having fun?" he asked.

"Always," I answered.

He reached out and played with the lock of hair that sat on my shoulder. "You looked like you were deep in thought."

I shrugged. "I was." He lifted his brow, and I continued. "I was just thinking of all the memories I've had here. How I've been a part of your family most of my life and have always been accepted." I glanced at him. "How even if I can't have kids, I have everything right here I could ever need. I'm glad you came home and chose to stay."

Rowan put his hands behind my neck and held me in a tight hug.

The warmth of his skin seared into my soul. He took in a deep breath and blew it out slowly. "I had to come back. Wherever you are has always been home to me, and there's no place I'd rather be."

My insides melted and my heart soared. "I love you, Rowan," I said.

His grin filled his face. "I never thought I'd hear those words from you." He leaned in and our lips met. It was one amazing kiss—until whoops and hollers from onlookers brought us back to reality. We had an audience, and if we weren't careful, this would be front page on the Orlinda Valley News for sure.

"Ignore them, Summertime," he said as he tilted my chin so our eyes met. "I love you back." He kissed me again, sweet and tender.

This time, when the cheers from the onlookers started up, I smiled against his lips, wrapped my arms tighter around his neck, pulled him to me, and said, "Damn, Rowan, that's not a kiss. If you're going to kiss me, kiss me like your fucking life depends on it."

And that's exactly what he did.

Epilogue

Summer- 7 Months Later

"You ready?" Rowan asked as he leaned over the fence.

"Almost," I answered as I spread the hay in the chicken coop. Big Red crowed next to me. "I think he likes his new house and his women," I said.

Big Red did a little side-shuffle and crowed again as six hens pecked the ground next to him. "He sure isn't complaining," Rowan agreed.

It was the end of May, and Rowan had been living in Kora's place as he waited to decide what to build on his own property. Big Red and Rowan became buddies, so we decided to get the cock some women to keep him company. Rowan was now the proud owner of six hens and Big Red.

I went home occasionally, but spent most of my time here. I loved the openness and fresh air, and had to admit, chickens had become my newest addiction—besides sex with Rowan, of course.

"I need to wash up quick and we'll go," I said as I shut the door to the coop behind me.

"Okay. I'll wait for you in the Jeep." Rowan gave me a kiss and a smack on my ass as I hurried away.

It didn't take long for me to wash up, grab my bag, and climb into the passenger side of the Jeep.

He hung up the phone when I got there.

"Who was that?"

"Just Kai." He put the Jeep in reverse, turned, and headed down the driveway. "He was wondering where we were. Everyone's already there. I told him they should be used to us being late by now."

I laughed at the truth in that statement. Rowan and I were always so busy with each other that being on time was not our calling card. "Do you have the present?" I asked.

"Yep. In the back."

It was Susie's birthday. She had just gotten into town and was planning on staying for the summer, so we were celebrating her at Kora and Kai's.

"Seems like we're the last ones, as usual," I said as we pulled up to the back of their property. Cars filled the driveway, so Rowan parked on the grass.

Before we got out, he pulled me to him. "If I could have my way, I'd have spent my day with you in bed." His lips met mine, and the now-familiar tingle traveled throughout my body as he devoured me with his kiss.

"We could go home," I whispered against his lips. "They'd understand."

He pulled away quickly. "Nope," he said. "We gotta go."

"Fuck, Rowan." I huffed out a breath. "Why the hell did you get me all worked up like that?"

He met me at the passenger door with my bag over his shoulder and the present under his arm and helped me step out. "A hot Summer is the best kind."

He smiled that sexy-as-hell smile I didn't think I'd ever get tired of, and I willingly let him pull me toward the noise of the party by the river.

We were greeted by everyone as we arrived. I found a seat by Kora and Darlene, and Rowan went directly to the kids, who were all wading in the river and splashing each other.

"Late again," Kora said.

"Get over it," I told her.

Darlene laughed. "Oh, don't worry, Summer. We aren't stressed by it. At least we know you'll show up in a good mood."

I rolled my eyes and accepted the drink Susie gave me. "Happy birthday, and welcome back." I gave her a hug.

"Thanks. It's good to be back," she said with a strange smile on her lips.

Tonya came over to us with a bundle of preciousness in her arms. Michelle Grace McKendry arrived in this world right on time the middle of February. Rowan and I had been at the hospital when she was born, as Rowan had refused to miss another niece's birth.

I stood and held my arms open. "Give her up, Tonya. I need some sugar."

She begrudgingly passed off her newest grandchild to me. Michelle Grace was the most adorable baby I had the pleasure of cuddling with—outside of Madeline, Darcie, and James, of course. I cradled her in my arms, lost in all her tininess. Her precious fingers, nose, and ears. She was perfect.

"Look who I've got," Rowan announced. I looked up to see him holding Adler and Leila's son, Donald—or Donny, as we called him—who was born exactly a month before Michelle.

"Now, Donny," Rowan said to the baby in his arms. "Michelle, there, can be your friend, and you'll need to take good care of her. Maybe you'll become best friends. Then," he said giving me a wink, "maybe if you're lucky, you'll fall in love."

The love in his eyes, directed at me and only me, made my heart swoon and stutter. "Only if they're very lucky," I agreed.

His gaze turned heated. "And, Donny," he continued talking to the baby, "if you are the luckiest man ever . . ." He trailed off and his gaze locked on mine. "She'd agree to marry you."

I froze. "What?" My heart fluttered wildly. He didn't just say . . .

Darlene and Leila, both grinning wildly, took their babies from us.

I turned back to Rowan, and my heart stopped at the sight of how much emotion filled his eyes. I'd seen him through so many of his life's ups and downs, but there was something about the look on his face now—a mixture of love, adoration, and. . . fear. "Rowan," I said. "You're scaring me."

"I'm sorry," he said as he clasped my hands in his. "I don't mean to scare you." He walked me closer to the edge of the water. "I fell in love with you on this very bank, and I've loved you just about forever. Summer, I know you have doubts and worry about what will happen in the future, but I hope these past months have shown you how much I love you."

A knot had lodged in my throat, and I was scared my heart would thump out of my chest. "Rowan, I do. I love you so much."

"I know," he said as he reached into his pocket and pulled out a ring.

My eyes popped wide, and my hands flew to cover my mouth.

"That's why I wanted everyone to be here when I asked you to marry me." He got slowly down on one knee and held the ring up.

My knees shook, and sobs broke free. I hated crying, but ugly crying? That was one thing I never did. Well, until now.

"Make me the happiest man ever and marry me, Summer," Rowan said.

"Dammit, standup and put that ring on my finger," I said through tears as I pulled him to his feet and crushed my lips to his. My body shook with sobs which I quickly got control of. "Yes, I'll marry you. Just don't fucking make me cry again."

"Hell yeah!" He slipped the ring on my finger and swung me in a circle. "Time to party, everyone! We're getting married!" Rowan held my hand in the air, showing off the ring on my finger.

Everyone hollered their congratulations.

"Wait," I said as my gaze locked on Susie. "It's Susie's Birthday. We can't hijack it."

Susie laughed and shook her head. "It's not my birthday. My birthday's in July. This was just a way to get you and everyone here without making you suspect anything."

"It's not your birthday?" I asked.

She shook her head and laughed.

Kora said. "All this was just a perfect plan created by Rowan."

I turned to him. "You planned all this? And no one told me? You know I hate surprises."

"I know," he said. "Trust me. But this was worth it. The only ones who knew were Kora, Kai, Darlene, Susie, and my brothers. Everyone else thought it was a birthday party."

"Kai told us when we got here," Adler said.

"Hell, Rowan didn't even tell me," Trevor said as he wrapped me in a hug. "But congratulations."

"You're marrying my baby," Tonya said.

I nodded, still in shock, and glanced down at my finger. The ring was a beautiful princess-cut diamond. I wasn't sure how large, but just enough to glitter in the sunlight and catch my eye. Like everything from Rowan, it was perfect. "It looks that way," I answered her. "Between you and me, this is overwhelming. I hate surprises, and he knows that."

Tonya laughed, and her cackle echoed off the trees. "You two are going to have an amazing marriage." She pulled me into a tight hug.

I didn't know what to do. First the surprise proposal, now this response from Tonya. This might be too much for one day. "What makes you say that?" I asked as I pulled out of her embrace.

"Carl proposed to me the same way. He caught me off-guard in front of everyone. It was a total surprise, and, like you, I hate surprises. This might be one of the reasons everyone says you and I are two peas in a pod."

I nodded. "So I hear."

Rowan came over to us. "What are you two talking about?" he asked.

"Nothing," I said. "Just how amazing of a man you are."

He glanced from his mother, back to me. "Why don't I believe that?" he asked.

Tonya laughed and strolled away. I took advantage of having Rowan here with me and wrapped my arms around his neck. "Let's just say your mom and I came to an agreement."

He wrapped his arms around my waist. "That's a little scary."

"Probably," I agreed. I kissed him long and deep, and when we finally broke apart, we were both winded. "Thank you," I said as I looked deep into his eyes.

"For what?"

"For sticking with me, and loving me through all my craziness and insecurities," I answered.

"Woman, like I've told you a million times. There's never been anyone else I've ever wanted as much as I've wanted you. I love you and I always have." Rowan's mouth crushed against mine.

My heart fluttered. Fear of those words was gone. This man was my home, and there was no where else I wanted to be.

ABOUT THE AUTHOR

Donna R. Madden has been married to her husband for over 30 years.

They have raised 3 amazing boys in a small town north of Nashville. They share their house with chickens, their dog Lilly, and cat King Marcus Henry XXII, who they all affectionately call "Kitty Kitty."

When Donna has spare time, she enjoys hanging out with her family and friends, relaxing by the pool or on the beach, and of course reading–mostly romance.

Notes to the Reader

Thank you for taking your time and reading *No Place Like Home.* I hope you enjoyed reading it as much as I enjoyed writing it.

If you loved the story and characters, I would be so grateful to you if you would take the time and leave a review wherever you purchased the book. Reviews help authors and are so appreciated.

Orlinda Valley is a fictional town, yet a culmination of many of the small towns around my home. The next book in the series is being written as you read this, and I hope you come back to Orlinda Valley again.

I'd also love it if you would join my mailing list to find out about new releases in the Orlinda Valley series, and other happenings in my writing career. Just scan the QR Code to find me everywhere, visit my Etsy shop, join my newsletter, and purchase my books.

9 798987 734391